Among the Lemon Trees

Nadia Marks (née Kitromilides, which in Greek means bitter lemons) was born in Cyprus, but grew up in London. An executive director and associate editor on a number of leading British women's magazines, she is now a novelist and works as a freelance writer for several national and international publications. She has two sons and lives in North London with her partner Mike.

Nadia Marks

Among the Lemon Trees

PAN BOOKS

First published in paperback 2017 by Macmillan

This edition published 2017 by Pan Books
an imprint of Pan Macmillan
20 New Wharf Road, London N1 9RR
Associated companies throughout the world
www.panmacmillan.com

ISBN 978-1-5098-1571-5

1 3 5 7 9 8 6 4 2

A CIP catalogue record for this book is available from the British Library.

Typeset by Palimpsest Book Production Limited, Falkirk, Stirlingshire
Printed and bound by CPI Group (UK) Ltd, Croydon, CR0 4YY

Visit **www.panmacmillan.com** to read more about all our books
and to buy them. You will also find features, author interviews and
news of any author events, and you can sign up for e-newsletters
so that you're always first to hear about our new releases.

To my sons, Leo and Pablo

Ancient Greek has four distinct words for love: *agápe*, *Éros*, *philía* and *storgé*. The Greek language distinguishes how the word is used.

Perhaps in the same way that the ancient Greeks worshipped twelve gods yet kept an open mind about a possible thirteenth deity, there could also be a word to describe a fifth kind of love.

Part One

Love on a Greek island, 1936

The power of the full moon has always been respected and revered by the people of the island. They believe that under the influence of an August moon, rational thought is likely to desert a person, especially those who have fallen under the spell of love. Anything can happen during such a time. It's a dangerous and wayward period; its effect on lovers, young or old, has no mercy. When the hot jasmine-scented air intoxicates the senses and moonlight fills the sky, human sap begins to rise and mischief is afoot. The moon shimmering over a balmy sea promises delights beyond the imagination and anyone can fall prey to its power and be led astray.

In days gone by, mothers of young girls would keep their daughters under lock and key anticipating this danger. It was on such an August night that an ardent, rebellious young girl managed to escape her mother's watchful eye and run to the seashore to meet the boy she loved.

She knew that by the time the moon had made its way high in the sky, the light would be too bright to provide shelter from prying eyes, so the young lovers arranged to meet after sundown but before moonrise. That was the magical hour when the world was cloaked in darkness and the sea was as still as glass.

For weeks the two sweethearts had planned their secret meeting to coincide with the twenty-eighth day of the calendar month and the day the girl would turn fifteen. Concealed by the blackness of the night they felt safe to kiss and embrace, lie in each other's arms and wait to witness the mystery of an August moonrise. They watched in awe as the glimmer of gold on the horizon rose gradually to become an enormous amber globe, hovering over the sea and bathing everything in its warm glow. But before the moon rose higher, illuminating the beach like a spotlight betraying the young lovers, they ran to take refuge in one of the many caves under the rocky cliffs on the beach. It was on that night, the night she turned fifteen and the full moon reigned in the sky, that she gave herself to the boy she loved more than anyone else in the world, while they both pledged eternal love to each other. He had turned sixteen three months earlier.

'I will love you for ever,' he said.

'I would die rather than stop loving you,' she said back.

1

London, 1999

Anna's mobile was on silent. She'd turned it off during dinner. It always irritated her if Max or the kids answered theirs while they ate. Dinner was a time just for them; anyone else could wait. After all, if they were all together what emergency could there be that couldn't wait? The only thing that Anna ever worried about was if her old dad might need her, but then again he always called on the landline.

She was emptying the dishwasher when she noticed the phone vibrating on the kitchen counter. Unknown number. She hesitated for a second before picking it up. Then came the stranger's voice.

'Mrs Turner?'

'Speaking.' Anna had an uneasy feeling. It wasn't often she was referred to by her married name, and the man's voice sounded serious.

'This is Dr Morris, from the Whittington Hospital,' he continued.

She stopped breathing.

'Dad.' Her whisper was barely audible. She nearly dropped the phone.

'We have Mr Turner here,' the voice carried on. 'He is fine, but you might like to come to the hospital. Your husband gave us your number. He is in A and E at the moment.'

Within minutes Anna had grabbed the car keys and was running upstairs for her coat, alerting Alex and Chloe who were both in their rooms. Max had apparently suffered a heart attack.

'Kids! Kids!' she screamed at the top of her lungs, as she ran two steps at a time to the bedroom. 'Your dad's in hospital. Let's move, let's go!'

'What happened?' they both asked in unison, rushing out of their rooms.

'He was fine at dinner,' said Chloe.

'He went for a run . . .' added Alex. 'He was OK.'

'I don't know what happened,' Anna said, out of breath, 'but apparently it's his heart, so let's go and find out. Chloe, you drive, I don't think I can.'

Max looked grim as he lay waiting to be dealt with in one of the A and E cubicles.

'Am I glad to see you guys,' he said, giving them all a weak smile as they rushed to hug him.

'What on earth happened, Max?' Anna squeezed his hand and kissed him gently on the lips. 'I knew running after dinner was a bad idea,' she said, worry etched on her face. 'It seemed you were gone a long time, but then again I thought you might have popped in on John.'

'To be honest,' Max replied, his voice rather faint, 'it's all a bit of a blur.'

He was having his usual sprint up the hill and around the block a few times, when he felt unusually short of breath, he began explaining. He had felt a burning sensation in his sternum. 'I just thought it was *heartburn*. I started blaming the Chinese food I had at lunchtime.' He cursed the fried bean curd: 'You know how I prefer it steamed.' He looked at Anna. 'It kept repeating on me and I thought I should never have eaten it. I was sure it was some kind of acid reflux. Then, next thing I know, I'm here and apparently being prepared for an *angiogram*.'

'Oh Dad,' Chloe said, fighting her tears, 'you gave us such a scare.'

'What's going to happen now? What's an *angiogram*?' Alex asked, looking at his mum.

He was a *lucky man* the cardiologist told Anna later on, and hopefully he might get away with a stent placed in his blocked artery instead of the alternative, which was open heart surgery. Max had always considered himself lucky and it was a matter of luck that when he collapsed, a woman with a mobile phone who was walking her dog saw him.

In the end he needed bypass surgery. His physical recovery was swift, and within a couple of months he said he felt like his old self again. 'Lucky escape,' he kept telling everyone. Max's brush with death was a big deal for the whole family. The children and Anna all rallied around him.

'Dad just needs to know when to slow down,' Chloe told her mother. 'He isn't as young as he thinks he is. You have got to tell him, Mum, I'm serious. I'm only seventeen and half, I don't want to be an orphan just yet,' she said, masking her anxiety with mock annoyance. Alex, on the other hand, decided it was his duty to keep an eye on his father, so when Max started to run again he joined him.

'I need an incentive to start exercising,' he told Max, 'it's so much better with company.' What Alex, a natural worrier, really meant was, 'I have to make sure you don't overdo it, Dad, and I'm the only one who can!' At fifteen he also had more obvious things to worry about, like exams and girls, and his father's possible demise was not on the agenda just yet either, so he was going to make sure he helped him back to health.

They were a close family, the marriage a long and

fruitful one; Max and Anna were happy in each other's company, never short of conversation and still doing things together. They would have been together twenty-five years next anniversary, for which Anna had been planning a surprise trip to Cuba. There was talk about going for the millennium and taking the children, the New Year's Eve of a lifetime. But then they thought about Anna's father and her siblings, and the trip was put on hold.

'Anyway,' Chloe had said, when they were discussing the alternatives for the anniversary, 'I hear that Cuba is celebrating the millennium in 2001, so we can always go next year . . .'

Both kids wanted a party, a big family affair for their parents, but Anna was reluctant.

'Go on, Mum,' they urged her, 'it's time we had a family celebration, we haven't had one since *Nonna* died. It'll be good for us all.'

'I know. You're right,' she said, 'but you know your dad, he's not one for parties. Besides, we've both been talking about Cuba for so many years, this is our chance, we want to get there before it all changes; we'll have a party another time.' So it was agreed. She was going to book the tickets and surprise him nearer the time.

His collapse had been totally unexpected. It really frightened Anna, and reminded her once again about the precariousness of life. Her mother's death four years earlier and Max's mother's death just a year ago, had also been a huge blow and she trembled with the thought of losing Max too; they had so much to live for, still so much more to do together.

Anna helped nurse him back to health with zeal, and everyone helped, especially Chloe. She and Anna had always been close, their relationship mirroring what Anna had with her own mother. In fact, the three generations of women had shared a close bond. *Nonna*, as the children called their grandmother, was Italian and bountiful in her love for her family. Her loss cost them a great deal so the near loss of Max made them appreciate what they had even more. It seemed to bring them all even closer.

'Silly old Dad,' Chloe said once he was out of danger. 'What did he want to do that for? His trouble is that he never knows when to stop!'

Despite all the reassurances that he was going to be fine, Max was devastated by what he regarded as the failure of his body. He had always prided himself at keeping it in tip-top condition, and he was fanatical about exercise and healthy eating, often arguing about it with Anna, who was much less neurotic about her longevity.

'Your genes and DNA have much more to do with how long you live, than how often you go to the gym,' she'd tell him. 'Look at my dad, he's never jogged in his life and he looks twenty years younger than his age.'

'You can look young but it doesn't mean you're healthy,' Max would argue back, and so the discussions went on. He was determined he was going to live forever or at least live like he was going to live forever.

The realization that he too was going to die at some point, and possibly soon given his recent collapse, hit Max with a force so powerful it felt as if he had collided with an iceberg. He was still so young. Perhaps not in years, he was going to be fifty-six next birthday, but certainly in spirit. He was full of vigour and zest, bursting with ideas, plans and schemes; death had no place in *his* life. Then it suddenly seemed to be all around him. First, his best friend; one minute the two of them were sharing a fine bottle of Bordeaux, the next he was gone, dead in front of his very eyes. That was a terrible shock but he put it down to the fact that Stewart was overweight and didn't take care of himself. Then his mother. No illness, no warning, she just went to bed and never woke up. Then again, *she* was eighty-six. But Max? What good reason was there for him to collapse like that? What good reason did his heart have to give way?

He might have boasted and tried to convince everyone that he was back to 'his old self again' and that everything was fine, but Anna wasn't fooled. His bouts of moodiness were now coupled with an uncharacteristic short fuse. His behaviour was not that of the Max she knew. Gone was the humorous banter, the gentle caresses. Anna had never known Max not to be physical with her. She had a lifetime of close tenderness with him. He'd always tell her that his favourite moment of the day was when he sat in bed at night watching her get undressed and ready to lie down next to him. Anna wasn't even aware of the effect she had on her husband. She didn't do it provocatively, no seductive underwear or lace, she could be simply taking off her jeans and T-shirt and he would put his book down to look at her.

'Ah! My moment of Zen!' he'd tell her laughing. 'I am one lucky man!'

Anna, always bashful, would joke back and make light of it but never tired of hearing it.

When Max took to staying up late or finding his book far more absorbing than his wife's naked body Anna started to worry. *Perhaps the heart problem has affected his libido*, she'd tell herself. *These things have consequences. Or maybe he's depressed.*

She wanted to help, be there for him, as was her habit with her husband; patience had always been one of her virtues, but nothing could have ever prepared her for what followed.

Max was leaning casually against the kitchen counter, one hand clutching a cup of coffee, the other plunged deep into his trouser pocket. It was approximately a year since his collapse. He was speaking words that she'd never imagined could come out of his mouth, words that didn't make any sense to her. She put her hand on the table to steady herself and swallowed hard to stop from crying. The trembling which first started in her limbs travelled inwards until it felt as if all her internal organs were ricocheting around inside her.

'She loves me,' she heard him say, eyes averted, his lips set in a hard line. 'It's a strong connection,' and 'I have come to a crossroads in my life.' She couldn't comprehend. The lump that rose in her throat grew bigger, making it hard to breathe. *He's not rational*, her brain screamed. *Mid-life madness, fear of dying!* it bellowed again, and then she remembered reading somewhere that every woman whose husband is having an affair believes he must be going through a nervous breakdown.

It had been months, she told herself, since his surgery. She'd been there for him, cared for him, supported him every step of the way. Surely he could see everything was going to be fine now? *I mustn't cry, just hear him through*, she'd told herself again, trying to muster some control.

13

'I don't understand. What are you saying, Max?' she finally said, her voice a mere whisper in contrast to the screaming inside her head. Was he confessing to an affair and about to beg for forgiveness, or was he saying he wanted to leave her?

'And you . . . do you love *her*?' she'd forced herself to ask.

'I'm in love with her . . . yes.' His reply landed like a fist in Anna's belly.

'*In love?*' she'd stammered, trying to imagine Max in love with someone that wasn't her. They had been married a quarter of a century and had two grown-up children to show for it. She'd never visualized the future without him. She always thought they were moving forward together, committed to each other, their families, their friends. Now here he was talking to her in another language, as if he was a stranger. *And what about last year?* Anna's brain screamed again. *How much love and support could a man have from his family, from his wife?*

'Who is she?' she whispered again.

'She is an academic, a lecturer at the university . . .' his voice trailed off. Anna held her breath. She didn't want to hear any more. It was more than she could bear. Max had hit her where it hurt; touched her most vulnerable spot. A woman with *brains*! An *academic*, probably beautiful, possibly younger *and* clever! None of those things really mattered to Anna, except the brains. It wasn't that Anna didn't have any; she was clever and talented and perfectly bright, but she'd never considered herself Max's intellectual equal; it was, she knew, her own hang-up. She had gone to college, *not* university, she had an art diploma *not* a degree; *he* was the brain, the brilliant professor. She admired him and deferred to his 'great' intellect. She knew she shouldn't, but she couldn't help it, she had always put him first.

'Are you *in love* with her, or do you actually *love* her?' she'd heard herself ask, tears blurring her vision.

'What's the difference?' Still he avoided her gaze.

Anna now flushed with anger. The disbelief, confusion and hurt she'd been feeling turned suddenly to fury.

'You know perfectly well what the difference is,' she hissed at him.

Of course Max knew; Anna teased him often enough about it.

'English is such a rich language,' she liked to tell anyone who'd listen, 'but in defining *love*, the Greeks have the edge.' It amused her and made her feel smart to elaborate on the subject of love. The Greeks, she'd explain, have four words for love and each one describes a different emotion. *Agápe* is the big love, *storgé*, the tender mother love, *philía* friendship, and *Éros* sexual love. '*Agápe*,' Anna would relate, 'encompasses all the other loves in one big absolute and supreme emotion. *Éros* on the other hand, according to the Greeks, is the love that in English is referred to as *falling in love*. It's all about passion, desire and obsession, it takes you over but ultimately it's ephemeral.'

So *yes*, Max should have known *perfectly* well what Anna was referring to. Her anger took hold.

'Max! Max!' she shouted. 'What is wrong with you? Listen to yourself!' She choked back her tears. 'It's me you're talking to, Anna, your wife, remember?' He stood rooted to the ground like a defiant child. He had no reply.

'Do you still want to be with me? Do you still love *me*?' she asked, after waiting a few moments for him to end the silence. She'd never imagined she'd ever have to ask that question of Max. He was her soulmate, her best friend, her lover, the father of her children. How could Max *not* love her?

'I think so . . . I don't know,' came his noncommittal answer, spiking her through the heart.

'You *don't know*?' she burst out again. 'After twenty-five years of marriage that's what you say to me? What about your children? What about Alex and Chloe, do you know if you love them?'

'I need space, time to think. I'm confused,' he mumbled.

In the weeks that followed, Anna felt she was living in a bad dream. Max was still at home but unable to make any decisions about the future. The two of them tried to behave normally in front of their children and then in private Anna would explode, frustrated with Max's inability to discuss or express his feelings. Time and time again she would catch Chloe looking at her quizzically.

'Mum, what is going on, what is wrong with Dad?' she had asked more than once, but Anna was determined to keep her children out of it until she herself was clearer about the situation.

Every time she was on the verge of telling him to pack his bags and go, she thought of all the years they'd been together. If Max was out of his mind, then she had to stay sane. A few months of madness versus twenty-five years of a good marriage; she had to give it some more time, but how long?

Determined that her life would not come to a complete halt, Anna tried to carry on as usual. She'd been walking down Piccadilly towards the Royal Academy of Arts. It was the final days of a major Monet exhibition and she'd talked herself into going. Thoughts of her life spinning out of control were clouding her brain. A concrete sky pressed down over the city, like a damp ceiling threatening to burst. As she walked along, all she could think of was: *Is this it? Is this really how all these years of a good marriage are going to end?*

She must have been distracted. The pedestrian lights had turned green; she was quite sure of it. The girl standing next to her stepped off the kerb, so she automatically followed her. The motorbike came from nowhere. The screeching brakes and deafening sound of the horn jolted Anna out of her daze and back onto the pavement with a jump. But the girl ahead of her wasn't quick enough and she took the vehicle's full impact. She was now lying on the tarmac, her body sprawled across the road like a broken toy. Her bag, and one of her shoes, had come off and were lying by Anna's feet. Anna looked at her in disbelief, her knees started to give way and she leaned on the traffic lights to avoid buckling over. Within seconds, a crowd gathered. A woman took Anna's arm and guided her towards a bench. The biker, apparently unhurt, was frantic and hovered over the girl. A man ran over saying he was a doctor and people were calling for an ambulance. Time lapsed. Anna thought it was like a film in slow motion.

The girl was still in the middle of the road. A pool of blood was now visible under her hair. Sirens could be heard in the distance.

Anna sat on the bench in a kind of trance, the woman

stayed by her side. People talked, paramedics did their job, police held back a gathering crowd of onlookers.

'Are you OK?' the woman asked softly.

'Will she be all right?' Anna said in a voice so weak she hardly knew it belonged to her.

'I don't know,' she replied and patted Anna's hand. 'I'm sure he was speeding. You were very lucky.'

When she looked back at the girl again the paramedics were putting her in the ambulance; the blanket that had covered her earlier to keep her warm was now over her face.

Anna sat staring into space. The crowd dispersed and she eventually collected herself and walked across the street to the Royal Academy. Heading straight for the ladies, Anna locked herself in one of the cubicles and burst into a torrent of tears. She cried silently for a long time. She cried because she was shocked and afraid, she cried for that poor wretched girl whose life had been cut down so suddenly and prematurely. She cried for Max, and for herself, and she cried because she knew how easily it could have been her now lying in a morgue somewhere. Locked in the cubicle in one of her favourite places in the world, Anna came to a realization. Enough was enough and it was time to try and take control again. If her husband was incapable of making any decisions, *she* had to do it. She would carry on, with or without Max.

The day after her lucky escape Anna felt an over-whelming need to see her father. She'd been avoiding him, cutting her visits short since the crisis with Max for fear of upsetting him, not trusting herself not to break down and until she knew what was going to happen there was no point involving him. Since her mother's death, she'd been left with a huge weight of responsi-bility, not only for her father but for everyone else in her family. As a daughter, a wife, a mother, and the sister of three brothers, Anna had, willingly or not, inherited her mother's role as the matriarch in the family by always having someone to worry about. But if there was ever a time she needed merely to be someone's daughter, it was right now.

They met in the grounds of Kenwood, her father's favourite walking spot. It was a sunny afternoon in May when the roses were in bud and the rhododendrons in full bloom and London looked its Sunday best. They walked arm in arm, Anna fighting back the tears.

'I feel the time has come to return to the island, I want to see the family.' Her father stopped walking to look at Anna. 'This could be my last chance.'

'What do you mean "your last chance", Papa?' she

replied, feeling her knees go to jelly, fearful that there might be something wrong with her eighty-year-old father.

'I don't know, Anna *mou*,' he carried on, speaking in Greek, which was always a sign that he was saying something of importance. 'I have a premonition this could be my last summer. These days, time is getting short and I want to be there.'

'Why? What's the matter?' The jelly feeling was spreading to the rest of her legs.

'No, no, Annoula *mou*, there's nothing really wrong. Not that I know of anyway.' He smiled, sensing her panic. 'I was thinking about things, and I just feel at my age it could be any time now, you know . . . I'm next in line. Remember what happened to your mother? Fine one day and then suddenly gone.'

Such uncharacteristic gloom from her father took Anna by surprise. She'd been used to him being optimistic, strong, and full of vigour but his wife's death had affected him badly.

'Don't talk rubbish, Papa.' She tightened her grip round his arm and carried on walking. 'You're perfectly fit and healthy, so don't think such nonsense. Anyway, it's a great idea. How long were you thinking of going for?'

'Two, three, maybe even four months, perhaps the

whole summer or more. I don't know, I just don't want to rush back.'

'OK. That's good,' Anna said slowly and immediately started to worry; *four* months was far too long for an old man to be on his own. 'It's a great idea, Papa,' she tried not to sound negative, 'but don't you think that's rather a long time to be there on your own?'

'Why don't you come with me then, like old times?' He stopped walking again and turned to her. 'The children are away this summer, aren't they? Didn't you tell me Chloe is going to America and Alex is travelling around Europe? Max won't mind if you spend some time with your old father, will he?' Taking hold of her hand, he looked his daughter straight in the eye. 'You haven't been back since your mother died, Annoula. Maybe it's time?'

Anna's reluctance to return to the island had much to do with wanting to preserve the memory of being there with her mother and with feeling that she couldn't face it without her. They'd all spent three blissful weeks together there that last summer, and then, two months after returning to London, she was gone.

Her father's unexpected wish to recapture the past stabbed Anna with a sharp nostalgia and a yearning to return to Greece. Her mother, she thought, had gone forever. There was nothing she could do about that, but her father was still here and he needed her. Besides, she was exhausted; she had spent so much emotional energy on Max in the last few months, she now felt totally empty and worn out. It was time to think of herself too.

2

The island was barely visible from the boat but Anna was already on deck, leaning out as far as she could, straining her eyes trying to see it. It shimmered in the far distance like a white dove floating on the liquid blue of the Aegean. Filled with the same happiness she'd always felt when approaching this place, she reverted to being ten years old again. Arms outstretched, hair blowing wildly in the breeze, face soaked by the salty spray, she screamed with joy, oblivious to anyone else around her. As they got closer, the rocky hills and mountains started to become visible and she could just make out the church of Agios Nikolaos high on a rock, glistening in the sunlight. This was *their* island and they were both returning after so much time.

The instant Anna stepped off the boat and onto dry land, she was flooded with a sense of familiarity and well-being. This place always had the ability to make her feel nurtured, cherished and loved.

When she was a small girl and they'd arrive as a family for their summer holidays, the entire village would gather at the little harbour to welcome them. That was the time before mass tourism, when visitors on the island were still a novelty. Anna always marvelled at how many people her father seemed to be related to in the village, and how much everyone who knew him from before he left loved him. People would rush to help with getting their luggage off the boat, and wish them a good stay. *'Kalosorisate,'* they called out, the customary welcoming greeting. Anna and her brothers spent several glorious weeks running wild on the island and, when it was over, none of them wanted to leave the freedom and their friends to return to a captive London life. They felt genuinely welcomed and liked there. *Philoxenia*, hospitality, is a matter of national pride to the Greeks and when Anna was older she often compared how this *philoxenia*, this love of the *xenos*, the foreigner, contrasted to the fear and suspicion of the unknown, of the *other*, so often demonstrated by certain British people.

The early July sun was already high in the sky and blisteringly hot when they finally arrived after the long boat journey from Piraeus. London had been wet and miserable and she stood at the harbour waiting for her cousin Manos to help with the luggage. The midday heat, beating down on her back, started to melt her English blues away.

The local people from Anna's childhood were long gone and there was no crowd to welcome them or to wish them a good stay, only Manos, beaming with joy at seeing his favourite uncle and cousin again. *'Kalosorisate!'* he bellowed, hugging them both. The once sleepy harbour was now transformed into a buzzing little port, full of pavement cafes, restaurants and bars. The only place that remained unchanged was the old *kafeneon* – or coffee shop – in one corner of the square, where for over a century the men of the village would gather to play cards, smoke and gossip. As always, the men – young and old – were sitting in groups, playing with their worry beads, smoking, drinking and surrounded by a forest of chairs.

Chairs are an essential part of *kafeneon* life. You would never see a Greek man drinking his coffee without a collection of them around him, it's impossible for him to occupy only *one* chair at a time; the allocation per person has to be at least three – one to sit on, another to put his leg on, and a third upon which to lean his elbows, leaving his hands free to make elaborate gestures. A fourth chair, where the coffee and a glass of water would be placed, is optional depending on the presence of a table nearby. This chair ritual is a peculiar Greek phenomenon which Anna had observed very early on in her life. She would often ask her father about it but for him it was natural and logical

– how else would a man drink his coffee and talk to his friends comfortably?

The dusty road up the hill to the house, not too great a distance from the village square, was too far on foot with all their luggage. It snaked through vineyards and olive groves with magnificent mountainous views, the bay and the little harbour below. The sight of the house always gave Anna a thrill. The shrubs and trees her grandparents had planted so long ago were inextricably linked with her early years.

The crowds hadn't welcomed them off the boat earlier, but they made up for it by being at the house when they arrived. Her father's first cousin, Thia – Aunt – Ourania, was there, along with a variety of relatives, waiting under the vine-covered pergola. It is possible, Anna always thought with amusement, that the Greeks have more relatives than any other nation. She had lost count of how many people she called auntie or uncle, and how many cousins she had. Strictly speaking, as Max never failed to remind her, no one is entitled to be called an aunt or uncle unless they are a sibling of one of your parents. But that is not the case in Greece; here on the island everyone is one happy family! The densely leafed vine, *klimataria*, twined and twisted over the wooden structure and covered the entire front of the house; it

27

was laden with huge bunches of green grapes that would soon turn a deep burgundy and be ready to eat in a few weeks. The organic roof made the space beneath it feel like an outside room. A big wooden table had been laid out with food and drink, ready for a welcoming feast in true Greek style.

Anna's father, Alexis, was an only child and very fond of his cousin, and since her grandmother had died before she was born, Anna considered her Thia Ourania her closest surviving female relative. Ourania had never married so had no children of her own, yet she was extremely gifted when it came to dealing with them and her life's work as a schoolteacher had been perfect for her. She loved her job, and the several generations of children she taught on the island loved her back. When she was young, and had first started teaching, there had even been a few youths who carried a lustful yearning for their pretty young teacher not so many years their senior. On some occasions, these young infatuations became troublesome, causing more than a flurry of gossip in the village.

'What does she expect if she looks like that!' tongues wagged accusingly. 'It is Greek island blood that runs through the veins of those boys!'

Her good looks were not Ourania's fault and nor did she flaunt them, but at the same time she refused to act like the formidable teacher. However, over time, not wanting to offend or give fuel to the youthful fantasies and narrow minds, she was forced to conform. Her floral summer dresses were put away and her dark curls tamed.

She was tall, taller than most of the women in the village, and her very name, Ourania – meaning *the one from the sky* – evoked in Anna's young mind celestial images and heavenly powers. She had kind eyes, the colour of warm chocolate, and as a little girl, Anna remembered secretly wanting to snatch the comb that held her hair in that tight bun and watch it tumble freely over her shoulders. She could, Anna used to think, be almost as beautiful as her own mother, if she didn't look so severe. They were quite similar in many ways, those two; about the same height and build, good skin and a profusion of dark hair. But the biggest similarity was their eyes. They both possessed the same wide, intensely dark, melancholic eyes.

Thia Ourania stood there under the shade of the *klimataria* with all the other relatives – nearly eighty years old, tall, handsome, and upright as ever. Even though her hair had now turned to silver, still pulled back in that severe fashion of hers, the eyes were the same as always: warm, deep and gentle. Overjoyed, Anna dropped her bags and threw herself into her auntie's arms, the way she had as a little girl.

'Welcome,' Ourania said in Greek, kissing her niece on both cheeks and enveloping her in a strong embrace. 'It has been too long!' She turned round to look at her cousin. 'You too, Alexis,' she said, her voice breaking.

It had indeed been far too long – over four years since they'd seen her, or any of the other relatives. It had taken them this long to make the journey back – a journey they couldn't face without Anna's mother. Until now.

3

Anna woke up to the distant sound of a dog barking. Within moments, a second one started up and pretty soon half a dozen more seemed to join in the chorus. This was not a sound you would hear in North London. Rubbing the sleep from her eyes, Anna slowly remembered where she was. In an instant she was out of bed and running barefoot through the house to the courtyard to find Alexis dressed, freshly shaven and sitting under the vine, drinking coffee and reading the newspaper.

'*Kalimera*, Annoula!' He peered over his glasses. 'You *must* have been tired!'

'Oh my God, Papa, what time is it?' Anna tried to gauge the time by where the sun was.

'It's nearly noon.'

'I missed the best part of the day.' She slumped down next to him. Early morning on the island had always been her favourite time, before the sun was high and the heat started to numb the senses.

'You must have needed the sleep, so don't worry, you'll have plenty of days to be up with the dawn.' He smiled and reached over to touch her hand. 'We are here now.'

The previous evening's celebrations had carried on well into the night and much food, wine and *raki* had been consumed. The stream of welcoming visitors continued until Thia Ourania eventually told everyone it was time to leave.

'It's good to be back, Papa. Nothing has changed,' Anna replied, breathing in the heady aroma of the garden and holding it in for as long as she could. This garden was completely different from the conventional English equivalent with its green lawn and regimented herbaceous borders. Here, anarchy reigned: no grass, or plan. Flowers grew haphazardly from pots or beds, scent beckoning a myriad of buzzing bees and butterflies, roses competing with freesias, pinks with arum lilies, bushes of scented geraniums, rosemary, lavender and pots of basil. A jumble of big old tins had been recycled as flowerpots, the writing on them still betraying that at some point they'd contained olive oil, olives, sardines, or any other foodstuff that might have been bought in bulk. No one had thought this garden through. It had evolved over the years, just like the island itself. Decades of history, generations of adults and children had passed through this house, this village, this island. For Anna, many happy memories and experiences were woven from the fabric of this place.

At that moment, sitting there with her father in the courtyard of their old family house, she experienced a kind of peace and tranquillity that she hadn't felt for months. The dappled light, filtering through the vine leaves, cast moving patterns on the table, the cicadas sang tirelessly, and a woman's voice drifted over the rooftops calling her child to the midday meal. How many times, she thought, had her own mother called her and her brothers to come to the lunch table in much the same way? For a split second Anna fooled herself and fancied it was *her* mama calling for her from inside the house.

'It's like she is here with us, Papa,' she whispered, and felt the memory hit her like a fist in the pit of her stomach. Emotion rose to her throat and filled her eyes until the tears fell one by one in great big drops on the brand-new oilcloth Thia Ourania had used to cover the outside table.

In just a few days in the old house, in the garden, with her father and daily visits from her aunt, Anna began to feel like her old self again, ready to explore the places of her youth. On her way down the steep path to the square, she met old Costis trying unsuccessfully to usher a goat away from somebody's garden. As soon as he saw her he waved excitedly.

'When did you arrive, Miss Anna?' he asked, hobbling towards her. 'Is your father here too? How long are you staying?' he continued, without waiting for an answer. She had known this man since she was a little girl. He must have been about the same age as her father and like Alexis still looked strong and fit, despite his tooth-less grin. He used to have a herd of goats that he brought to some fields near their house, and was obviously still doing the same.

'It's good to see you, Costis.' Anna smiled, glad to see that little seemed to have moved on since she was here last. 'Where do you take the goats, now that all these houses have been built up here?'

'Oh, no problem, Miss Anna,' he chuckled. 'I always find somewhere, and you know goats, they'll eat anything!'

Costis used to bring buckets of goats' milk to the house to give to Anna's mother for the 'babies', as he had called the children when they were small. 'Goats' milk is as good as mother's milk,' he told her, 'it makes them healthy and strong.'

'Shall I bring you some milk?' Costis asked. 'Remember how you loved it when you were a baby?'

'I wouldn't know what to do with it, Costi,' Anna laughed.

'Ask your Thia Ourania, she'd know!' he said, waving goodbye.

She had forgotten how everyone knew everyone here. In some ways, she thought, making her way towards the village, it must be comforting to have the support and help of your community. But, then again, not being able to do much without the whole village knowing, must be suffocating. Anna remembered how oppressive it had been for her as a teenager. Alexis was always worrying and anxious about what people would think if any of the children misbehaved.

The village square too, was unchanged. The pedestrianized centre accommodated chairs, tables and umbrellas laid out by the three cafes doing business. No matter how hot it was elsewhere, a cool breeze always blew from the sea there. No sooner had Anna sat down than a small crowd gathered; the woman from the kiosk where Anna always bought her newspaper, the three waiters from the cafes, and the baker's wife. All stood around her smiling and firing questions. 'How long were they staying? Where were her husband and the children? How did they all cope without her dear mother? What about her brothers, and how was her father? Was he well?' The questions kept coming and she barely had a chance to reply.

'Why don't you all calm down, and let the lady speak,' said a warm, throaty rasp of a voice behind Anna's back. 'And, Stavro, where are your manners, get the lady a drink.'

Before she could turn round to see who it was, the owner of the twenty-unfiltered-Carelia-a-day voice was standing in front of her, shaking her hand. He was tall for a Greek, with a strong, rough, earthy body and a big, broad smile. *I've never seen him before, he must be a fisherman*, she thought, shaking his hand. The sun-baked skin, strong hand grip and developed muscles could have been a fisherman's, or those of a man who worked the earth, but the whiff of his cologne, well-cut Levi's, expensive black T-shirt and fashionable loafers told a different story.

'My name is Antonis Zevros.' He flashed even white teeth and pulled up a chair.

'May I?' he asked, already sitting down. 'I own the taverna over there.' He gestured to the restaurant across the street with his chin.

He spoke English with a heavy Greek accent tinged with American. 'Pleased to meet you, Miss Anna, and very happy to speak English with you. I was living in Chicago for twenty years and I miss it. I came back to the island last year because my old mother got sick and needed me. She thought she was going to die,' he said, taking his turn, not letting Anna get a word in, which was fine by her. She was glad to be let off the hook. 'I came rushing back and took her off to Athens to see the doctors. We were all scared she wasn't going to make it.'

'Did she get better?'

'Oh yes, she's just fine! I think it was a trick to get

me back,' he laughed. 'Which was probably just as well. It was time to leave.'

'What happened? Didn't you like Chicago any more?'

'You could say that. The American sweet dream turned a little sour. American wife, American house, American business, the full catastrophe, as Zorba would say. It didn't work out.'

Baffled by so much personal information, Anna sat there listening to this complete stranger talk about his life. The rest of the crowd slowly dispersed, returning to their work. Stavros brought Anna ice-cold lemonade and Antonis Zevros sat with her as she sipped it in the cool shade. He wasn't young, but not old either; she guessed somewhere between forty and sixty, she couldn't tell. He had smiling eyes the colour of treacle, a strong, firm, square-jawed face, etched with deep laughter lines; lines that betrayed a life history, which she was now learning about whether it interested her or not. His thick hair, long enough to cover his ears and fall in soft curls over his eyes, was still quite dark, flecked with only a touch of grey. Max's hair, Anna thought, had already gone almost completely grey.

'Are you glad to be back home now?' she asked.

'For years I was missing this island really badly, but now I'm here, I miss it there.' He laughed again. 'Eh, human beings, we don't know *what* we want!'

Antonis Zevros was spontaneous, boisterous and full

of Antonis Zevros; so Greek, Anna thought, and smiled to herself. But despite that, she liked him; the sparkle of his eyes and easy smile were infectious. She was amused by the way he referred to her as Miss Anna and by the way he drew her into his conversation.

'So, Miss Anna, you too are divorced, yes?' He asked this in that blunt way Greeks have in these parts that guarantees to shock the English.

'No!' she heard herself reply sharply, a sting in her heart and irritated by his presumption; her marital status was *not* something Anna wanted to discuss and at this point divorce was not in her vocabulary. She knew of this particular characteristic, 'Greek tact', as Max called it; it's not meant to offend, but nevertheless, it usually did. No matter how many times Anna tried to explain to her husband that nothing was said with malice, somehow or other someone managed to get his back up.

'OK,' Max would often complain, 'I know I put on a bit of weight, but does your uncle really need to draw attention to it?'

'Anyway,' Antonis went on, affably oblivious to Anna's reaction, 'how long are you staying? You must come to my taverna for dinner, you'll be my guest. Tonight!'

'Thank you, I promise I will,' she replied and meant it. 'But tonight I'm with my father.'

And then, to her astonishment, Anna found herself revealing to this over familiar man she'd just met, feelings she would only ever share with her closest friends. She told him about her mother's death, about not having come back to the island for so long and about how her father wanted to make this journey his last.

But she didn't tell him everything. She held back from spilling out to this stranger that she had also come to the island to escape the melancholy and confusion which Max had plunged her into and to put space between them in order to work out what they both wanted from each other and their life.

But then again, maybe she didn't mention any of those things because for the first time in months, during the hour Anna sat in the cafe with Antonis Zevros, those things had actually slipped her mind.

4

'I must tell you who I met today,' Anna said with a mouth full of salad, a few hours later over lunch with her father and aunt. They were sitting at the table under the vine tree, feasting on Ourania's homemade *spanakopita*, which she brought along with crusty bread, a bottle of red wine and a salad of ripe tomatoes and rocket. Her aunt had been turning up every day since their arrival with a cooked meal and produce from her garden that tasted of the sun. It was wonderful to be looked after and Anna could see her father was beginning to find his old self again in his cousin's company.

'I met a man this morning in the square,' she continued, hungrily stuffing a piece of bread in her mouth. 'He used to live in America, his name is Antonis Zevros, do either of you know him?'

'So I hear,' Alexis replied looking over the rim of his wine glass at Anna, 'but no, I don't know him.'

'What do you mean, *so I hear*?' she asked, absolutely astounded that her father could know what she'd been doing or who she'd been talking to that morning while he'd been sitting in his garden at the top of the hill.

'How big do you think this island *is*, Anna?' Alexis replied, glancing over at his cousin.

'Leave me out of this!' Ourania protested, turning round to smile at her niece. 'I don't mind who Anna talks to; don't take any notice of your old dad.'

'I heard it from your Uncle Spiros,' came Alexis's reply, interrupting his cousin. 'He came by for a coffee after you left and told me he saw you when he drove past the square.' Anna looked at her father in disbelief.

'And what exactly did he say he saw?'

'That you were having a drink and talking to a man.'

'And what *exactly* is the problem with that?' she asked, irritated.

'I didn't say there was a problem but you have to be careful here, Anna; people talk.'

Suddenly lunch looked less delicious as memories of teenage squabbling with her father started to surface. Being there alone with his daughter must have sparked off something of the old over-protective father again. For more than two decades Anna had been coming to the island as a married woman, usually with a husband and two children in tow, and therefore there'd been no cause for any local gossip or concerns from her father. Once again she was forced to remember this aspect of small-island living. Now, even if still a married woman, she was there on her own and apparently causing a stir, or so Alexis would have her believe.

'For God's sake, Dad!' Anna said sulkily sitting back in her chair and folding her arms. 'I was only *talking* to the man, not dancing naked with him.'

'Anna! Please,' Alexis replied, wide-eyed. 'There's no need to over-react!'

'Well, really, you are *all* being ridiculous. I'm a grown woman; I can talk to whoever I like and do whatever I want!' Anna's reaction was a surprise to all three. Her father was apparently provoking long-forgotten feelings, making them emerge with unexpected force. How was it possible, she thought, that at her age her dad could make her behave like a hormonal youngster, triggering this utterly childish response? Before coming away Anna had wished to relinquish her matriarchal status and be a child for a while but she had apparently forgotten the inevitable consequences. Once she became aware of what was going on, she regained control, and burst out laughing.

'Sorry, Dad, and don't worry,' she said and reached over to squeeze his hand in an apology, reverting back from fifteen to fifty-three again. 'I know what I'm doing, I'm grown up now, I won't embarrass you or the family, I promise.'

Promises, even if full of good intentions, are often made to be broken. But breaking the promise Anna made to her father that day, was *never* her intention. However, sometimes unforeseen circumstances prevail and meddle with all the best-laid plans.

Dinner at Antonis Zevros's taverna was not only inevitable, as he wouldn't take no for an answer, but desirable too. The first time Anna accepted his invitation she took cousin Manos along in an attempt to keep to the island's protocol and her father happy. She loved her cousin a lot, and he also liked Antonis Zevros. Manos, seven years Anna's junior, was the family's baby; as a little boy he was adorable and impish, qualities he never lost, along with a sense of humour. Over the years the two cousins had become good friends, and even closer when he came to live with Anna's family in London as a university student. He was now engaged to a girl from Crete and about to go and live there, much to his mother's distress.

'She'd still have me in my school uniform if she could,' Manos said when he first told Anna about his plans. 'She's beside herself that I'm leaving the island. I keep telling her, "It's a boat-journey away, Mother," but she keeps crying. What can I do?'

Thia Asimina, Manos's mother, whose name translates as *the one made of silver*, was Thia Ourania's younger sister and another one of Alexis's many relatives. On some of the Aegean islands it's customary to give girls names with elaborate meanings. Anna always found it amusing that the island was full of unsuitably named women, like *the beauteous one*, when clearly she was not, or *the fair-haired one*, who had dark hair. However, in this case Anna's two aunties were both aptly named, and if you didn't know they were sisters you'd never have guessed. Whereas Ourania was heaven-sent, a gentle soul with a kind disposition, never quick to judge or gossip, her sister was the opposite. Fetching and carrying was her favourite pastime, she had a tongue as sharp as a broken seashell, and a cold hard edge like the silver she was named after. She considered all children an irritation apart from her precious only son, whom she had had at an advanced age, having almost given up hope of ever becoming a mother. The rest of the family she considered unworthy of her, her husband included; Alexis was the only exception because he lived in England. Luckily for him, Manos had inherited his Aunt Ourania's good nature and his Uncle Alexis's looks. It wasn't surprising then that he had found a wife from another island and was eager to move.

Going with Manos to the Black Turtle, Antonis's taverna, soon became a regular habit for the two cousins, along with a few other things. By day they would go swimming, hire bikes or go hiking, and by night, stay up very late, usually in the Black Turtle, recapturing something of their lost youth. During her first few weeks on the island, Manos took time off to be with Anna and they had more fun than either of them had had in years, while being all too aware that many things were about to change for both of them. Manos would be leaving for Crete at the end of the summer to embark on a new chapter in his life, and Anna . . . well, she had *no* idea what she was going to be doing. She hadn't spoken to Max since she arrived; they had agreed that what they both needed was time to think and reassess. They had also decided that until they knew how things would go they would not bring the children into their mess.

Apart from making sure his dad didn't overdo the running, Alex was getting on with his life and seemed to be oblivious to any tensions between his parents, but Chloe was acutely aware that things were not as they should be.

'What's going on with you and Dad, Mum?' she had asked, giving her mother one of her looks while they were shopping together for her trip to America.

'Oh sweetheart, it's nothing,' Anna had lied. 'It's a bit of a rough patch. Your dad is still trying to adjust to his health issues.'

'It's been long enough, Mum,' Chloe replied, feeling irritated yet fearful. Too many of her friends' parents had separated and that was one option she had never contemplated for them.

'It'll all be fine,' Anna carried on and changed the subject. 'Now, let's go and get a cup of coffee!'

Once on the island Anna made up her mind that what

she needed was to stop thinking altogether. For at least a while she needed to forget her life, forget Max and his madness and rebuild her emotional strength. Of course it was easier said than done. There were many days when the island's energy and the wine which she drank in quantities acted as a *nepenthe*, chasing away her sorrow and making her forget, but there were also days where it was impossible. Would this life crisis that Max had singlehandedly caused result in her family dismantling? She couldn't bear to think about it. Her family had been her central fusion, her axis. When awake she often managed to banish those thoughts and focus on herself but she was not so successful in her dreams. She would often wake up crying having dreamt of her children and her mother; Max was absent from those dreams.

The Black Turtle buzzed with life, energy and noise. Most nights a couple of men sat in the corner singing, one of them playing a bouzouki and the other a guitar, while people ate, drank, and at regular intervals got up to dance. Although the tables and chairs in the little courtyard were a cooler option, they were colonized by the English and German tourists, and the cousins preferred to stay in the smoke-filled room, with its ceiling fans, music and dancing.

Alexis was now resigned to his daughter's friendship with Antonis Zevros, since cousin Manos vouched for his respectability and acted as her chaperone. Anna knew that her Thia Ourania had much to do with his change of attitude and was grateful to her. She managed to get him to relax a little about her social interactions, much like her mother used to do when she was young. Anna knew that her mother's absence from her father's life had taken its toll and she was glad to see him being fussed over once again. Like Manos and Anna, Alexis and his cousin were now spending most of their time together; they too had a lot of catching up to do. Ourania's love was doing them both the world of good.

In a weird sort of way Anna had reverted to some kind of past life, a state of mind that disengaged from the London fifty-something-year-old-mother-of-two, rejected-wife-of-Max, who is going-through-a-mid-life-crisis, and stepped back into the much-needed, young overprotected girl-of-long-ago, daughter-of-Alexis, on-holiday-with-her-dad. On the island with her father and auntie, Anna started to feel loved again, cocooned and entirely separated from her other life. London and Max seemed a distant galaxy away.

However, as much as she tried to avoid it, thoughts of her husband filled Anna with anger, disappointment and sadness, but thoughts of her children, Chloe and Alex, filled her with longing, which inevitably led to thoughts of her mother. So many things around the place linked Anna to her, and them: old toys, books, clothes and a million photographs. When her mother was alive

47

she was a keen photographer. She loved to be photographed with her grandchildren and Anna would snap at anything – documenting and capturing moments now gone forever. After her mother died, the camera lay untouched. The hardest thing for Anna to accept when she was gone was that she would never be able to ask her the questions only *she* had the answers to, or hear her voice again. Anna would close her eyes sometimes and try hard, but could just about hold on to the sound of her laughter. With her loss, a part of her, a chunk of Anna's history, of her essence, had vanished with her mother too, forever.

'Come with me on my boat, Anna,' Antonis whispered one evening while the bouzouki played an old melody and they drank ice-cold ouzo. 'Just you and me and the moon,' he breathed into her ear, pulling her closer in the noisy restaurant. 'It will be full in a few days. You haven't lived till you see the full moon from the sea.' The hairs on his arm brushed the back of her neck and the strong grip of his hand on her shoulder gave her goosebumps. Anna inhaled his scent. He smelled of cinnamon and mastic, a heady exotic blend that triggered in her memory-bank something distant and delicious.

'Yes . . .' she heard herself say, and couldn't believe that she said it.

If her father's attitude towards her since they had arrived on the island made Anna involuntarily revert to being fifteen again, then her friendship with Antonis was doing something similar. Whereas her father made her behave like a sulky teenager at times, Antonis made Anna's heart beat faster, caused her to blush whenever she saw him and start to regain her self-confidence. When she left London she was bruised and emotionally battered. Antonis's attentions were going a long way to helping heal the shock and rejection she'd brought with her. Max's mid-life crisis, his declaration of love for another woman and doubts about their marriage, even if feeble and hesitant, had shocked her and hurt her deeply. Whenever she thought of him now she flared up with anger.

Manos and Anna were sitting in the square drinking their morning coffee when they saw Antonis walking cheerfully towards them.

'*Kalimera*, my friends!' he shouted across the tables. 'It was a beautiful night last night.' He stood over Anna and bent down to kiss her cheek. 'Our full moon will be here soon,' he carried on, flashing her a smile. 'Don't forget, Anna!'

'Every night is a beautiful night here,' she replied feeling flustered.

'Anna wants to go shopping,' Manos interrupted.

'What sort of shopping does she want to do?' Antonis asked, looking at Anna.

'I want to buy some art materials,' she said and picked up her coffee. 'Do you know any shops around here that might sell them?'

In her few weeks on the island, its perfect light and colours, the house, the garden and the beach had all inspired Anna to start drawing again. She hadn't picked up a crayon or a pencil in months. Illustrating was how she made her living but she never considered it as *work*, it was her passion. She was never happier than when she had a sketch pad in her hand but in the months that followed Max's confession, Anna had lost all desire for it.

From a very young age she'd dreamt of becoming a children's book illustrator. After leaving art school and marrying Max she even wrote some stories which she took along with her illustrations to publishers. The verdict was unanimous; Anna had to accept that she was a much better artist than writer so she gave up the writing and began a career as a freelance illustrator. She did well, working regularly for most of the women's magazines and for quite a few children's book publishers. She kept busy all through pregnancies, babies, family, and when the children went to school she got even busier. It suited her. She loved being at home but she often got the feeling that Max was a little envious of her 'easy' existence. He never went as far as to tell her, but she felt it. She wondered if he wished she was more academic, more like him.

He was a professor in Electrical Engineering; an academic, a brain. He travelled a great deal for his work but that didn't bother Anna, there was always great excitement when he returned. She admired and respected him, was always proud of his achievements even if what he did was beyond her comprehension; Max's grasp of art wasn't huge either, but it didn't matter.

'The artist and the scientist,' he would joke, giving her a kiss. 'We couldn't be more different. I'm methodical and analytical and you are disorganized and emotional!' Anna liked their differences; she thought it made their life more interesting.

'I don't know about a shop, but Nicos Varnavas would be the best person to ask about art,' Antonis replied, looking at Manos. 'What do you think, my friend?'

'That's true.' Manos nodded in agreement. 'Nicos! *He* should know.'

Apparently – they both took turns to explain to Anna – Nicos Varnavas was an artist who had recently moved back to the island from Athens and was now living and working in the nearby village of Elia.

The idea of a fellow Greek artist living on the island

appealed to Anna and she was curious to meet him, so when the two men offered to take her up there by car the next day, she was more than happy to accept. The village of Elia was very small, just a cluster of houses really, way up in the hills surrounded by orchards, vineyards, tamarisk trees and pines. The drive was a delight and once again Anna was transported back to her childhood, as so many things had the power to do on this island. The village was cool and fragrant, especially when the lemon and orange trees were in blossom and perfect for a respite from the heat below. As children during their summers on the island they would all gather, her brothers and cousins, just after sunrise and hike up to spend the day there. The climb by foot used to take them all morning; the car journey in Antonis's Mercedes took less than fifteen minutes.

Anna had suggested that they telephone prior to turning up, but was told that Nicos Varnavas had no telephone line in his house nor even a mobile.

'He's a bit of a hermit,' Antonis said when she expressed surprise at this. 'He just sits up there by himself and paints all day long.'

'According to village gossip,' Manos laughed, 'he lost his heart to a Viennese trapeze artist, but according to my mother, it was his *money* and his *mind* that he lost and that's why he's run away to hide in the hills. If you ask me, it's people like my mother that he is running away from.'

Nicos Varnavas's house was nothing like she imagined; built on the side of a hill, surrounded by trees and shrubs, it was less of a house and more of a studio-cum-workshop. Anna had expected to see a small low-rise whitewashed typical island house hiding away from view with a shed, at most, serving as a studio. Instead, the building they saw or rather build-ings, as it was in two parts, were clearly visible from the road and not at all hidden away. The first building, a simple rectangular structure painted a warm shade of terracotta, was connected by a stone path to another, circular structure, a shade lighter than the first building with sweeping curved walls and a sculptural chimney which created a wonderful shape against the Grecian sky. The whole edifice looked unexpected and as improbable on that plot of land as a UFO. It was no wonder the islanders considered the man who lived in it as something of a mystery and had spun all kinds of stories around him.

'Let's go and find him,' Antonis said, slamming the car door shut and turning towards the building.

'He's got to be around here somewhere,' Manos called out and beckoned her to follow. Walking through a big metal door they entered an open-plan space. Judging by its contents it was obviously Nicos's workplace. Masses of light poured in from a huge skylight and canvases of all sizes were either hanging or leaning against walls. Every surface seemed to be covered with tubes of paint, brushes, bottles and jars. An exciting colourful chaos prevailed. Apart from the room's visual treat, Anna was intoxicated by the familiar smell of paint and turpentine which filled the air.

'He's over there,' they heard Antonis shout from the back of the studio. 'He's feeding his chickens.' To Anna's further surprise she was soon to discover that Nicos Varnavas was not just a prolific artist but something of a farmer too, who apart from growing his own vegetables and fruit, kept hens, rabbits, bees and a goat. Eager to meet him, Anna followed the others who were making their way noisily towards him but instead of the customary friendly open-arm local welcome she was used to, their host, who had his back turned to them, nonchalantly carried on with his work, ignoring their calls. Feeling as welcomed as a fox in a chicken coop the thought occurred to Anna that perhaps this particular Greek was not so thrilled at being invaded by a bunch of unwanted visitors. Thankfully and luckily, as it turned out, Nicos Varnavas was far from rude and antisocial. What transpired was that although he didn't own a telephone or a TV, Nicos *did* own an MP3 player to which he was well and truly plugged in at the time of their arrival. Once he actually saw everyone he was as warm and hospitable as any other local and very pleased and willing to help Anna with her quest.

Over coffee, ice-cold water, home-grown grapes and figs, which Nicos served under the shade of a lemon tree, Anna was able, after their initial tricky start, to observe him and try and get a handle on this unexpected Greek.

He had a quiet, easy way of talking, which was in total contrast to Antonis's boisterous manner, or Manos's gregarious personality. He emanated calm. When asked a question he took time to consider his answer and held you with his eyes as if measuring the response. In fact, Nicos's eyes were the first thing Anna noticed about him; his gaze was intense, his eyes deep set and so brown they were almost black. He was around the same age as Manos and looked every bit the bohemian artist; he probably hadn't changed his style since art school. He had a lean body, dressed in paint-splattered loose-fitting khaki trousers and T-shirt and his height was on the short side – he wasn't quite as tall as Manos and was a lot shorter than Antonis. Anna noted that if she had been wearing heels she was sure she'd tower over him. Tanned of course, his skin, the colour of warm caramel, was also unlike Antonis's, which was fiercely dark and sun-baked. He wore a red bandana, probably in order to keep his mass of raven-black hair in place while he worked, giving him a Native American look.

Greek men *like* their long hair, Anna thought with amusement, looking at both Antonis and Manos, who by English standards had more than average length too. Most of her male friends in London either had cropped hair or had shaved it off on account of going bald, but here were three men who weren't in the first bloom of youth with long tresses, even if, as in Manos's case it had started to thin on top. Nicos had slim elegant hands and long fingers, which, as he delicately rolled a ciga-rette, Anna pictured playing the piano or strumming a guitar rather than mixing paints or feeding animals. He was, she mused, very *sympathitikos*, as the Greeks say, very likeable, this fellow artist, who lived on his own with his animals, his art and his broken heart. The four of them stayed chatting for the longest time, eating juicy grapes, drinking thick sweet Turkish coffee and smoking endless cigarettes. Smoking is like a national sport on this island, thought Anna. You'd never have believed it was the ancient Greeks who lived by the rule of *pan metron ariston*, everything in moderation. These modern Greeks seemed to live by another rule altogether; *everything in excess!* She hadn't smoked for ten years, yet being with these guys she found it hard to resist.

'Have you been working since you've arrived on the

island, Anna?' asked Nicos at some point, in pretty good but heavily accented English.

'Anna speaks perfect Greek, you know, Nicos,' Manos informed him proudly. 'She might live in London but her heart belongs here.'

'I don't doubt it,' Nicos replied, this time in Greek. 'I'm sorry, Anna, do you mind? It's not often I get the chance to speak English here.'

'Of course not,' she said amused that yet another person wanted to try their English on her when all *she* wanted to do was practise her Greek.

'If I had actually *brought* any material with me, I could do it anywhere,' she obliged, this time in English, embarrassed to confess to her total work inertia of late. 'But sadly, so far since I arrived here,' Anna continued, darting a quick look at Antonis and Manos, 'I have done nothing but enjoy myself.'

'Not sadly!' Antonis rushed to add. 'Enjoying yourself is a happily thing, Anna!'

'True, true,' Nicos replied, smiling and shaking his head in agreement.

'The problem is that my work always gave me a lot of enjoyment,' she replied, putting her cup of coffee down on a chair provided for the purpose. 'What makes me sad is that lately I've lost it.'

'But why, Anna?' Manos said, looking alarmed. 'Where's it gone?'

'It happens sometimes.' Nicos smiled again, giving Anna a knowing look. 'You will get it back again, don't worry. It happens to me often and when it does I stop and spend time with my animals and my plants, or I go to the sea, to swim or fish, and when I start again, it's even better. So, Anna, are you ready to start again?'

'I am,' she said and for the first time in months she knew it to be true.

5

For the next few days all Anna could think of was getting on with some work; her meeting with Nicos had fired her up and she couldn't wait to get started.

In a matter of a few weeks on the island she had begun to feel more hopeful, more or less in control of herself again. Her marriage was definitely in crisis and only time would tell how life was going to progress, but she was feeling less anxious about it galloping towards a dark unknown. Gradually Anna started to live for the moment and not for what *might* happen.

Antonis's attention had catapulted her back to the hot island summers of her youth. A little adolescent flirting was doing her the world of good, but she decided it had to stay there. Accepting an invitation for a moonlit boat ride alone with him was out of the question; she feared it could lead to where she wasn't prepared to go.

Once Anna started working, her friendship with Nicos began to flourish too and he'd regularly come down to the village to have a coffee with the three friends. The first time he did that, the whole village seemed to pass by the cafe in the square to take a good look at him. According to rumour it was the first time anyone had actually seen him close-up and his presence caused an even bigger stir than Anna's arrival on the island. In his nonchalant way Nicos took it all in his stride, pretending he hadn't noticed.

'Do you blame the man for wanting to live alone in the hills?' Manos laughed, giving Nicos a friendly slap on the back as they all watched in amusement the stream of locals parading, as if by chance, in front of the cafe to look at the legendary hermit. 'They're a bunch of small-minded peasants, that's what I say,' Manos complained. 'Why do you think I'm leaving? Everyone knows everyone's business around here and worst of all they're mean about it.'

'If you want to live in paradise you have to put up with a few snakes,' Nicos replied with a little smile. 'It really doesn't bother me, Manos. I live my life according to my rules. I pick and choose who I want to spend time with. Do you think the big city is any better?'

'Chicago was full of snakes but it was *no* paradise,' Antonis added with a big sigh, leaning back on one of the several chairs he had accumulated around him.

'And what about London, Anna?' Nicos asked, turning round to look at her. 'How is living there?'

Living in London? The question startled her. Apart

from her children, her *life* in London was something she had finally managed to stop thinking about.

'Why don't you come up to Elia sometimes with your sketch pad, Anna?' Nicos asked one day when they were all having an early evening drink in the square. 'It's very peaceful there.'

Anna had started work on a botanical theme and had spent her first week in the garden with her father and Thia Ourania, evoking childhood memories of sitting in that same spot, with colour pencils and paper, her mother by her side. She'd been so busy with Manos and her new friends that she was hardly ever there, so Alexis too was delighted to have his daughter to himself, even for a little while.

'Your mother loved to see you work, Anna,' he told her the first day she laid out her crayons on the table under the *klimataria*. 'You know she kept all your drawings since you were quite small.'

'I know, Papa,' Anna replied, her head filled with sweet recollections.

'I think you might find the olive groves and fields around the house interesting,' Nicos continued. 'Maybe the flora and fauna is sparse this time of year, but don't forget, Anna, I have a little menagerie in my back yard!'

It was an unexpected offer since Anna knew how

much Nicos valued his privacy. His proposal was touching and flattering, yet, instead of eagerly accepting, she was hesitant. Her father's inevitable disapproval was one reason for dampening her excitement, but then she realized there was also something else. The distance from Anna's house to Elia was quite impossible to make on foot with her art equipment, especially in the summer heat, and she was all too aware that Manos or Antonis would offer to take her there by car. She'd had enough of being chaperoned and, besides, if she was going to work and be serious about it, having Manos, Antonis, or anyone else around wouldn't do. She had to find another solution, a way of getting up to the studio on her own.

Finally, after much consideration, and to no one's approval, Anna came up with the answer. She hired herself a little scooter. Everybody, including the baker and his wife and even old Costis the shepherd, was against the idea, insisting that it was a sure way to get herself killed. As always, the only person on Anna's side was her Thia Ourania.

'If you managed to drive a car and ride a bicycle in London for all these years, I don't see how going up a few deserted hills is going to get you killed,' she'd said one afternoon when her niece called round to see her.

The two were sitting in her back yard under a lemon tree laden with fruit soon to be ready for picking, and drinking her ice-cold lemonade made from last year's crop.

'I wish you'd say something to get them off my back,' Anna begged, leaning back into her chair and taking a lung full of lemon-scented air. 'You know you are the only one who can talk some sense into my dad.' It was a rare treat to enjoy some time alone with her favourite aunt in her own home. The loving childhood memories connected with her house were numerous. Ever since Anna and Alexis's arrival she'd been spending most of her time with them up the hill, cooking, cleaning and generally fussing over her cousin. Her back yard, which was almost an extension of the kitchen with its table and chairs under the lemon tree, led into a small orchard which, when Anna and her brothers were small, they used to call the secret garden. A swing made of thick rope that she'd put up for them, and then years later, for Anna's children and others that followed, still hung there frayed and tattered. Two generations of cousins had passed through this woman's home; this woman who bore no children herself yet treated them all as her own.

'I miss their sound, Annoula *mou*, I long to hear their voices and laughter again,' her aunt said, following Anna's gaze towards the orchard. 'Don't the children want to come to the island any more?'

'They do, of course they do.' She was quick to justify

their absence. 'But they're older now, *Thia mou*, they want to be with their friends. Alex has gone to France this summer and Chloe has gone to America. Maybe next year. . . but, you know . . . even if they were here you wouldn't be hearing *children's* voices any more.'

Alex's deep tones had been for a while hardly distinguishable from his father's and Chloe was very much a young woman now. If only she could turn the clock back just a few years. To be sitting under the lemon tree with her aunt and her mother while the children played around them, happy shrieks and laughter resonating from the orchard. She had hoped that her children would have joined her for a few days but not only had they decided not to, they'd both gone off on their travels with only the odd email from their various holiday destinations.

Who was it, Anna thought, that told her once that being a mother you had to learn to be forsaken? Perhaps it was her own mother round about the time Anna used to go off without even sending a postcard back home. But then again she doubted it; one thing her mother avoided was the guilt trip on her children, so perhaps she'd read it somewhere. Even if her London life was out of her mind her children were always there and Anna would have loved more contact with them, but she too was not into the business of guilt-tripping them. They would soon be together again and they'd be full of their travel stories as usual.

'I know, Anna, the years pass . . . the children grow . . .' her aunt said with a sigh. 'Look at *you*, my angel. For me it's hard to think of you as this grown woman. You will always be my little Annoula and your children are still babies to me.'

'I guess that's why my dad still treats me like a child.' Anna smiled at the memory of her father's disapproval of a few weeks ago. Ever since that disturbing little scene around the lunch table she had been very discreet about what she'd been doing, and with whom, in fear of another outburst.

Anna had made a decision not to discuss her life crisis with her father in fear of burdening him and altering his opinion of Max. Alexis loved and respected his son-in-law and Anna couldn't bring herself to shatter his view of him. Not just yet anyway. Besides, she didn't know what she'd say to him or how she felt. They hadn't talked of divorce or even separation. She was hoping that the time apart which they'd given themselves would bring clarity to both their minds.

She wished she could have confided in her aunt, but Ourania too, like Alexis, considered Max an exemplary husband and held him in great esteem.

'I've never had a husband myself, Anna *mou*, but from what I know of them your Max puts them all to shame.'

Anna's idea of marriage, a blueprint she aspired to based on her own parents' union, was one of love, loyalty and dependability. She knew that her father had met her mother in Italy during the war when Alexis was stationed there with the British army and that they had fallen passionately in love and that her mother's family fiercely disapproved of the match. Once the war was over the lovers had no option but to elope in order to marry. Anna had mythologized her parents' love story all her life; it was impossibly romantic and as magical as any Hollywood movie.

'I'm very happy you and Alexis decided to come back, Anna *mou*.' Ourania reached across and took her niece's hand. 'The island is not the same without him, you know. I think even the trees miss him.' Anna knew that her aunt loved both of her parents, Alexis especially, who was like the brother she never had.

'We all miss your mama, Anna *mou*,' she carried on. 'Rosaria was a good woman. It must be lonely for Alexis in London without her. I'm glad he's returned home.'

Home, Anna mused. She'd often wondered about the idea of home. Did her father consider the island *his* home even though he'd lived away from it three times longer than he had actually lived on it?

'Do you think Alexis considers the island more his home than London?' she asked her aunt.

'I feel yes,' she replied, looking thoughtful. 'I think the place you were born and spent your early years is where you truly belong.'

So, Anna wondered, is *that* what constitutes home; where your roots have been laid from birth? Maybe for some it is, but for others it might also be possible to pull those roots up and replant them somewhere else. Her mother seemed to have done just that. She started her life in Italy but was able to happily transplant her roots where her husband took her. Unlike Alexis, Rosaria apparently never yearned to return to *her* birthplace.

In Anna's case, even though she was born in London and loved it, she decided that this island was as much of a home too; she always missed it when she wasn't there, longed for it, dreamt about it. So, she pondered again, can there be more than one place we call home? Perhaps, she thought, through the journey of our lives we acquire many homes and maybe we *don't* have to make a choice. Anna liked that idea a lot. The way she was feeling, she found it very liberating and comforting.

'It's possible that we can choose where that place we call home is,' she said, thinking out loud. 'My mother obviously did.'

'Perhaps, Annoula *mou*,' her aunt said, reaching across the table to take her hand again, '*home* doesn't always have to be a place. For example, for Rosaria I think home was where your father was because her own home had been a difficult and hard place for her. So you see? Maybe sometimes what we call *home* can mean different things.'

'I know very little about Mama's home, *Thia*,' Anna

said, hoping her aunt might fill some gaps for her. 'She never talked about it and I stopped asking. I think the fall-out with her family was too painful for her.'

'I believe so, Anna *mou*,' Ourania replied. 'Maybe in time Alexis might tell you more. But Rosaria never talked about it, not to me, not to anyone and I never pried. Your father told me some things but he is the only one who *really* knows what happened.'

'And for you, *Thia*? Where is home for you?' Anna asked, knowing perfectly well that she'd never lived anywhere else apart from this island.

'My home has always been here, Anna *mou*. I never left it for long; I chose to stay. There was no option.'

Anna thought that her mother on the other hand had been given an option for a new life, by her father, who came to her rescue at a time when the future in her country was hopelessly bleak. Italy at the end of the Second World War was a place of appalling devastation so perhaps it was easier to turn her back on it and follow the man she loved.

'And what about you, Annoula *mou*? Is London *your* home? Is that where *you* feel you belong?' her aunt asked, searching her face for an answer as if she'd guessed what was troubling her niece.

'I don't know, Auntie,' Anna replied, feeling her throat tightening. If what her aunt had said was true then her family was what had always constituted 'home' for her but now, with the insanity her husband had plunged her into, she felt vulnerable and doubtful and in danger of losing her stability, her home. 'Right now,' Anna carried on, 'London feels a very long way away.' Not wanting to alarm her aunt but feeling she wanted to unburden a little, she continued. 'At this moment, this, here, the island, is what feels like home to me. You, Papa, Manos, the house, my new friends all feel very much like home. It brings me closer to my mother too. I sense her presence much more strongly here than in London. London right now doesn't feel like it belongs to me.'

'I know I'm no substitute for your mother, Anna *mou*. But you are like my own. And remember that whatever it is you are feeling right now, whatever sorrow you have, it will pass; it always does.'

6

As it turned out, work was just what Anna needed. It infused her with energy and her creative juices began to flow again. Her day would start with an early morning swim in the bay, then breakfast with Alexis under the vine before jumping on her scooter to ride to Elia and work till late afternoon. Nicos would work in the studio and tend to his animals and land while Anna combed the surrounding countryside with her sketch pad in search of inspiration and shade. Every day the two would stop and have lunch together amongst the olive trees and inspect each other's work, which could not have been more different. His was bold and abstract, broad expansive brushstrokes exploding with colour on giant canvases, while Anna's sketches were delicate and organic in pastel crayons and pencils. In the evenings Anna would meet Manos and Antonis at the Black Turtle and gradually Nicos started to join them too.

Her new routine meant that she hardly spent time with her father any more, but he was far from lonely. Apart from Ourania, who was with him most of the time, there were all the other friends and relatives. Father and daughter were both happy; Alexis was spending quality time with the people he loved, which was what he had come to the island for, and Anna's healing process was well on its way.

They'd all been drinking in the taverna for hours, a whole lot of them. The usual crowd, plus a couple of friends of Manos, called Rita and Giorgos, and some people visiting from Athens. Nicos was in the middle of an animated conversation about politics with a man sitting at the next table when the musicians began to play a particularly poignant melody, an old tune, a kind of Greek blues, guaranteed to stir the blood and move the soul. As soon as he heard it, he stopped talking, stood up, walked to the middle of the little dance floor and began to dance all by himself, oblivious to anyone around him. He danced a *zeimbekiko*, the 'lone lament', as the Greeks call it, which every man worth his salt and manhood had to get up and dance at some point in the course of an evening when the night wore on and the alcohol flooded the brain. Over the weeks that Anna had been on the island she'd seen them all do this dance in their own particular way, but she'd never seen Nicos take to the dance floor before.

The *zeimbekiko* is not a dance to be taken lightly. It's serious stuff, it's a man's dance. The urge to dance is apparently not something you can suppress. It takes you suddenly, it leaps from the heart to the feet and propels you onto the floor almost beyond your control. Everyone has their own way of dancing and no two people move the same, because it's not a dance that you *learn*; it's a dance that you *feel*. Through the steps and moves, which are mainly improvised, you express your feelings, usually unrequited love, grief, sorrow and pain, depending on your state of mind when the urge takes you.

Anna sat in the smoke-filled taverna, watching Nicos dance for the first time. He was graceful, almost balletic in his movements, lost in the complicated rhythm of the dance. Arms outstretched, head bowed to the ground, he moved with fluid agility, in a sort of less harsh, less rigid form of Spanish flamenco. His movements were unlike others she'd seen; he displayed none of the usual macho bravado, peacock-like stances and proud acrobatics that boasted raw manhood. Yet he looked as strong and masculine as any of them. As Anna looked on she got a glimpse of Nicos that she never expected. She'd thought of him as cerebral and reserved, not earthy or sensual, but what surprised her most about his dancing was to see him dance at all.

He wasn't showing off to anyone, he wasn't dancing for an audience. He was dancing for himself, which in fact is the whole essence of the *zeimbekiko* – you dance away your pain, you exorcize your demons. He danced as it was meant to be – with a kind of introspection and modesty.

Nicos continued to rise and fall like a tidal wave to the soulful sound of the bouzouki, a song that talked of love and heartache. Anna was transfixed. She watched and wondered what pain and sorrow *he* might be exorcizing. Was it that of the frustrated artist, or perhaps the lost love of a Viennese show girl?

Éros
(ἔρως érōs)

is 'physical' passionate love, with sensual desire
and longing. Romantic, pure emotion without the
balance of logic. 'Love at first sight'. The modern
Greek word *'érotas'* means 'intimate love'.

7

That night as Anna lay in her bed, images of Nicos on the dance floor flickered through her mind. The night heat that came through the open window fuelled her imagination and filled her with confusion. She hadn't felt like that in years; she burned up with an intensity she recognized as sexual longing. For the most part of the twenty-five years with Max he had been the object of her desire, the one she yearned for. This was new to her. Through the open window she watched the August moon, with its thousand and one erotic promises swelling its way towards full. It hovered over the scented night, bathing the world in its glow. This time it was not an innocent flirtatious fancy she was gripped by, no child's play like she'd had with Antonis. This was a raw sexual yearning which consumed her body like a flame for a man who, until a few hours ago, she'd considered just a friend but whom now Anna apparently desired more than anything else. Flooded with erotic anticipation, and an intense sense of apprehension at what this full moon might bring, she stayed wide awake, unable to sleep and hoping that by morning her irrational feelings would have passed.

By five o'clock, as the first sun rays eased their way through the wooden shutters into the room and onto her bed, she gave up trying to sleep, got up and sneaked out of the house towards the beach. Still in its infancy, the sun covered everything it touched with a rosy blush, and only the faint chill in the air betrayed that this was dawn and not dusk.

This time, instead of diving from the rocks into the clear blue as she always did, Anna walked into the sea slowly, immersing her body in the cool water in an attempt to soothe her lust-induced fever. After a long swim she climbed up on the rocks and stretched out on the smooth surface. Surrendering her limbs to the sun, eyes tightly closed, Anna imagined it was Nicos who caressed her with his burning touch. The cool waters of the early morning sea had done nothing to diminish the path her brain and body had taken. Her skin tingled as the sun, now higher in the sky, banished her chilly start. She couldn't tell how long she had lain there drifting in and out of a delicious trance when she was startled out of it by a familiar voice. For a moment, before Anna opened her eyes, she thought she was dreaming, then, squinting against the bright light, she saw Nicos standing over her dripping seawater in a puddle round his feet.

'*Kalimera*, Anna,' he said softly as he sat down on the rock next to her. 'Isn't this a little early for you?'

'Nico!' she said with a start, sitting up in a fluster, trying to rearrange her bikini. 'Where did *you* spring from?'

'I was already in the sea when you came in,' he replied, shaking his hair like a puppy-dog, releasing a myriad of water droplets which landed on her like tiny jewels.

'Did you want to catch the sunrise, or couldn't you sleep either?' he asked as he stretched his body on the smooth rock beside her.

'Couldn't sleep,' Anna whispered, flushing with embarrassment at the memory of her earlier thoughts. 'What about you?' she carried on for something to say. 'When did you come here?'

'I didn't go home after we left the taverna last night. I love the beach at dawn,' he said and then fell silent.

For the longest time they both lay on the rock side by side without saying a word. The seagulls and the crashing waves were the only sounds. The heat rising from Nicos's body made her head swirl. He was so close she thought that if she touched him she would burn her fingers, which, at that moment, she longed to do more than anything else. Instead she lay perfectly still, barely breathing.

*

Anna felt embarrassed and foolish. Nicos had been nothing but a friend ever since they met and she had no reason to think he saw her in any other way. Shifting slightly away from him she tried to regain control.

'We underestimate the power of sex, Anna,' an old friend had said to her once in the midst of a heated discussion about a Greek politician who was involved in an inappropriate sexual relationship.

'We are rational beings, we have control,' she protested, but the friend shook his head in disagreement. 'There are some things that are beyond control, Anna.'

She knew about the power of *Éros* and its consequences; although she'd married Max pretty young, Anna had had a small share of it, but this was the first time it had hit her so unexpectedly. It was like the thunderbolt. It seems that when you have been targeted by Aphrodite's baby boy you are done for, even if it's only for a while. At that moment, lying next to Nicos with a sting in her heart, she wanted to keep Cupid's little arrow lodged there forever. *I'm such an idiot, an old fool*, she kept thinking; *burning up with desire at my age and for a man who is oblivious, and what's more in love with someone else.* She desperately wanted to say something funny, something flippant to break the spell. Unable to move she continued to lie there with her eyes tightly shut until instinct made her open them again and she saw Nicos leaning on one elbow, staring at her face. A troubled look clouded his eyes, a frown edged between his brows.

'What is it?' she said, alarmed, springing up to a sitting position. 'What's wrong?'

'Oh. It's nothing . . .' he started, but then stopped.

'What, Nico? What's the matter?' Anna said, surprised to see him reaching out to her. She moved closer and put her hand on his arm, their bodies nearly touching. 'Do you want to talk about it?' she said, encouraging him to open up.

'No, Anna, I don't think it will help.' He ran his fingers through his hair, took a long deep breath and exhaled slowly. He didn't have to tell her. She was quite certain of what was eating Nicos up, and what had provoked last night's 'lone lament' of a dance. She'd heard it often enough from people in the village and, no matter how much Anna *didn't* want to hear about his love for another woman at that point, Nicos was her friend, and if he wanted to confide in her, which apparently he did, she felt duty-bound to listen.

'How long has it been since you last saw her?' she asked, tightening her grip on his arm to let him know she understood. 'Do you miss her terribly?'

Anna had no idea what effect her questions would have on him or what his response would be, but his reaction was definitely not *it*. He simply gave her a look

that could only be described as a cross between astonished, bewildered and amused.

'*Who* is *her*?' he asked, looking quizzical, a smile
starting to play on his lips. 'Who are you talking about,
Anna?'

'Erm . . . I don't know,' she said, confused, embarrassed and lost for words. 'Your Viennese girlfriend?'
she blurted out and wished she'd kept her mouth
shut.

'*What?*' he asked, breaking into a broad smile now,
the deep furrow vanishing. 'Where did you get *that* idea
from, Anna?'

Mortified, like a child who gets the facts wrong and
feels humiliated, Anna flushed with embarrassment.
Apparently what she'd just said had nothing to do with
Nicos's mood, and adding to her discomfort he seemed
to find it rather amusing. *That's what you get for listening
to village gossip*, she scolded herself. The legendary Viennese trapeze artist she thought was most likely a figment
of the overactive imagination of her Auntie Asimina,
who had nothing better to do but weave stories around
people she didn't know.

'Well . . . it's just . . . it's just . . . what they said about
you when we first met.' She stumbled on her words and
wished she could stop talking but realized it was too

late. 'They said you have a broken heart so you live on the hill alone . . . to forget.'

'I see. What exactly did they tell you I was trying to forget?'

'I don't know,' she said, sounding idiotic, feeling even worse, and desperate to put an end to the conversation which Nicos seemed to find entertaining.

'It's funny how people like to fantasize,' he said, laughing, and started to roll a cigarette. 'I suppose I asked for it. Keeping myself so separate from the village was bound to fire up the imagination.' He lit the roll-up and passed it on to Anna before starting to make another one for himself.

'Anyway, she was not Viennese. Ava was German. From Berlin. She danced with the National Ballet of Hamburg and I met her when I went to work there ten years ago.'

Anna could not begin to imagine what her face must have looked like, but going by what Nicos did next she was sure it must have been a picture of confusion and embarrassment.

'Don't look so upset, Anna,' he said. 'Village gossip is not *your* fault.' Then, in an uncharacteristic gesture, he lifted her hand to his lips and gently kissed it. 'This is what living on a rock in the middle of the Aegean is like. Get used to it, *I* have.'

I should have known better, and I should never have

believed their fanciful stories, she thought. If only she'd listened to Manos; he'd warned her it was all village tittle-tattle.

'Anyway, I haven't seen Ava in seven years, that's plenty of time for a broken heart to heal, don't you think?'

Anna didn't dare say anything else for fear of making herself more ridiculous. She held on to his arm, the back of her hand pulsating from his kiss, and just waited to see what else he might tell her.

'So there it is, Anna,' he said at last, stubbing his cigarette out on the rock. 'My heart is not broken and if it aches it is not for Ava.'

A pang of jealousy hit the pit of her stomach with the thought that Nicos's heart was aching for someone. She was feeling conflicted by their conversation. She was more than pleased that Nicos was talking to her, taking her into his confidence after all this time, but on the other hand she had no appetite to learn who he was in love with. She waited a while before responding to his comment, anxious that she should not say the wrong thing again.

'So who is the lucky woman then, Nicos?' she said, bracing herself and trying to sound cheerful.

'Do you really want to know, Anna?' he replied, ignoring her attempt at light-heartedness. The vertical line on his forehead appeared again.

Did Anna *really* want to know? Probably not, she thought; but it was too late. She should never have asked the question if she didn't want to hear the answer.

'If you want to tell me, yes,' she replied reluctantly.

Nicos took a long deep breath and fixed her with a searching look.

'The trouble is, Anna,' he said, almost in a whisper, 'it's not that simple. The problem is . . . it's *you!'*

What Anna had missed more than anything from all the months of physical distance and rejection from Max was to feel cherished again. The sense of that blissful merging into one being that comes with making love; that loss of self, time and place, and the feeling that nothing else mattered. All the time Anna was in Nicos's arms a single word spun around in her head: *surrender!*

At long last, after all this time of feeling unloved, her body was responding and surrendering again to the joys of sensual pleasure, physical contact.

Neither of them could tell how long they had lain in each other's arms on that rock, but going by the sun's position in the sky and the intensity of the heat it must have been a while. Suddenly an overwhelming array of conflicting feelings – pleasure, passion, shame, desire – washed over her, making her feel wretched.

They seemed to hit her like a water-jet, paralysing her with fear. *What did I just do?* her brain screamed. It was one thing, she thought, to engage in a little erotic fantasy and another to be totally consumed by raw, penetrating sexual desire and act on it. Abruptly Anna jumped up, grabbed her things and started to run away from Nicos. She ran and ran and didn't stop until she got to her Thia Ourania's house at the edge of the village.

8

She didn't know what made her go there. Maybe it felt like a sanctuary, a refuge. The safe place of her childhood, the last place where temptation, adultery and carnal desire would reside. She called out for her aunt to let her in, pounding on her door, but there was no answer. *Probably visiting Alexis as usual,* she thought, and walked round to the garden in search of some shade.

Heart thumping, drenched in sweat and gasping for air, she sat under the shelter of the lemon tree to calm herself. She didn't want to go back home, she wanted to go inside her aunt's house and be on her own, something she hadn't done since arriving on the island. Being alone, Anna was reminded, is not a Greek concept and to actually *want* solitude signals a problem. A solitary Greek is a sorry Greek. *Alone* is usually mistaken for *lonely* and to leave someone on their own for too long means to have failed them. But right then, all she wanted was to be away from the usual crowd, she needed her own space. She needed to gather her thoughts.

Anna found her aunt's back door key under a pot of

basil. She always kept it there – in her absence she'd let herself in many times. The door opened straight into her kitchen. Inside it was deliciously cool, dark and soothing, and a tantalizing smell of vanilla and cinnamon hung in the air. *She must have been baking biscuits, Ourania's famous koulourakia, to take to her cousin for his early morning coffee*, she thought, and imagined them both enjoying their breakfast at that very moment. It felt safe and calm in there. Anna's heart gradually started to regulate its beat again. She poured herself a glass of cool water from an earthenware jug her aunt always kept on the kitchen counter; a touching old island habit which she still observed. A white linen cloth – its edges weighted down with tiny beads and shells – lay over the mouth of the jug to keep the dust off.

'I love the earthy taste the water gets when it comes from the jug,' her aunt explained when Anna asked why she didn't keep the water in the fridge. 'It makes me think it came from the old well.'

Sitting at the kitchen table in the cool darkness she started to play back like a film in her head what had happened earlier on the rock with Nicos. Anna could smell him on her skin, her body ached and throbbed from his touch. She breathed in the heady, musky scent, the smell of sex, and her head started to swirl again. She remembered reading once, when she was young, that Marilyn Monroe never washed after sex because she wanted the smell of sex to linger on her skin. Now she understood why. A delicious pain travelled from the pit of her stomach to her gut, making her double over with its force. She could hardly believe what had happened to her. She'd just made passionate unbridled love that engaged all her senses, in the open air for the first time in her life. It was the sort of sex that she hadn't experienced in years and the power of it hit her like a bullet.

Anna poured herself some more water and with glass in hand went in search of her favourite room. It was not only her Thia Ourania's sewing room but also the play-area for two generations of children. Nothing much had changed in almost forty years. It looked just as it always did when Anna was a little girl. Her aunt's old Singer sewing machine was still under the window, at its feet a big basket piled high with a rich variety of embroidered textiles and fabrics. Next to that were the cotton reels and yarns her aunt had neatly arranged in order of colour. At the other end of the room, in a corner, was a big box jammed full of old toys, and above that, four shelves laden with all kinds of books, mainly Greek myths and legends. On those shelves lived nymphs and gorgons, gods, heroes and villains, who came alive year after year, to spellbind, amuse and often terrify the children. Next to the bookshelves stood the big red wooden dressing-up trunk, which dominated the room along with the sewing machine. The trunk was a treasure-trove.

Once opened it would unleash a fantasy world that had no limits to the childish imaginings. Its contents had the power to transform any child into whatever it wanted to be. The moment Anna laid eyes on it, a kind of calm washed over her. For the first time that day she ceased being a woman in crisis and became a time traveller. She sat cross-legged next to the trunk, and with trembling hands opened its lid. A musty smell emanated from it and in an instant she was engulfed by the past. The deeper she dug into the trunk, the deeper the memories. She pulled out dressing-up outfit after outfit, which her aunt had lovingly preserved: the cowboy suit Manos always insisted on wearing, which caused endless fights with the other boys, the clown costume Thia Ourania made for one of Anna's brothers, a beaded waistcoat, leather belts, scarves and hats all came tumbling out. Old lace and silks for the girls, bangles and headdresses and a princess gown, pink and sparkly, which the girls took turns in wearing. Anna inhaled their musty smell, hugged them tight and soaked them with tears; their young voices echoed around the room like ghosts.

The last time Anna was alone in the house with her aunt she told her of how she missed those voices. It was now Anna's turn to feel bereft. In that room surrounded by her past, she wept not only for her lost self, but also for her children's lost childhood. Those innocent little beings that she unconditionally loved and showered with a thousand and one kisses every day of their infancy, had gone forever. They had vanished into the ether to morph into sulky adolescents with grown-up voices. Yet, more than anything, she thought, it was their childish sounds that would always stay with her, and it was their voices that would reverberate in her head forever. Anna remembered her mother telling her once that she believed motherhood was all about loss. 'First terrible loss for a mama,' she'd said in her strong Italian accent, 'comes when the baby leaves your body. But this is the life and we must accept it.'

As the memories raced through her head the tears kept pouring out of her. Anna cried for everything that had been lost. For her aunt's lost youth and life of solitude, for her mother who was lost forever, and her father who was lost without her. Anna cried for Max who was slipping away from her and the love they were now both in danger of losing.

An image of Nicos drowning her in kisses flashed through her mind. How did she ever end up in this situation? She had just committed adultery, which made her no better than Max, so why wasn't she feeling guilty or ashamed of what she had done?

What Anna felt was a huge sadness. In all their time together, being unfaithful to Max had never crossed her mind, she loved him and was perfectly content with her life, but his betrayal had left her bruised and disillusioned and now she too was pulling away. Over the years, she often considered the question of sexual betrayal, a subject of discussion with girlfriends. Her belief was that it didn't necessarily have to destroy a marriage but it was something that could be worked through. So as much as Max's affair pained Anna, she would have liked to be true to herself and forgive him. But it was his declaration of love for the other woman and his doubts about *her* that broke her heart. Could she ever forgive him and could they ever find a path to unite them again or would the distance between them carry on growing for ever?

Finally, sitting in the stillness of her aunt's house, surrounded by the relics of her childhood, Anna stopped crying. There were no more tears to shed, she'd used them all up. She hadn't cried that much, and for that long, since her mother died, and even then she had tried to keep herself in check for the sake of others.

In the course of her emotional voyage she had practically emptied the dressing-up trunk and was now surrounded by its ragbag of contents. Rummaging around to make space for their safe return, Anna's fingers stumbled on a hard object which she quickly pulled out to inspect. A distant memory of a highly coveted jewellery box which her aunt kept on her vanity table made her girlish heart skip with joy. The box was wrapped in a white linen cloth held together with a yellow satin ribbon tied into a neat bow. Although it was old and fraying the ribbon still retained its golden brightness as if betraying the treasure within. With eager hands she undid the bow and started to unwrap the box like a baby in its swaddling clothes. The legendary jewellery box Anna remembered well was made of a black lacquered wood, so shiny you could see your face in it; the box which was now lying naked on her lap was of a reddish brown wood and intricately carved with exotic African scenes. This was altogether a very different box. Disappointed but at the same time curious at what it might contain, she lifted its lid.

To Anna's surprise, instead of a long forgotten childhood treasure, inside the box was a pile of old envelopes held together with the same fraying yellow ribbon as before. It didn't cross her mind, not even for a second, that perhaps she shouldn't be looking in that wooden box, or that it could contain something private belonging to her aunt. Anna simply took it for granted that it held yet more mementos from her past. She lifted the bundle to examine it, assuming that the letters must be the ones she and her brothers used to send as children to their aunt from London. For years their father insisted they write regularly to her in Greek.

'She loves you and wants to know your news from England,' he'd repeat over and over when they protested.

'It doesn't cost *you* anything, but it makes *her* very happy.' He'd struggle patiently with them for hours over these letters, which Anna realized years later was Alexis's attempt to teach his children his language. When she was young she resented the task, but as an adult she never stopped being thankful for his persistence. Once more that day emotion rose up to choke her, and she braced herself for yet another journey into her past.

She started to pull loose the yellow ribbon.

9

There have been many times when Anna was grateful for the hours her father spent trying to teach her his native tongue, but never, *ever*, as much as on that fateful morning in her aunt's house. The words that leapt out at her like flames from those old musty letters had nothing to do with the writings of four young children to their maiden aunt, but everything to do with the scorching passion of a young man for his lover. The wafer-thin paper was yellowing with age, the ink was blue and the writing was the work of a calligrapher. Those were not words scribbled in haste; it was the hand of *Éros* that guided the pen that wrote them. The letters were arranged backwards in chronological order, with apparently one of the earliest to be received on top of the pile.

2 May 1937

My beloved, the letter began,

Every day that passes I miss you more and more.

This is torture, a life sentence. How can I live away from you? I will not survive without your love, your burning kisses. Each night before I sleep I look at the sky. I sit on deck and gaze at the stars and think of you, my love, my life. I imagine you are doing the same and that we are united once more for a moment on a distant galaxy. I love you, my Ourania, you are the sky and the stars. You are my whole world.

I go to sleep with your name on my lips, imagining you are in my arms, in our hideout on the beach. My life is empty without you. I kiss your mouth a thousand times and long to feel your soft skin once more next to mine . . .

As if in a trance, Anna read on. Letter after letter continued in the same desperate passionate tone. Letters mainly of love, loneliness and longing. Brief accounts of life on board a ship, descriptions of distant ports and cities.

Each letter was dated, they spanned over two years, from around 1937 to 1939, and always began with *'My beloved . . .'*

. . . Today our ship docked in Cardiff, which is the capital of Wales in the United Kingdom. After the beauty of the Mediterranean, this city seems so grey

and unfamiliar. Oh my love, how I wish I could show you all the places I have sailed to. Venice is exquisite, by far the most beautiful place I have ever seen. You would not believe your eyes if you saw it. Can you imagine a city that has instead of roads, canals, and instead of cars, boats? People go from one place to the other by what they call a gondola. Italian people are friendly and many of them remind me of our people. The language too seems familiar, and I'm picking it up quite easily; many workers on the boat are Italian.

The buildings look like the palaces in the fairy-tale books you used to read when you were a girl. I bought you a postcard so you can see a picture but we didn't have time to post it so I will keep it and show you when we are together. How I long to hold you in my arms again, Ourania mou. What wouldn't I give to have you in my arms and make love to you till sunrise? The mere thought of you is more intoxicating than the bellyful of wine we are allowed to consume when we dock in some foreign port. But we have to be patient. This time will soon come for us.

There were so many letters in that little bundle. Most of them were well over three or four pages long, and all full of colourful images, love and desire. Lost in the story

Anna wished to devour each and every one. Finally, right at the bottom of the pile, she came across a lone single page with just a few words on it. She held her breath while she read.

Sept. 1939

My beloved,

My heart has been broken in a thousand pieces. I feel bereft and more unhappy than I know how to express. I will pray every day that you might change your mind and still want to come to be with me, but I have to accept your decision. I respect your courage and bravery. You are a wonderful, remarkable girl, Ourania mou, and you will always be my love.

My only regret is that I will not be there to support you and protect you all from this war that has broken out in Europe at this time. My heart trembles for your safety. Please take care, my beloved.

I love you now, and forever . . . till we meet again,

L

The rollercoaster of emotions got the better of Anna and once again her tears returned. She was gripped by a sense of gloomy curiosity. Apart from the date, none of the letters gave any detail as to where they came from or from whom. The language was sensual and lyrical, the love, desire and yearning for Ourania genuine. Who was this passionate young man with the broken heart? Each letter was simply signed off in a beautifully scripted *L.* Who was he and what had become of him? Why had her aunt put such an abrupt stop to the affair? What had happened to all that love and lust she ignited and why did she end it?

The fact that her aunt had at some point in her life been struck by the thunderbolt and had felt that vault of electricity pass through her body pleased Anna and saddened her at the same time. Ourania had apparently been deeply in love, yet had chosen a life of solitude; all that had remained from this love were those letters. How could such strength of feeling vanish? Does time really cure *everything*? Anna's brain was a scramble of questions. The only consolation to this story was that at least the two lovers had been able to spend some time of passion together no matter how brief before parting. For over sixty years her aunt had preserved the memory of her love affair, a memory of fierce longing and sensual pleasure, locked away in a wooden box like a faded photograph or a lock of hair in a silver locket.

Anna was completely engrossed in this story of tenderness, desire and separation. By now her hands were trembling, her throat was dry, yet she was perspiring profusely; her heart pounded so hard she could hear its frantic beat. She knew she had to stop reading but couldn't. She felt like a cheat, or even worse, like a thief, but kept on. Suddenly a sound outside the window made her jump so hard it sent the letters on her lap onto the floor. Anna started scrabbling around in a frantic effort to gather them, and in her haste knocked over the glass of water next to her. Now she was not only drenched in sweat, but water too. What if her aunt had returned? What if she found her sneaking like this, betraying her trust? How could Anna ever look her in the eyes? What would she say to her?

With a superhuman effort, adrenalin working overtime, she managed to put letters in envelopes, tie yellow ribbon, wrap swaddling-cloth, and place the wooden box back into the trunk in minutes. Shaking with nerves and exertion Anna started to clear up the room, preparing to face whoever was outside. She waited, barely breathing, but nobody came; it had probably been a stray dog circling the garden. Finally, shaken, exhausted and emotional, she left the house.

Head swimming, she walked in the blazing heat to collect her scooter, which in her earlier haste she had forgotten at the beach. Anna needed to talk to someone, but who? Manos? Would he know about their aunt's secret? If not what would she say to him? Possibly his mother knew, but if that was the case Anna was sure everyone else would have known by now, including her. Also, knowing her Thia Ourania's relationship with her sister, it was doubtful. Anna thought that her own mother would have been a more likely confidante than her Aunt Asimina. But if her mother had known would she have also told Alexis? Anna couldn't imagine that either; even if her mother knew, she was fearlessly loyal and would never have betrayed Ourania's secret. Full of unanswered questions, Anna found herself heading up to Elia. The only person she wanted to see was Nicos.

She found him at the back of the studio feeding his chickens. This time he wasn't plugged into his music so as soon as Anna called his name he responded.

'Anna *mou*!' he shouted, dropping the enamel bowl full of chicken feed, sending the hens into a pecking frenzy round his feet as he rushed towards her.

'I thought you'd run away from me forever,' he whispered, scooping her up in his arms, and covering her in kisses. Anna could feel the shape of his arm muscles under his shirt, the rough bristle of his chin on her face. Desire started to rise in her again. His lips travelled from her mouth to her throat and, cradling her like a baby, he carried her into the house and onto his bed. Without a word he started to undress her. Sand, salt and sweat still on their skin, they tasted of the sea. His body hard and heavy on top of hers blissfully blocked out any rational thoughts she tried to hold on to. Nothing mattered; she felt that she had no past or future, just the *here* and *now*. Anna shuddered in anticipation and once more the delicious rush of sexual energy ran through her veins. As they rolled around on the softness of the bed, under the white haze of the mosquito net, she gave herself up to pleasure for the second time that day.

'Perhaps he was killed in the war,' Nicos said over the deafening mid-afternoon noise of a million cicadas who'd taken occupancy in the tamarisk tree just outside his bedroom window. This time Anna didn't run away. She stayed willingly and lay languid in Nicos's arms until their breathing returned to normal and their hearts resumed their regular beat. This time she couldn't tear herself away from him; she lay enveloped in the milky blur of the mosquito net, his head resting on her thigh, damp tendrils of his hair spread across her belly.

'That might also explain why she never married,' he said again, caught up in her aunt's story.

'It's so sad, Nico. So much love, so much passion. What happened to it? It's very unclear from the letters,' Anna said, stroking his face, sadness clouding her vision again. 'There was obviously so much love between them yet she renounced her love and ended up living her life alone.'

'I keep telling you, Anna, this is a small island with

a handful of small-minded people; even *now*. Can you imagine how it must have been then?'

'But they were so young and if they were so in love, why couldn't they be together? What made her forsake him? From the last letter I read it was Ourania who stopped the love affair.'

'Perhaps he had to go away before they could marry and since they were so young this would have been frowned upon . . . or he couldn't marry her. What if he was already married to someone else . . . like you, Anna? Don't you see? In that kind of society if they'd been lovers she had no option but to keep it a secret.'

Once, a few years ago, when she spoke with her aunt about love, marriage and children, Anna had assumed she'd been deprived of all three.

'What one has never had, one cannot regret losing, Anna,' she told her niece and as always Anna marvelled at how wise and philosophical her aunt was being. The thought that this wonderful woman had lived a loveless life had troubled her a great deal but now in the light of the new revelations Anna hoped that she had only been alluding to marriage and children and had not missed out on love and passion. It's all very well to say, *what you haven't had you don't miss*, Anna mused, but how can a person feel fulfilled if they have never tasted passion, which is the absolute essence of life?

She ran her fingers through Nicos's hair and started to overflow with joy and gratitude for the passion this man so unexpectedly lavished on her.

'I want to know what happened to them, why they parted,' Anna told Nicos, with a sudden pang in her heart at the thought of separation. Now, like her Thia Ourania all those years ago, she too had a secret lover, and a secret which Anna had to protect.

'If you really want to know what happened to your aunt you might have to ask *her*,' Nicos replied. 'You never know, Anna, she might finally *want* to talk about it. Especially to you.'

10

It was almost dusk by the time Anna got back to the house. The sun had already set the sky on fire and the sound of birds settling for the night surpassed the deafening midday noise of the cicadas. She parked her scooter at the side of the house and breathed in the heavenly scent of jasmine which had started to infuse the early evening air. Anna never ceased to be astonished by how this tiny, delicate, modest white flower can exude such a powerful aroma. She was sure the ancient Egyptians must have modelled their painterly representations of stars on the simple jasmine. Each drawing of a star appears to resemble the shape of a single flower, a whole plant like a constellation. During the day when the sun is high in the sky it's as if he steals the bashful jasmine's thunder so it retreats away, it holds back. But when the sun begins his descent and the sky turns to ink, then the jasmine flower explodes with a scent so beautiful that merely breathing it in is never enough.

The sound of singing and laughter coming from the garden intrigued Anna, and as she walked through the gate she was greeted by a heart-warming sight, a scene of love and friendship. Her father and aunt were sitting round the table under the *klimataria*, a bowl of ripe red grapes freshly picked that morning in the centre, drinking wine from a carafe and singing along to an old melody which was spilling out from the house – a Greek song, but with a Latin refrain, a song from the 1930s and '40s, the popular music of their youth. Anna had heard these tunes, tangos, waltzes and serenades, countless times. Her parents loved them, and over the years she had sought to buy new recordings so they'd have a collection of tapes and CDs instead of their old records.

'Annoula!' her dad shouted, enthusiastically clapping his hands as soon as he saw his daughter. 'Come and dance with me! I've been trying to get your aunt to but she won't.'

'Why not, *Thia*?' Anna asked, glad not to be reprimanded for once for being so late. Dropping her beach bag on a chair she took the hand of her father, who was already up and ready for a dance.

'My knees hurt, that's why,' Ourania laughed, and sat back to watch the two of them waltz around the table. Anna felt like a little a girl again in her father's arms. He had taught her to waltz and tango under this very vine to the sound of these very tunes during their summers on the island and it was here Anna had watched Alexis and Rosaria dancing together, demonstrating intricate moves for her benefit. Fighting back the tears, she held tight onto her dad and wondered how much more emotion she could take in one day.

That night she was quite prepared to lie awake torment-ing herself, like the night before. Instead she fell into a deep continuous sleep. When she came to, the next morn-ing, she was unsure if the events of the previous day had actually taken place or had been an elaborate dream. Did she really do all that yesterday; make love on a rock and then again once more with such abandon? Was that really her? The scent of sex still lingered faintly on her skin. She ran her hands over her body as if to check that her limbs were still the same, still hers, but nothing seemed to betray what had gone on twenty-four hours previously.

Anna got out of bed and stood in front of the full-length mirror on the old wooden wardrobe. After such intensity shouldn't some physical mark have been left on her body? Shouldn't she at least have grown a pair of wings or something? Taking off her nightdress she started to examine herself further. Apart from a few bruises from rolling around on the rock and Nicos's strong embraces, she looked like the same old Anna. She stood looking in the mirror for ages trying to imagine what Nicos saw to like in her. She realized that she'd stopped looking at her body like that years ago. When younger she'd kept a close eye on it, made sure it was in good shape; that was probably because she quite liked what she saw then. Now it was always such a disappointment. What, she wondered, had happened to that lovely young woman that was Anna?

Just because what she saw wasn't to her liking any more she assumed that perhaps no one else would like it either. Max obviously didn't, otherwise why did he do what he did? Suddenly Anna was looking at herself with a new pair of eyes. Admittedly what reflected back was a far cry from the young nubile body of long ago; it may no longer have the lustre and smoothness of youth but it was still her body, still healthy and robust. A body that was still functioning perfectly well and still capable of giving and receiving pleasure; which, apparently, a man younger than herself liked well enough to make passionate love to, even if her husband didn't.

She continued to gaze at her reflection and wondered what Nicos saw in her. She was often told she had good legs and she knew she had a small waist, or at least she had when she was young. Her mother always said that she took after Alexis's side of the family and that she inherited her Thia Ourania's smile, but all she ever saw these days was a tired middle-aged woman.

As she looked in the mirror Anna decided that perhaps all those hormones released while making love might have had *some* positive effect on her, because in the soft morning light, with her deep suntan and minus her glasses, she didn't look *so* terrible. She always maintained that the only possible upside of having to wear reading glasses – yet another reminder of the ageing process – was that when not wearing them the blurring effect made everyone looked so much better. The only consolation to the fact that Nicos didn't need glasses and most likely had twenty-twenty vision was that his eyes were shut all the while they made love. The memory triggered another thought which nearly made her buckle over with laughter: if her teenage self or even her twenty-something self had ever imagined what she'd been doing at her advanced age, they would have both died with embarrassment. She remembered how at that age she dismissed anyone over thirty as past it. Do we *ever* get past it, she wondered; does the body *ever* give up on sex?

Suddenly the loud ringing of the telephone made Anna jump out of her naked skin. It vibrated through the house, shattering the early morning peace and making her feel anxious. The phone hardly ever rang there and if it did, it was always for an emergency. Who could that be? She stood pinned to the floorboards as if paralysed, her heart pounding. It carried on ringing for ages until finally Alexis picked it up. Anna strained to hear what he was saying but it was impossible. His hushed tone filled her with panic. Who could be calling so early in the morning, and why was her father speaking in a whisper? Grabbing her dressing gown she ran into the living room.

'Here she is! She is awake after all!' Alexis said, raising his voice to its normal pitch again. 'Good morning, Anna. It's Max,' and giving her a big smile he handed her the receiver.

At that moment in time, the last person on earth Anna expected, or *wanted*, to hear from was her husband. Before parting they pledged to give each other space, time to think, and they had both kept that promise. This phone call was not part of the plan. So, why was Max calling now? Anna took the receiver with trembling hands.

'Anna!' Max's voice was deep and serious and vibrated down the line. 'How are you? Alexis said you were asleep.'

'Yes, I mean no. How are *you*?' she said, her heart beating furiously. 'Have you heard from Chloe and Alex?' she carried on at a loss as to what else to say.

'No, not a thing, but I'm sure they are fine.' Max continued in the same serious voice. 'Chloe is back from California and she's met up with Alex somewhere in the south of France. They are with Charlie and Emma now, camping.'

Charlie and Emma were the children of Anna and Max's closest friends and the four of them had been inseparable since childhood. Their parents, Pam and Jo, had spent many a summer holiday with them on the island when the children were young. Now the teenagers were happy to leave their parents behind and make their own holiday arrangements. When they had first announced their camping intentions Anna had been anxious.

'How safe will it be with no adults around?' she worried.

'Mum! Get a grip!' Alex teased her. 'How old do you have to be in your opinion to be considered an adult? Chloe is eighteen now, she's practically a pensioner!'

'Chloe sent a couple of emails from San Francisco and Dad had a postcard,' Anna said, amazed at the banality of the conversation. 'They both seem to be having a great time.'

'Yes, well, how are you, Anna?'

'I'm fine, Max,' she replied, trying to sound normal. 'And *you*? How are *you*?'

'I'm OK, yes, OK. I've done a lot of thinking, a *lot* of it. I'd like to come to the island; I'd like to see you, Anna. We need to talk. I've missed you. What do you think, will you see me?'

11

Anna could feel her stomach twisting into a tight ball, making her want to double over with pain. Stress always hit her that way; either she doubled over or felt like throwing up. This time it was both. The phone call from Max unsettled her more than she could ever imagine. Her mind was racing and so was her heart. Anna couldn't remember a time that she hadn't been delighted to hear from her husband or happy to see him. Now, all that came to mind was that this was such bad timing. Max couldn't come now, *not now*, she couldn't face him, she didn't *want* to face him. *She* was the one confused now. There was so much to think about, deal with, work out. Every cell in her body screamed, 'NO MAX, DON'T COME. NOT YET!' She had been on the island for two months and quite a lot of days, but to her it seemed like only a couple of weeks. She needed more time, she still didn't know how she felt about everything and she definitely wasn't ready to make any decisions. But she said nothing; she couldn't.

'Is everything all right, Anna?' Alexis asked after she

put the receiver down. Her face had betrayed her. 'The children? Are they OK?' He asked again in Greek, worry etched on his brow.

'No. I mean yes, everything is OK, Papa, there's no problem, nothing's wrong,' she replied, trying to recover her composure and steady her voice. 'Max said he'd like to come and visit us for a few days, that's all.'

'Oh, but that's wonderful news,' he said with relief.

Had Max sensed that something was up, Anna wondered? She knew all about *a woman's intuition* or *a woman's instinct*, but she had never heard it said of a man. When Max told her of his affair she had been oblivious to it, she didn't sense a thing. Did Max have an intuition about her? Is that what made him pick up the phone? All kinds of slightly paranoid thoughts whizzed through her mind while she hurriedly got dressed, anxious to leave the house before Alexis started chatting and asking questions.

In a state of mild panic Anna made her way down the hill, trying to put her thoughts in order.

The walk was doing her good. She needed to be alone. The morning breeze was beginning to clear her head and calm her nerves. In an attempt to exercise reason she kept telling herself that she was being a touch melodramatic. Max couldn't know or sense anything; he was two thousand miles away. *And what if he did?* She concluded, *he didn't have much of a right to say anything to her anyway!* Max had told her he'd done a lot of thinking, but then so had Anna. Perhaps now it was time to get serious; time to share those thoughts and take charge of the situation.

Halfway down the hill the sound of a car and the blast of its horn made her turn round. Antonis's Mercedes was thundering down the road in a cloud of dust after her, making sure her solitude wasn't going to last long.

'*Yia sou*, Annoula!' he said, leaning out of the window as he pulled up. 'Where have you been? I've been trying to find you. I called Manos and he said he didn't know.'

'I haven't been anywhere,' she replied, looking at him in disbelief. If she wasn't so discombobulated she would have burst out laughing. She'd been out of sight for just over twenty-four hours, and everyone was looking for her? But, as she was constantly reminded, this *was* a very small island.

'Jump in, we'll go to the square for coffee. Have you had breakfast?' he said, reaching for his mobile. 'I'll call Manos to join us.'

Anna felt a pang in her heart. Dear Antonis, she thought, always cheerful, always good-natured and always generous. What a ridiculous situation to be in.

As much as she wanted to be alone she didn't have the heart to refuse him. In years to come, she thought, as she was getting in the car, perhaps she'd look back at all of this and even manage a smile. Right now though, Anna felt she had very little to smile about.

When they arrived at the square Manos was already sitting at their usual table.

'Finally we see you!' he teased, standing up to give his cousin a kiss. 'Where have you been?'

'What is it with you two?' Anna replied, feeling irritated but trying to adopt the same jovial tone as him. 'I've been doing what I've done every day for the past few weeks, *working*! Remember?' she lied.

'It's just that you left the taverna in a hurry the other night and we haven't seen you since.'

'Precisely! It was just the other night, the night before last to be exact. Do I have to account for all my movements to you too? Don't you think I've got enough with my dad on my case?'

'Enough of your arguing, little cousins,' Antonis interrupted, laughing. 'We have more important things to discuss.'

Over coffee and freshly baked *tiropita*, which Anna couldn't eat, her stomach still tied in knots, Antonis informed them excitedly that he was busy arranging a moonlit beach party to take place soon.

'There are only a few days till August's full moon,' he said, giving one of his dazzling smiles, 'and since *you*, Miss Anna, refuse to come on the boat with me we'll do it on the beach and everyone is invited. Remember what I told you about August moon?'

'Of course I remember, how could I forget?' she replied, but hoped that perhaps *he* had.

All Anna could think of after she left the cafe were the words of Stan Laurel: *'Here's another nice mess you've gotten me into.'* Laurel at least had Hardy to blame for all his mishaps, but who did she have? The only person she could blame was herself. What was she thinking of? She'd come to the island to be with her father and sort herself out, not get into a ridiculous mess. How was she going to get out of this? Her husband turning up any day now, presumably to discuss where they were going with their life; Antonis planning romance and celebrations on a moonbeam; and Nicos expecting her in his studio to make passionate love any minute. It was all too much. Where was this all going to end and did she actually *want* any of it? Her brain was a scramble. She'd been so wrapped up with herself for so many weeks she was beginning to lose the plot, whatever the plot was. She'd been furious with Max for behaving like a juvenile and now she was doing the same.

When Anna finally left her friends, who gave her no

alternative but to agree to meet them that evening in the Black Turtle, she discovered that she had walked to her aunt's house again. Her feet just took her there without her even realizing it until she arrived on the doorstep.

This time her aunt was at home, her back door open. Anna followed the gentle hum of the Singer sewing machine and found Ourania busy mending one of Alexis's shirts.

'Hello, Anna,' she said without looking up until she finished the stitch. 'What brings you here this morning? Are you not working today?'

'I'm not sure, *Thia*, I don't think so . . .' Anna's voice trailed off.

'What is wrong, Annoula *mou*?' Ourania said, turning round to look at her niece. 'You look upset. Did something happen? Is Alexis all right?' She started to get up. This time Anna could hear alarm in her voice.

'No, no, he's fine, *Thia*, don't worry, there's nothing wrong with him,' Anna said and realized that she must have given her poor aunt a fright appearing out of nowhere like that.

'Then what *is* wrong, Annoula *mou*?' she asked again and taking both of Anna's hands in hers she gently pulled her towards the window seat. Anna knew she was feeling upset, but she had no idea she also showed it.

'Nothing's wrong, *Thia*, I promise, I just wanted to see you,' she hurriedly replied and then quickly added, 'Max is coming for a few days, he phoned this morning.'

'Well that's good news, isn't it?' Ourania said, looking at her niece with surprise. She held her gaze for a while, searching her face.

'Are you happy he's coming, Anna?' she added, and reached across to stroke the younger woman's cheek. Anna found this gesture, this loving touch, which reminded her of her mother, too much to bear. The emotion made her heart ache and once more, for the second time in that very room, the tears started pouring out of her.

'Do you want to tell me what's the matter, Annoula?' Ourania said softly.

'Oh *Thia mou*, it's nothing. It's just that . . . it's just that I'm so confused,' she said through her tears, like the little girl her aunt had made her feel with that simple gesture of hers.

'I understand if you'd rather not talk; you just have a good cry if that makes you feel better,' she said, stroking her hair.

Anna stayed in her aunt's soothing arms for a long time; neither of them said or did anything. She let her tears flow and her mind gently drift and thought of how this woman had surprised her yet again with her understanding and compassion. Anna had assumed that her aunt would press her to talk, to confide, to try and find a solution to whatever her problem was. That's what her mother would have done. But Ourania, even though Anna considered her as *almost* her mother, was not her. It also occurred to Anna that perhaps only a woman who herself has had a secret to protect would be so understanding, so stoic, so discreet. As her mind drifted, Anna's eyes lingered on the old dressing-up trunk across the room.

Did her Thia Ourania still feel somewhere in her heart that love of long ago and did her lover's letters still make her heart swell with joy when she read them? Why should age, Anna wondered, diminish what her aunt had once, or take away the memory of the young vibrant woman she'd been, so full of passion and sexual desire, capable of inspiring words of love to be written about her?

After what seemed like a long time of contemplation, Ourania got up and went to the kitchen to bring them both some coffee and food. When she returned she set the tray down on the little wooden stool by their feet and while they ate, they started to talk. They talked for as long as they were silent, and more; they talked well into the late afternoon.

They spoke about loss and sadness, about separation and love, about family and the passage of time. Two women from two different generations, different times, different worlds, but nevertheless two women with shared emotions. It would seem that fundamental human feelings never change, no matter how many years come to pass. To Anna's surprise she discovered she was able to talk to her aunt like never before. The knowledge that she had been moved by love and passion and had known conflict and sadness in her life made Anna really open up, believing that her aunt might understand her better than in the past. She didn't talk about Nicos of course, or go into too much detail about her problems with Max. But she did tell her about how their marriage was going through a crisis, her sense of confusion and how she came to the island to give them both space to think.

'I do feel love for Max,' she said taking a sip of water. 'We've been together for so long, we are family, we have two beautiful children, we have built a life together, we have shared so much so how can I not care, yet . . . I don't know if you can understand this, *Thia*, but sometimes things happen and everything changes and so do your feelings.'

'There are times,' Ourania said and cupped her warm hand over Anna's, 'that even if you love someone very deeply, you need to leave them, get away from them, no matter what the reasons are.'

Suddenly, looking across to the trunk, Anna decided that maybe this was the time she *could* ask her aunt about the letters. Own up to her about her unexpected discovery, apologize for her indiscretion. If she didn't want to talk about it then Anna would understand, she too would be stoic; but she felt she had to at least try and find out; she needed to know. Anna felt the knowledge would bring them even closer.

At first she said nothing. The silence was acute; it hovered in the room like mist. All the while Anna held her breath and waited, unsure how her aunt was going to respond to the question. Still she said nothing. Then, after a time, she slowly stood up and walked over to the trunk. She knelt down as if in prayer, opened the lid and plunging her arms into its depth pulled out the box. She held it in both hands and, cradling it, walked back to the window seat. The only audible sound for many moments was the clock on the wall.

'These letters,' she finally said, pointing to the box on her lap, 'kept me alive for many years. It was a powerful love. There was no escape from it.'

'Did he ever come back?' Anna asked, uncertain if she should.

'He never really left, Anna *mou*; you see, he stayed always in my heart.'

'Did anyone know? Did you tell anyone about it?' Anna asked again, wondering what consequences a secret love affair would have had in that society over sixty years ago.

'It was no one's business,' she said and pulled the box closer.

'Not even years later? After a time, did you not want to speak about it? What about my dad or my mum?' Anna asked, hoping she wasn't overdoing the inquisition. She knew Ourania and Alexis had always been good friends and Anna wanted to think that perhaps she'd had an ally in her father, like she had in her cousin Manos.

'Your father and my sister Calliope were the only ones who ever knew, the only ones I ever trusted,' Ourania said.

'Would you tell me about him?' Anna asked again, gingerly.

'I don't think so,' she replied, reaching across to squeeze her niece's hand. 'Not now, Anna *mou*, not yet, perhaps another time.'

Even though Ourania didn't reveal very much, Anna was overjoyed to have been told anything at all. She had taken a gamble, she had crossed the line, in asking her all those questions. It was obvious that her feelings about her love affair were deeply private and that she had spent a lifetime protecting them. Anna felt privileged and lucky to have been allowed even a little glimpse into her aunt's past. What also pleased her was the discovery that Alexis had indeed been as good a friend to her as she'd hoped.

By the time Anna left her aunt's house, all she had time to do was rush home, say hello to her father and get changed in time for Manos to pick her up and drive them to the Black Turtle. She would have liked to visit Nicos beforehand but there'd been no time and she was pleased to learn from her cousin that he was joining them that evening. She felt excited and nervous about seeing him again.

Nicos was already sitting on a bar stool scanning the door with an anxious expression when they walked in, a glass of red wine in one hand and a cigarette in the other. The minute he saw Anna a smile spread across his face.

'There you are!' he said, jumping off the stool to walk towards them. As much as Anna would have liked to have given him a great big hug, she held back, they both did, and instead gave each other the customary kiss on the cheek.

'Where have you been?' he said, taking her arm. 'I hoped you might have come to see me.'

'It's a long story,' Anna replied, 'and now I could really do with a drink.'

That night they had one of their best Black Turtle evenings. There was a big crowd and everyone was in high spirits. The music played on, all the old island favourites. The food kept coming, delicious dishes of *meze* appearing on the table all night. The highlight was a plate of chicken livers cooked in what Anna thought tasted like nectar but eventually, after much probing, Antonis revealed was pomegranate juice, a secret recipe handed down by his grandmother. The wine flowed, ice-cold retsina, Anna's favourite, and so did the bonhomie between everyone. The place was packed with not only the usual foreign tourists but also with Greek visitors from the mainland on their August break. Antonis, busy helping with service, didn't sit with them but made sure there was never an empty bottle on their table. They all sang and all danced that night, and Anna got thoroughly drunk. She did not remember the last time that had happened to her. 'As a rule,' she kept telling everyone, 'I'm not given to drunkenness, *not* because I'm such a good girl but because it makes me feel ill if I overdo it.' But that night, *overdo it* she did!

The side effects of her overindulgence stayed with Anna for the whole of the next day, which ended up being a very good thing because it forced her to do something she hadn't managed since arriving on the island. She finally spent some quiet time at home *and* with her father. One of the reasons she'd gone there was to be with him, but instead she'd run around like a teenager, gone out all the time, argued with him, and stayed up late. The most she'd done was to spend some fleeting moments together instead of the quality time she had promised herself.

That day, suffering from a mild hangover, turned out to be the most pivotal day of her entire life. Prompted by the previous day's conversation with her aunt, Anna decided to also ask her father some questions about the past. What followed was completely unexpected. Once he opened up, Alexis spoke to his daughter for three whole days. He spoke of things she could never have imagined, or believed. He began to talk as never before. The words poured out of him, unleashing a torrent of events that took place in Greece, Italy and England long before Anna or any of her siblings were born. They talked sitting under the vine, walking in the garden, over dinner, late into the night, and then again the next day over breakfast, lunch, dinner and in between.

Alexis spoke of people Anna had never met, including her grandparents, and then about his childhood and early youth. He told her the reason he had to abruptly leave the island at the tender age of seventeen was in order to protect his family's honour, and about his painful years in exile; he spoke of love, and longing, of secrets and passions, of cruelty, war and courage. Over those three days Anna's father took her by the hand and led her on a sometimes painful and other times joyful voyage. He talked to her of things that had never been spoken of before, things that changed her world and her understanding of who she was and where she came from forever.

Part Two

Love on a Greek island, 1936

'I will love you for ever,' he said.

'I would die rather than stop loving you,' she said back.

They lay perfectly still in each other's arms, hearts beating in unison. They dared not move lest the spell be broken. Guided by their young bodies, as natural as breathing, they made love for the first time, a gentle, sweet love, slow and tender.

Outside the cave they could hear the sea's steady murmur against the shore, promising them sensual pleasures yet to come. But dawn was approaching and they had to part before the sun, like the previous night's moon, would unwittingly become a lover's traitor. Ourania reached across and took Alexis's face in her hands, giving him a final lingering kiss.

'I must go,' she whispered. 'In an hour my father will be awake.'

'I will keep watch while you go,' Alexis replied without showing any signs of letting her go.

'I *must* run,' she said again softly, but this time she got up to leave.

Agápe
(ἀγάπη agápe)

 ˙ means love in a 'spiritual' sense. In the term
s'agapo (Σ>αγαπώ), which means 'I love you' in
ancient Greek, it often refers to a general affection
or deeper sense of 'true unconditional love'. This
love is selfless; it gives and expects nothing
in return.

1

The twin brothers Andrikos and Costandis Levanti married their sweethearts on the same day, in the same church, in the early spring of 1919, when the almond trees were in full bloom and the island was covered in a carpet of wild flowers. Their blushing brides were young and virginal in their traditional white lace wedding dresses handed down by their mothers. Both carried bouquets of wild flowers and orange blossom. The brothers, also dressed in the customary male wedding attire, walked tall and proud as peacocks next to their brides.

Some mornings in early spring on the island the chill lingers in the air and you could be fooled into thinking there'd been a sudden snowfall in the night. The delicate white almond blossom flowers tend to blow off the trees with the slightest gust of wind and pile up on the hill slopes masquerading as snowflakes. It was on such a morning that the wedding procession snaked up through the groves to the little church of Agios Panteleimon.

Leading the procession was the village priest, old

Father Euthimios, followed by four young bridesmaids each carrying a giant white candle, flame trembling in the morning breeze. The prepubescent girls, dressed, like the bride, all in white, in the tradition of a Greek Orthodox wedding, were the dutiful custodians of the candles which they had to keep alight till they reached the church. Behind the girls and in front of the couples followed the musicians who, with their traditional instruments – a fiddle, a lute and a drum – accompanied the wedding procession on its way.

The line of people that followed was longer than anyone had ever seen before or since. The marriage ceremony was to be performed by Father Euthimios, who had known all four since their baptism in that same church, which according to his memory seemed only just a few years ago. The little church overflowed with guests, and everyone strained to get a glimpse of the priest bless the *stefana* garlands and place them on the couples' heads. The blessing of these delicate white crowns made of satin and pearls joined together by a white ribbon is a central moment and one of the pivotal points in the sacrament of marriage, symbolizing the couple's unity.

The wedding celebrations lasted three whole days and three whole nights; guests came from villages all over the island and for many years to come people talked about the double weddings of Andrikos and

Chrisoula, Costandis and Aphrodite. There was much dancing and feasting to be had over those three days, and since the second day of the celebrations fell on a full moon many a love match was to be hatched too. Apparently, the story goes, nine months later the island saw something of a baby boom.

Andrikos and Costandis, like their father and grand-fathers before them, were fishermen – the main occupation of the inhabitants on the island and most of its neighbours. The brothers learned their trade from their father, who took his sons from a very early age out to sea with him. By the time the boys finished elementary school, around the age of twelve, they accompanied their father full time. Working in numbers was in their favour, allowing them to triple the amount of fish their competitors caught. With his sons on board, the family business thrived and then when their father became ill the boys took over from him.

The brothers married well, both brides coming with generous dowries and happy dispositions. Not long after the wedding night, Aphrodite was the first to break the good news to the family that she was with child. Chrisoula was soon to follow. Alexis Levantis, named after his paternal grandfather, was born almost nine months to the day after his parents' marriage, and made his young father the happiest man in the village. What more could a man wish but to be blessed with a son? A few months later Chrisoula had a daughter. A raven-haired, dark-eyed little beauty of a baby girl called Ourania, who made her mother's heart fill with joy and her father's with disappointment.

'Next belly-full will be a boy,' Chrisoula had said, shrugging her shoulders as she cradled her baby lovingly to her bosom. As it turned out, Chrisoula's next belly-full was also a girl, and so was the next one and the one after that. In fact, Chrisoula went on to have five daughters without managing to produce one son and heir for Andrikos, while Aphrodite, after her initial success, never managed to produce any more babies at all.

'One boy is worth ten girls,' Costandis would boast good-naturedly to his brother.

'Girls will look after me in my old age,' Andrikos would retaliate.

In truth, after the initial disappointments, everyone settled down to what they all called *God's will*.

'We have no control over what children God grants us,' Andrikos would say in way of justification for his failure to plant a male seed in his wife's belly. 'If God *wanted* me to have a son he would have given me one.'

In the meantime, young Alexis, or Lexi, as Ourania chose to call him, was growing up in a sea of love, pampered and adored by all his family, especially by his five female cousins. He was the rooster in the hen-coop, and even though there were plenty of boy cousins elsewhere in the family Alexis was the favourite.

His favourite was Ourania. Not only because he thought she was the prettiest of all the girls but also because he thought she was feisty and strong-minded and played as well as any boy.

Alexis and Ourania, being the closest in age, always had a strong bond between them and had loved each other for as long as they could remember. At first it was through games and toys, no dolls and girlish stuff for Ourania. Hide and seek in the orchards with Alexis was her preference, fights with sticks and pretend swords and guns. It was all laughter and play, but then it changed. Neither of them could say exactly when it happened, but it was probably around the age of eleven or twelve when they both seemed to be struck simultaneously by a new feeling. No one noticed at first, and they carried on as before, spending every minute they could together. Games, laughter, play, but now the playing had changed, it was more physical, and they seemed to be drawn together by a magnet. When they touched now, it felt different; it was thrilling. They would steal away from the other kids to be together, to feel the delight of being alone.

Everyone was used to them being close, so it seemed quite natural until the time came when Ourania started to menstruate; then *everything* changed. She was forbidden to be in the company of boys, and even with Alexis she was expected to be chaperoned. She tried to rebel, as was her nature, but it did her no good. The two cousins still longed to be together as always, even if they knew that what they felt for each other would be considered inappropriate. Love on a small island, under the watchful eye of *everyone*, was a difficult thing but, as they say, where there is a will, there is always a way. Ourania's and Alexis's way was now going to be that of secrecy.

2

Unlike their parents and grandparents before them, who all left school as soon as they could, or never went to school at all, Alexis, Ourania and her favourite sister Calliope, just one year younger than herself, decided they wanted to continue their education beyond the free-school age of twelve. Ourania was particularly fond of learning and by the time she was ten she had already made up her mind that she wanted to become a teacher herself.

The village had only the one-teacher-for-all school which was adequate enough for the first six elementary years, but any child wanting to continue with secondary education had to travel to Limny, the biggest town on the island.

At first there was much debate and discussion about whether the girls should be allowed to follow the path of academia, or whether they should stay at home to learn the customary craft of housekeeping, preparing themselves for marriage. For Alexis, of course, there would be no debate; he was a boy. But Ourania was adamant and Calliope, who adored her sister, was determined to follow suit. Chrisoula, too, was in favour of her daughters getting an education, something she had wanted for herself but was never allowed. The village schoolteacher, who considered the two sisters her prize pupils, was also in favour.

'It's only once in a while I find a girl as clever and willing as your Ourania,' she told the girl's parents. 'She has a good brain in that pretty head of hers and a thirst for knowledge. The younger one, too; she's as bright as a little pearl that one. It would be a sin not to allow them to go further.'

The teacher's words struck a chord with Chrisoula, who was determined to give her girls the opportunities she never had.

'We can afford it, Andrikos,' she said to her husband, 'the other girls have no interest in learning, they'll stay here and help me, but these two have been blessed with brains and we can't stand in their way. We don't have sons, but God has granted us two daughters as clever as any boy!'

Bursting with pride, Andrikos nodded in agreement. It was true, his two older girls were bright sparks and they seemed to absorb knowledge like those magnificent sponges he fished out of the Aegean and sold in the markets at such high prices. But he was troubled with the prospect of letting his daughters out of his sight, and worried what the rest of the village would think.

'How can we let them go to town on their own without a chaperone?' he asked his wife. 'What would people say about us?'

Nobody at that time thought that education was a quality a man looked for when searching for a bride. What was expected from a daughter was to stay close to home, be modest and obedient, and learn to be a good wife and mother; too much knowledge was undesirable. Marriage was the only priority. But luckily for the sisters, their mother was on their side and their father was an amicable man who was willing to listen.

Since she could see no other way round it, Chrisoula decided that Alexis would have to be the girls' protector.

'Your nephew is like a brother to our daughters,' she told her husband. 'He is not like other boys, he'll look after our girls and if people's tongues start wagging, then shame on them!' Andrikos loved his brother's son as if he was his own and knew that the boy would give his right arm to protect his cousins. His trust was implicit.

The journey took over an hour on a bus that stopped in the village square every day except Sundays to pick up its passengers.

Time-keeping never played an important role in the life of the island, except when it came to catching the bus. It always arrived at *exactly* six twenty-five each morning, returning at four in the afternoon with precisely fifteen minutes for embarking and disembarking, no matter what. This anomaly regarding punctuality was all down to Philipos, the bus driver, who having been given a timetable when he first started the job, was determined to keep to it religiously. Everyone knew that if they wanted to go anywhere by bus they had no option but to abide by Philipos's rules, because very few people had cars in those days and their journey by the only other form of transportation – a donkey – would not be as speedy or as comfortable.

Philipos, who had been driving his bus for over twenty years, had a big belly, a kind heart, and a big, soft spot for the young cousins. Ourania reminded him of his own daughter and he felt personally responsible for their safe return home each evening.

'If she was my daughter I wouldn't let her out of the house,' he'd mutter to himself. 'Education! What does a girl need that for?'

O Aetos, The Eagle, as Philipos named his bus, was his pride and joy and he took almost as much care of it as of his own house. At the top of the steps inside the entrance of the vehicle he had placed a doormat, insisting on clean footwear from all his passengers before entering. On the dashboard he had erected a little shrine to the Holy Virgin to provide protection and guarantee a safe journey. A small icon of the *Panayia*, the All-Holy Mother of God, stood on the right-hand side of the driving wheel surrounded by bright-coloured plastic flowers, while an artificial electric candle was wired up to stay alight at all times in front of the shrine. From the rear-view mirror, just to be on the safe side, he'd also hung a selection of other good-luck trinkets. Amongst them was a crucifix as well as a big blue glass evil-eye stone, a pagan symbol to ward off envious spirits. On the front bonnet of his bus, Philipos had commissioned a local artist to paint a picture of the bus's namesake in full flight, with the name underneath, inscribed in beautiful calligraphy, which by the end of the day would be hardly visible under many layers of dust. Each night on his return to his own village, Philipos would wash and polish his bus and only then, when *The Eagle* was spick and span, the colours of the bird gleaming bright again and the bus ready for another day's journey, would he consider coming into the house to wash himself, eat dinner with his family and rest.

Alexis and Ourania started high school at the same time, and Calliope, thirteen months younger, the following academic year. School started early so in the winter months they would leave their homes before sunrise and arrive back after nightfall. If the weather was bad, permission was granted to any children waiting for a bus to stay in the schoolhouse until its arrival, but in the summer the cousins would take advantage of the free time and run to the beach.

The two cousins couldn't believe their luck; the switch to the new school came about the time when Ourania had reached puberty and the veto on boys had already started. If one was to try and pinpoint the moment the two fell truly in love it would probably be around that time. Although Ourania and Alexis already knew that their feelings for each other had altered, and that something else had taken hold, it wasn't until that first school year, before Calliope joined them, that these feelings became clearer.

They also understood that this was a completely forbidden love, and must be kept secret. No matter how much Ourania tried to fantasize when she lay in bed at night that love would conquer all, or Alexis told himself that Ourania was *not* his *sister*, they both knew all too well the rules of their land and that there was no way they would ever be allowed to marry. The Greek Orthodox Church and the law have never allowed marriage between first cousins and union between them is considered a sin, a social disgrace.

Unlike other children, the two cousins didn't particularly look forward to Sundays and holidays, they much preferred school days. They always made sure they were the first to arrive and board the bus, making their way to the very back of the vehicle. Alexis sat next to the window and Ourania next to him, taking care to place their two bulky satchels, which not only contained heavy books but also their food for the day, by her side, thus ensuring nobody else could sit with them. Later on, when Calliope started school, she would always take the seat in front of them. For the hour or so that the journey took to reach the town they were blissfully happy. At the beginning they were the only two children from their village to go to town, so for the duration of the journey they savoured their proximity, taking care not to draw too much attention to themselves or let anyone see that their feet under the seat were always entwined.

The early sexual awakenings that Alexis and Ourania experienced were as innocent and chaste as their young years. Ourania, especially, was happy to just sit as close as possible to her beloved, feel his warmth, and listen to his voice. Alexis, aged thirteen, already had his full influx of testosterone, with a voice as deep as his father's, a smudge of hair growth on his upper lip promising a budding moustache, and the physique of a young athlete. He was growing up to be as handsome as Ourania was beautiful. But even if his hormones were telling him what to do about his love for his cousin, he wasn't going to listen, unless Ourania gave him a sign.

In those days by the time a girl reached the age of fifteen she was considered ready for marriage. Even if Ourania was still at school and not fifteen yet, the offers for marriage were already starting to come in. The custom at the time was that if a girl agreed to a proposal of matrimony, the marriage would not take place until the bride was old enough. If both parties agreed to the match, this was called *giving the word*, which meant they were both spoken for and considered betrothed.

Not a month went by that a third party acting as a go-between – the so-called *proxenia* – didn't come knocking at the Levantis' door with offers. Ourania was quite a catch. In fact all the Levanti girls were desirable brides; good family, nice girls, with a sizeable dowry. But according to the cultural code the older girl had to *give the word* first before the others could take their turn. Ourania would not even listen to marriage talk and would run out of the room covering her ears when her mother brought news of a fresh proposal.

'All she cares about is school and books,' Chrisoula told her concerned husband, who, in reply, reminded her that it was *she* who had been so keen for their daughters to be educated.

'Yes, for two or three years,' she replied, shaking her head in despair. 'How could I know she'd want to carry on?' Turning down good *proxenia*, Chrisoula thought, was bad luck; it was like closing the door on the face of good fortune. 'School is fine, but so is finding a husband,' she carried on. 'Besides, there are the others, they need to take their turn; we have five of them to marry off, Andrikos, and luck doesn't come knocking all the time.'

'I would rather die than be someone else's wife, Lexi,' Ourania told him in tears one day as they walked by the seashore while they waited for the bus home. Calliope, who by now was the only one privy to the sweethearts' secret, was sitting on the beach reading a book while the two took a stroll. 'Besides, I'm too young for marriage. I want to finish school first and then I want to marry *you*.'

The sisters were as close as twins and had an implicit trust in each other, so when the time was right Ourania had had no hesitation in disclosing her secret to Calliope.

'No one else must *ever* know!' was the younger sister's wide-eyed alarmed response when she first found out.

'Don't worry, Calliope *mou*,' Ourania reassured her, taking both of her hands in hers, 'you are the only one I would *ever* trust.'

'Do you really love each other?' Calliope asked with a worried expression.

'Yes we do! And some day we will marry. I know we will!'

'How could you *ever* do that?' Calliope asked again with a sharp intake of breath. 'You will never be allowed!'

'I don't know how,' Ourania replied, 'but we'll find

a way; so long as I have you with me and Alexis, everything will be fine.'

With an anxious heart, Calliope pledged to keep her sister's secret safe and that she would do everything in her power to keep it that way.

3

As the two cousins grew older they found that the journey to school was no longer sufficient to sustain their passion. Basking in each other's proximity as they sat together on the school bus was not enough. But with Calliope willing to provide cover, it was sometimes possible to escape the watchful eyes of the family and be alone.

'It's an unfair world,' was their mantra, 'why did we have to be born related?'

In the meantime, the offers for Ourania's hand were still coming in, although now people were starting to wonder what was wrong with the striking young beauty who had no interest in marriage but only cared about books.

'I'm still young,' she told Alexis one day when they managed to sneak away and hide in the hollow of a tree to kiss. 'I can still keep them at bay, but for how long?'

'You mean there might be a time when you have to accept someone?' he whispered and pulled her closer to him.

'Never!' she cried. 'I *told* you, Lexi, I would rather die than marry someone else. If I can't be *your* wife I will *never* marry. They can't force me.'

'I've been thinking,' he said, 'that the only way for us to be together is to elope.'

'Yes! You have to steal me, we can run away to another country where the rules are different,' she agreed enthusiastically.

'People do it all the time.'

'I know!' Ourania's eyes flashed with excitement. 'My father's uncle stole his girl because everyone thought she wasn't good enough for him, and they went to live on the mainland. No one saw them again.'

'We'll do the same. I will leave school and get a job and save enough money, and then one day I'll come and get you and never come back.'

'Then when we are settled we'll send for Calliope. Otherwise they'll marry her off too, to someone she doesn't love.'

The idea that once a match was agreed by the family, a girl would be expected to marry a man she hardly knew or loved, and would be forced to lie in his bed and give her body to him, enraged Ourania. There were other things too, mainly about the way they lived, that Ourania now started to question. Her love of books, which went further than the school curriculum, was allowing her glimpses into a world beyond the island's small horizons.

'I won't abide by their barbaric customs,' she'd told Alexis, referring to the age-old custom of proving a bride's purity after the wedding night. The ritual required that after the first night the groom would appear at the bedroom window to proclaim his bride's virginity by beating his chest like a Neanderthal and firing three shots in the air with his hunting-gun. Then, as if that was not enough, the blood-stained marital sheet would be hung out of the window like a flag of victory for all to see.

'People on this island are still living in the Dark Ages. I won't have some man shouting to the world whether I'm a virgin or not!' Ourania said with fury.

'You won't have to!' he said smiling. 'You'll be marrying me!'

'When *we* make love it will be no one's business but ours,' she told Alexis, and a thrill rushed through his veins with the thought of making love to her.

Then finally, one day in early summer, while walking on the beach after school, Ourania took Alexis by the hand and with a mischievous smile reminded him that soon she was going to have her fifteenth birthday.

'If they think I'm fit to marry at fifteen, then I'm fit to be yours forever,' she said and kissed him.

They planned everything. Calliope was going to pretend to be ill and would take herself to bed, which she shared with her sister, and ask for Ourania to keep her company. Once night fell Ourania would climb out of the bedroom window and run to the deserted beach to meet Alexis before the full moon could betray them.

'Hurry,' Calliope whispered, her heart in her mouth as she held the window open for her sister. 'Be careful,' she whispered again, but Ourania was already running into the night and to Alexis's arms.

The two sweethearts had talked and talked about how it would be and they were prepared for their first night of love. Alexis, who by now often made little trips to the city on his own, had furtively visited a barber's shop and purchased, for the first time in his life, a condom. Their lovemaking was as awkward as any young lover's first attempt but tender and sweet as they let their instincts guide them. Afterwards they lay in each other's arms, closer than ever before, and pledged their love forever.

Later that summer, other secret love meetings were to follow and each one was better than the first. Apart from being Ourania's ally, Calliope was also her best friend and confidante. Late at night as the two sisters lay together in the same bed she would ask Ourania to tell her about the mysteries of sex.

'It's like two bodies becoming one,' Ourania told her.

'Did it hurt?' the younger sister asked after the first time, with fear in her voice.

'Like a red hot poker,' Ourania giggled, 'but I didn't care. It was worth all the pain. You'll see, when you fall in love you won't mind either.'

Tales of excruciating pain experienced during first-time intercourse had always frightened the young girls, not to mention the terror induced from stories about childbirth. For every bride-to-be, the joy she felt on her wedding day was also marred by a sense of dread of what was to follow.

Although the age difference between them was small, Calliope looked much younger than her sister. Shorter and delicately boned, she was less womanly, less mature-looking than Ourania. Her hair, the colour of chestnuts, was a mass of dense curls that framed her intense little face, and her huge brown eyes seemed to carry the troubles of the world. Since neither Ourania nor Alexis appeared to be particularly anxious about *anything*, lost in their own universe of bliss, Calliope was often fearful for them.

'What if you get found out?' she'd whisper in her sister's ear when they were together in their bed. 'What will they do to you?'

'Don't you worry, my sister, they won't find out, and if they do, we have a plan,' Ourania would whisper back, alluding to their talk of eloping.

The two lovers managed to continue their clandestine meetings for most of that summer, but once they returned to school things changed. The workload had increased and every evening they had hours of homework. Alexis had a talent for mathematics, whereas Ourania had a problem with numbers and needed his help. When she spent time going over homework with him in his room, concentration would prove a problem and the desire to touch each other was beyond their control. It was on such an evening, knowing that they had the house to themselves, that temptation proved too much.

The light had started to fade and the room was getting dark. Alexis had turned on the reading lamp on his little desk but it only faintly illuminated the books in front of them. The heat that emanated from their bodies was intoxicating; Ourania's lips seemed redder, fuller and moister than ever; her hair smelled of rose water, and her dark eyes glistened in the semi-darkness.

The mere brush of Alexis's thigh on hers made her breathless and heady. The atmosphere was electric. They knew it was risky, they knew it was madness, but they couldn't help it. They fell on each other and rolled, for the first time, on the softness of a bed. Oblivious to the world, lost in each other's bodies, nothing else mattered, and nothing but the sound of their lovemaking reached their ears.

Deaf to the world, they didn't hear Alexis's mother,

Aphrodite, return home. They didn't hear his door open just enough for Aphrodite to glimpse inside the room and almost buckle over, as her knees gave way beneath her, at what she saw. Nor did they hear her walk away, the back door creak open, or the rustle of leaves in the yard as she stumbled out thinking there had been an earthquake and the roof had fallen on her head.

'*Panayia mou*,' Mother of God, Aphrodite murmured, with fear in her heart as she crossed herself three times. 'What did I just see?' She put her hand out on the wall to steady herself and very slowly sat down on a small wooden stool by the back door. The unacceptable image she'd just witnessed made her dizzy, blurring her vision. Aphrodite sat motionless; she took a deep breath of autumn air that smelled of firewood, and held it in for a long while before letting it out slowly. '*Panayia mou*. How? When did this happen?' she murmured again, and crossed herself once more. What she had just seen on the bed, in the twilight of the room, was a calamity of huge proportions, for which, she started to think, she must accept some blame. When the two youngsters were first thrown together on their journey to school she had great reservations; now she was blaming herself for not raising stronger objections.

When Chrisoula first suggested that Alexis was to be the girls' chaperone, Aphrodite had been concerned. She knew that a man's desire is a hard thing to master and her boy was a hot-blooded male like any other. She'd been surprised that Costandis didn't share her apprehensions, and she had told him as much!

'Ourania is a beauty and I've seen the look in our boy's eyes when she is around him.'

But Costandis didn't listen. 'Don't blaspheme, woman,' he bellowed at her. 'The boy loves her like a sister, they've been together since the cradle.'

Since no one else seemed to share her worries, Aphrodite stopped thinking about it and said no more. But she knew her boy, she knew him well, and now she realized she had been right, and she should have spoken up more, acted on her instincts. And why, oh why, knowing this, did she go out and leave them alone? She should never have left the house, she'd always made sure she was around when the cousins were there; that was her fault too.

Consumed by fear and guilt, she wondered what was to be done *now*? Carnal relations between cousins was a grave sin in the eyes of God, not to mention the shame and the disgrace it would bring to them all. Theirs was a good family, a family with reputation and standing in the village. Such things didn't happen to them – *incest* – the mere thought of the word, because for her that was what it amounted to. The thought made her cross herself three times again. Aphrodite sat out in her back yard, not daring to go back inside, long enough for the rosy evening light to fade and the first stars to appear on the inky sky. She sat long enough to decide that no one must ever find out about what she had seen. She would talk to no one except Alexis himself. She must hurry and do it as soon as possible, because whatever this thing was, it *had* to be stopped.

But Aphrodite was not to know that putting a stop to what had begun would be the hardest thing she'd ever had to do in her life and that it would break her heart.

That night, Aphrodite spent sleepless troublesome hours praying to the Holy Virgin for guidance about what she must do. Before she went to bed she lit a fresh candle in front of the *Panayia*'s icon, a little shrine in the bedroom, and burned some olive leaves and incense.

'You are a mother. You have a son,' she prayed silently in her bed to the All-Holy Mother of God. 'Show me the way and forgive them their sin, they are too young, they don't know what they are doing,' she begged.

The next day she got up before sunrise, still lost in thought and prayer, and busied herself with making the breakfast and food for Alexis's lunch. By the time her son and husband were up she had decided she must act quickly and speak with Alexis as soon as he returned from school. She needed to be alone with him, away from his father or anyone else. No one must hear what she had to say to him. She spent an anxious day counting the hours for his return, and then, when the time came, she wrapped herself in her shawl and walked to the square to wait for the bus.

Seeing his mother waiting, a solemn dark figure at the bus-stop with a grim expression on her face, Alexis was overcome with a feeling of dread. He knew all too well the dangers of the sea and how many fishermen drowned each year. This was a scene from one of his childhood nightmares that had plagued him all his life. Each day when he said goodbye to his father he wondered if he'd ever see him again.

'What is it, Mother,' he said, leaping out of the bus before Philipos had a chance to pull the hand brake, Ourania jumping out at his side too. 'Where is Father?' he asked anxiously, an invisible hand twisting his gut.

'Your father is fine,' was her abrupt reply, 'I want to speak with you.' And looking at Ourania she added, 'Alone!'

Alexis sat silently at the kitchen table listening to his mother's words. The colour drained from his face, his mouth was dry, his knuckles were white. He wanted to block out everything she was saying to him. He didn't want to hear any of it.

She spoke seriously and sternly; someone he didn't recognize. His mother had always lavished love and tenderness on him, cherished his every word and never chastised him. This was an altogether different person from his soft and gentle mother. He had never seen her like this, unyielding and stern.

Finally, leaning his elbows on the table, he took his head in both hands, and shielding his face from his mother, he spoke.

'I cannot live without her.'

'You can't live *with* her.' Her reply came back quick and sharp.

'I love her!' he responded, his throat tight as a fist, shocked that his gentle-mannered mother could be so hard.

'It makes no difference, Alexis. Don't you see? You have no option.'

'Please, Mother, you don't understand,' Alexis begged. 'I want to marry her.'

'Alexis, my son,' she said, her voice softening a little, 'this love of yours is a sin in the eyes of our God and the eyes of the world; it cannot exist. No priest will marry you and you will be outcasts, your children will be born monsters. The same blood runs through your veins. Your fathers are not only brothers they are twins! Do you hear me?'

'She is *NOT* my sister,' Alexis shouted and covered his ears.

'Listen to me, Alexis, she is as good as a sister to you,

and you know it. There is no other way, you have to stop it now, before it's too late.'

'Then, if there is no other way we'll run away together. It might be a sin here, Mother, but there is a world out there that doesn't think so.'

'God is everywhere, Alexis. *He* sees.'

'We will go away,' he carried on, ignoring her. 'Or *I* shall go away, and send for her. We will be together, one way or another, whatever you all say; away from here, away from your shame.'

'Alexis, shame will follow you wherever you go if you make this union. What must not be, cannot be, no matter how much you want it.' Aphrodite's eyes filled with tears now. She loved her son like nothing else in the world and the last thing she wanted was to see him unhappy or to lose him. 'With time you will get over it, you'll see,' she told him. 'You are both so young, you have your whole life ahead, you are just infatuated; together we will find a way.'

'She saw us, Ourania *mou*!' he told her the minute they had a chance to be alone. 'My mother *saw* us on the bed!' and the thought made his face flush with fury and embarrassment.

Ourania had been very anxious to learn why her Thia

Aphrodite had been so uncharacteristically stern with them the previous day, and finally Alexis was explaining.

'She says it's a sin, and we'll be doomed, and our children will be born monsters.'

'Do you believe her?' she asked with a gasp, covering her mouth with both hands.

'Of course I don't believe her! I love my mother but she talks like an old peasant woman sometimes. It's all a lot of old wives' tales,' he said and shifted closer to her. The two of them had gone to their favourite hideout, the place where they first consummated their love, the cave on the beach. Darkness fell much earlier now, making it easier to steal away unnoticed, and although the autumn breeze blowing from the sea was biting, they didn't care, they just held on to each other and tried to work out what they were going to do.

'But I can see that we can't stay here,' he continued, 'we might believe in each other, but no one else here will.'

They hugged in desperation, but they both knew that they had been fooling themselves to imagine it could have ever worked out any other way.

'By the time you finish school I will have made enough money to send for you,' he said full of conviction, stroking her hair.

'I'll study hard to be a teacher so I can work too,' she replied.

'I will hurry,' he promised. 'I will find a place for us to settle down and get married, away from here and the disgrace they say we'll bring them.'

'If I can't come with you, then I will be here waiting for you,' she said, 'for as long as it takes. Trust me!'

'I will write to you every day,' he promised. 'I will tell you my adventures and always think you are with me.'

'I will think of you every day and will wait for you to send for me,' she told him and gave herself to him one last time.

So it was, on a crisp winter's day in 1936, that the whole family, and most of the village, gathered at the seafront to see Alexis board a boat destined for the Athenian port of Piraeus in search of his new life; a life in which he hoped to be with the girl he loved more than his family or the island he was born on. Everyone else, and that included his father, thought that young Alexis had decided to go and seek his fame and fortune in foreign parts, a common enough practice on the island, to return in a few years, older and wealthier, back to the fold of his family. The only people who knew the real reason he was leaving were Ourania, Calliope and Aphrodite, who, with a pain in her heart and a secret she took to her grave, had to bid farewell to her one and only son, the love of her life, the light and joy of her world.

They all took their turn to kiss him and wish him a speedy return, and when the time came to kiss his mother Alexis held her tight in his arms, kissed her forehead three times, asked her to look after herself and his father, and promised her that he'd take good care of himself. His young heart was too keen and full of life's anticipation to even contemplate that perhaps this could be the last time he would ever embrace her.

Family and village stood at the dock waving their white handkerchiefs and cheering him on his way as they watched the boat slowly glide into the Aegean. United in their loss, Aphrodite and Ourania stood motionless side by side, each in their grief. But whereas the young girl's heart was full of hope, Aphrodite's was breaking into a million pieces with the knowledge that she might never see her beloved boy again.

4

Aphrodite was a kind, God-fearing woman, and even though her pain was unbearable, she still found it in her heart not to hate or blame Ourania. In fact, if anything, she felt that they were now linked by a common bond – their love for Alexis. Besides, she kept reminding herself, *she* was largely to blame for what had happened, so she tried to be strong and brave, and kept her tears for when she was alone.

'Don't cry, woman,' Costandis would tell her if he ever caught her weeping, 'the boy will be back before we know it.' But Aphrodite knew different.

Ourania, for her part, didn't entirely blame her aunt for the separation either; she knew there had been no other option. But still she cried herself to sleep every night in her sister's arms. Gentle Calliope would kiss her and stroke her hair and rock her to sleep.

'He'll send for you soon,' she soothed her.

'I feel as if I've lost a limb,' Ourania lamented. 'Sometimes I honestly think I'm going to stop breathing.' This was the first time that the cousins had ever been apart for any length of time, and their separation hit Ourania like an avalanche.

'You'll soon be together again, my sister,' Calliope reminded her. 'You must be patient; at least we have each other, can you imagine poor Alexis? He is all alone!'

'I know, Calliope *mou*, I'm so frightened for him,' she said through her tears. 'I'm so lucky to have you, and I know Alexis will soon send for us both.'

As much as Calliope wanted to believe in her sister's dreams that they would all be together again, she had her doubts. She truly wished for Ourania to be happy and even if she couldn't imagine life without her, deep down she felt that some day she might have to.

Alexis had been gone for three intolerable months when at last the first letter from him arrived. The mail at that time was delivered only once a week and people in the village had to collect it personally from the post office. In fact on that day, there were *two* letters awaiting collection from Alexis – one was addressed to Ourania, and the other to Aphrodite. Their arrival caused great excitement and news travelled fast. Ourania collected her letter with a pounding heart and then rushed home to open it alone. The envelope looked as crumpled and as distressed as she'd imagined her beloved Alexis would be after his long months of travelling. She held it in her hands for a while, savouring the thrill of anticipation.

She turned it this way and that, ran her fingers over the foreign stamp, the colour of wild violets, which looked to her as exotic and unfamiliar as a precious jewel, and finally, with trembling hands, started to open it.

Gingerly she pulled out several sheets of pale blue paper, fine as butterfly wings, and with them, another, different piece of paper fell out onto her lap. This, she was to discover, was a separate letter, the official letter addressing all her family, something which Alexis was to continue doing for as long as he wrote to Ourania.

Holding her breath, she started to read the long-awaited news from her beloved.

6 March 1937

My dearest love, Alexis began,

I miss you more than words can say. In this envelope you will find two letters. This one is for your eyes only. Keep it next to your heart. The other one is for everyone else, my uncle and aunt and the girls, please give it to them too.

My sweet love, without you I feel as if the sun has been eclipsed from my sky but the knowledge that we will be together again some day soon keeps me going. I want to see you, touch you, kiss you. I want to know how you are, and hear your voice, but I know I must wait. Every night since I left you, before going to bed, I write down something to you even if I know I won't be able to post it. It's the only thing that has kept me sane.

I want you to know that I am well enough, so you must not worry about me. I'm trying to keep my body and spirit strong so I can work, make money and send for you as soon as possible.

My journey has been eventful and hard and I have missed you all very much, but most of all I miss you, my love. So much has happened to me since I left the island, I don't know where to start. I feel as if I have been gone for years, not months.

The best thing that's happened so far, is that soon after I left you, I met a young man, three years older than me, who boarded our boat at Chios. His name is Costandis, like my father, and in many ways, especially his love of the sea, I am reminded of him. He is fun to be around, and like my father he is very kind. We've become very good friends. I know you'd really like him . . .

As Ourania read on she was lost in Alexis's words; she could hear his voice and feel his presence in the room with her. She imagined it was Alexis himself speaking to her, as if they were sitting together in their hideout at the beach, telling her about his new life, his new friend, his plans.

. . . Costandis was planning to look for work on a merchant ship and head for the United Kingdom, Alexis went on. *He has an uncle living there, in Wales, in Cardiff, one of the largest ports in the country and where many Greek ships go to dock. He asked me if I wanted to come along with him, and said he was sure his uncle would help us both. So we started looking for a job together and soon found work on the same merchant ship, which is where we are now, heading for Cardiff. I've been hired as an apprentice carpenter and Costandis is working in the kitchens, which is good for extra food.*

The ship is called The Doric, *and we've been on board for six weeks now. It's the hardest work I have ever done in my life but I don't mind because I know why I'm doing it – for us! Tomorrow we will reach our first port destination, in Italy, and we'll be allowed to go on land so I'll post this letter to you.*

*Even though the work is hard I'm enjoying it and
learning a lot . . .*

Alexis's letter went on for several more pages; his
voice echoed loud and clear in Ourania's head. She
continued to read and re-read it at least four times and
then, when Calliope came home, they read it together
all over again. She couldn't get enough of it. She wanted
to visualize everything. He sounded so far away in his
exotic new worlds, new horizons, new skies and seas.
The promise of a new life seemed closer than ever and
she couldn't wait to get a taste for it herself.

The next day, after everyone had a turn to read their
letter from Alexis, she put it back in the envelope, and
carefully placed it between the pages of one of her school
books and took it with her. The other one, the one
addressed to her, she folded into a small square and
placed inside her undergarment next to hcr left
breast.

She knew that everyone at school, including
her teachers, had been waiting to hear news from
Alexis.

'It's sent from Italy,' Miss Eugenia her geography
teacher said with delight after Ourania asked her to
decipher the writing on the stamp. 'It's been stamped
in Palermo, in Sicily,' she said, putting on her reading
glasses to examine it better. 'Can you believe it! Our

Alexis is seeing the world!' Her voice was full of admiration.

The months that followed after the first letter from Alexis and before his next one were unbearable. To alleviate the pain, Ourania decided to replace crying herself to sleep each night with sitting down and writing to him. It was something like a diary, a virtual conversation with her sweetheart, which lifted her spirits and gave her hope, although she had no idea if he would ever read it. She would read it out loud to Calliope and together they would dream about the time when they'd see him again.

Once Alexis's ship finally arrived in Cardiff and Costandis's uncle turned out to be as kind and as helpful as his nephew had promised, Alexis was able to give Ourania an address where she could send her letters. He had been anxious and uncertain at what kind of reception he'd receive from his friend's uncle but his worries were unfounded. Georgios Mendrinos could not have been kinder and more hospitable. Georgios had arrived in Cardiff some thirty years earlier in much the same way as the two boys and felt that giving them a helping hand was the least he could do. He too had benefited from the kindness of others when he first arrived fresh off the boat in a strange country, with no knowledge of the language or much money in his pocket.

The Greek community, although small, was visible even then, and he gradually found his feet. In fact Georgios Mendrinos's favourite anecdote was telling people, as often as he could, exactly *how* he found his feet in Cardiff.

'I found a job in a cobbler's shop!' he would roar with laughter when recounting the story.

Soon after he arrived in the city he was hired as an apprentice by a Greek shoemaker who taught him the trade, and after a few years helped him on his way to open his own shop. Now thirty years later he was considered one of the best cobblers in the city. His shop was proudly named *Bespoke Footwear* and was popular among both Greek and local people. He'd done well for himself, and helping his sister's son and the boy who came with him was a duty he took seriously. He too had left his island as a young man and his biggest regret was that he'd never gone back, or seen his mother again before she died. He'd meant to, but he didn't, and now it was too late.

Georgios Mendrinos's house was a small, two-up, two-down Victorian terrace, not far from the docks, and the boys had never seen the likes of it before, not even in a picture. Everything looked impossibly crowded. Their strapping physiques were in total contrast to the two narrow beds and cramped room they had to share, but they were both more than grateful for the kindness and hospitality they were given.

Georgios, for his part, was delighted to have the boys stay with him for the short while they were in town. The last three years had been very sad for him. He'd been happily married for a quarter of a century to Marika, a bubbly, nurturing Greek woman, whose sudden death left him lonely and bereft. Georgios and Marika had been desperate to have children, but their union had been fruitless.

'You would have liked your Thia Marika,' he told his nephew when he first arrived, 'and she would have *loved* you! She wanted a son more than anything.'

The voyages back and forth across the Mediterranean were repetitious and tiring, and although *The Doric* briefly docked at various ports, which at first the two boys found interesting, they soon began to look forward to the few days' breathing space that Cardiff offered. Georgios's house became something of a bolt-hole for both of them and on arrival they always found a big pile of letters waiting for them with news from home.

As time passed, life on the island also resumed its routine. Ourania and Aphrodite still ached from their loss and although they were never hostile towards each other they preferred to keep their distance. Even so, an unspoken truce seemed to keep the two women connected and when news from Alexis was being discussed at family gatherings, they both felt the sadness in each other's hearts. Alexis wrote regularly not only to Ourania but also to his mother. Distance was now beginning to make him see the impossibility of the situation and he stopped blaming her. He just kept his head down and worked hard towards making it possible to send for his beloved.

For Ourania too, schoolwork was beginning to be all absorbing and the volume of studying she had to do allowed little time for wallowing in sadness. With the entrance exams for the teachers' training college she wanted to attend looming ahead, she had her work cut out. By the time she finished revising, did her share of house-chores, and wrote a letter to Alexis she was all too ready to collapse into bed with Calliope and promptly fall asleep.

I'm determined to pass with good grades and win a scholarship to the college, she wrote to Alexis. *I want to be able to work and earn my share whatever we do in the future. I'm having a hard time convincing my parents that this is truly what I want from my life. Obviously I have to go to Mytilini if I'm to attend college, which in itself is a big problem. Remember what it took for them to agree to let me go on a bus ride to school? And that's only because you were there! Allowing me to go to another island might be too much to hope for. Still, they are getting used to me being difficult and as I keep telling my mother, if I'm old enough for marriage, I am old enough for college.*

Which reminds me . . . the proxenia *are still coming in, but be absolutely certain, Lexi* mou, *I'm taking no notice of them. My mother thinks I'm crazy and she is constantly trying to get me to change my mind. I have a feeling she is beginning to give up on me. I told her she should move on to one of the other girls if she is that frantic about getting one of us married off. Asimina seems as desperate to find a husband as my mother is at finding one for me, so I'm hoping she'll start focusing on her soon and leave me alone. Of course Calliope is next in line but as you know she's not that interested in marriage just yet either. She wants to go to college too, which is a good thing, because together they'd probably agree to let us go. Can you imagine if we both end up being teachers? We would be a great team!'*

Alexis would read Ourania's letters with relish and amusement. He anticipated them with great pleasure and excitement, loved her sense of humour, and they cheered him up. He knew she longed to see him and missed him as much as he did her, yet she always managed to be upbeat and full of positive spirit.

The closely knit Greek community in Cardiff was more than happy to welcome both young men into its fold. Their church of Agios Nicolaos, patron saint of seafarers, built in the Byzantine style some years earlier, was something of a meeting place, with a small community centre attached to it. This was soon to become a regular haunt for the two boys who when in town preferred it to the city's many rowdy drinking establishments. Gradually, the Welsh capital and its Greek community was beginning to feel like a home to them both.

Each time their ship docked, on the very first morning Alexis would habitually take himself off to Agios Nicolaos, where he would light a candle, give thanks to the saint for watching over them, and sit for a while in the sanctuary of the chapel absorbing the calming smell of incense, and pray. He prayed for a speedy reunion with Ourania, for his mother's forgiveness, his father's safe keeping, and for himself. He asked the saint to grant him patience, courage and wisdom, all of which he knew he desperately needed in order to cope with whatever was yet to follow in his life.

5

November on the island is the start of the olive harvest. At the beginning of this annual gathering the place would be gripped by what can only be described as *olive fever* and a festive atmosphere would dominate villages and countryside alike. Although the work was hard and laborious it was an activity that everyone, young and old, always wanted to take part in.

As most families had several olive trees growing in and around their land the harvest spirit affected everybody and not just those with the big olive groves. Very much like the production of homemade wine, producing olive oil was a tradition that went back centuries, passed down from family to family.

The Levanti brothers had more than two dozen trees between them and in a good year, when the rains were plentiful, the trees would reward them with a healthy crop and keep both families in oil for a long while.

Alexis had been gone a year when the olive harvest was once again in full swing. There had been plenty of rain in the spring and autumn, and the trees were heavy with fruit. The family would come together for a few hours in the early evenings and after church on Sundays for olive gathering. It was on such a Sunday morning, when the sun was as warm as a May day, and the fat juicy olives glistened amongst the silvery leaves, that Ourania and Calliope decided to postpone their school work till the evening and join in the family fun.

Everyone, friends and relatives, would team up and get involved in the picking of the olives, although, strictly speaking, *picking* was not what the harvesting entailed. *Beating* the fruit off the trees would be a more accurate way to describe what they did. Nets and sheets would be spread underneath the trees to catch the olives that were brought down with long poles, sticks and rakes. Fit adults and older boys would take turns to climb the wooden ladders propped up against the trees to shake or saw off branches that landed with a great thud on the nets below. It was dangerous but exciting work, which was performed with good humour, laughter and song, anticipated each year with as much excitement as the great pyre constructed in the churchyard at Easter to burn the effigy of Judas.

Ourania and Calliope were glad to be outside again participating in physical activity, away from their pens and books for a time. With just a few months to go before Ourania's entrance exams to the teachers' training academy, and the volume of homework, neither of the girls had much time for anything else. Ourania was feeling particularly happy; Alexis's last letter had been very positive and full of plans for what he hoped would soon be their reunion. The fresh air and warm November sun was exhilarating and both sisters were in high spirits.

'Remember that year when Alexis bashed his hand with the rake so hard he broke his wrist and he was running around screaming like a girl?' Ourania told everyone, laughing.

'How can I forget?' Aphrodite replied, stopping to catch her breath. 'I was ready to break his other wrist for being so stupid!'

'That boy never listened!' shouted Chrisoula from where she was standing. 'He always did dangerous things when he was young.'

'What about that time when my old dad picked up the sack full of olives which split open and spilled them all over the place?' Costandis reminded them from halfway up a ladder.

'That was funny!' one of the cousins replied. 'You all started shouting at him . . . Poor *Bappou*, he was so embarrassed!'

'Oh yes, do you remember? We had to pick up all the olives one by one,' another relative laughed, reaching out to beat a branch that had just landed in front of him.

'It wasn't really his fault,' Ourania said, 'poor Grandfather! The sack got caught on the rake and ripped without him noticing.'

The good-natured chatter and reminiscing went on as people worked, and the mood on that November Sunday was jovial and happy.

'All right, everyone! I need a break now,' Andrikos suddenly shouted, looking down from a gnarled old olive tree he was sitting on, wiping his brow with a big white handkerchief. He'd spent most of the morning either up a ladder or on a tree and he'd now had enough.

'Well come *down* then! I'll take over,' Calliope shouted to her father, eager to climb the tree before one of the male cousins got in before her.

'I'm next!' shouted Ourania, always competing with her sister when it came to tomboy tactics.

'You wait your turn!' Calliope shouted back and started climbing the ladder.

Each person had a task, everyone knew exactly what they had to do and they all worked together in peaceful synergy. At some point, someone began to sing and gradually one by one they all joined in. Young voices and old voices all melted together in a lilting island song that spoke of the sea and her fishermen, the fishing boats and their precious load of coral and pearls. The humming of the bees, the twittering birds and the singing voices, all merged into one while the sun beat down on

177

everyone's back and the sky rained big hard purple, black and green olives.

The loud dull thud which made the ground vibrate around everyone's feet was quite different from the sound of a branch hitting the earth. Abruptly the singing stopped. Everybody froze. An icy silence brushed over them. There, right in front of everyone, amongst the leaves, branches and fallen olives, lay Calliope. She was sprawled out like a broken doll, having just fallen out of the tree, and still clutching the branch she had been sitting on.

Everyone stood mute and very still. Chrisoula was the first to break the silence: with a piercing scream, she rushed towards her daughter. As if a spell was broken people jumped into action and rushed forward, apart from Ourania, who was rooted to the ground unable to move. She blinked several times, expecting that each time she looked again the scene in front of her would be different. But what she continued to see was her mother kneeling over her sister's apparently lifeless body.

'*Panayia mou!*' Chrisoula was screaming. 'She's not breathing! Quick, someone get the doctor.'

All at once everyone started yelling and crying, jolting Ourania out of her trance. Panic and adrenalin kicking in, Ourania turned on her heels and started to run and run and didn't stop until she was pounding at Dr Doumas's front door.

'My sister, my sister! Doctor, doctor!' she yelled through sobs and tears. 'Come quick! She's stopped breathing!'

Calliope's fall wasn't fatal. When the doctor arrived he was relieved to discover that she was in fact still breathing and thankful that no one had attempted to move her. She was, he said, suffering from concussion and had to be taken to the hospital immediately. A make-shift stretcher was constructed from the nets and sheets on the ground, and under the doctor's instructions, slowly and with great care, Calliope was placed in his car and driven to the hospital, her mother and Ourania by her side.

Apart from a fractured elbow and three broken fingers, Calliope had suffered no other apparent injuries. However, despite the doctor's initial assumption that she was merely concussed, she had in fact fallen into a coma. No further diagnosis of her alarming condition could be made until she recovered consciousness. The whole time Calliope slept, Ourania would anxiously scan her face for the slightest movement, but she remained motionless and pale, her chestnut curls a halo around her head. For sixteen days and nights Ourania refused to go home or to school and stayed by her sister's bedside, until finally one morning Calliope snapped her eyes open and started talking to her.

'Ourania! What's going on? Why am I in bed?' she asked, bewildered.

'Good morning, sleepyhead!' Ourania replied, trying to sound cheerful for fear of betraying her worry. 'Do you remember falling out of a tree?' she asked and bent down to cover her in kisses.

'I remember flying,' Calliope replied, looking around the ward, 'but why am I in hospital?'

'You weren't very successful at flying and you fell to the ground!'

'Ouch! That must have hurt!' Calliope smiled. 'Am I OK?'

'Yes! And now that you have woken up you'll be even better, but you gave us all such a fright.'

'I'm sorry about that. How long was I asleep?' she asked, lifting her hand to look at her bandaged fingers.

'A little longer than your usual lie-in.'

'Can I go home now?' she asked again and tried to sit up.

'We have to wait for the doctor. He told me I had to get him the minute you opened your eyes.'

'Can I sit up and wait for him?' Calliope asked as if everything was back to normal.

'Perhaps we should wait.' Ourania was hesitant. 'Dr Doumas has been looking after you.'

'I'd like to move a little, I feel so stiff,' Calliope said and tried to shift herself up to a sitting position but her elbow gave way beneath her, causing her to fall back again.

'Help me sit up, Ourania *mou*, I've no strength,' she said and reached out for her sister's arm.

'It's not very surprising you are weak.' Ourania put an arm round her sister's waist to help her up.

Leaning on Ourania, Calliope tried to shift herself into a sitting position on the bed but found it impossible.

'That's strange,' she said, 'I don't seem to have any strength at all.' Suddenly it hit her. 'My legs . . . it's my legs!' Calliope said in an almost inaudible whisper. 'I can't feel them!'

6

Contrary to what everyone had hoped, Calliope's fall had been a very bad one. She'd been too foolhardy and high-spirited that day and had climbed way up into the tree's top branches. Her bones might have been able to withstand the force of impact with minimal injury, but the trauma and damage to her spinal cord resulted in a neurological condition causing total paralysis of both of her legs, and partial paralysis of her left arm.

Chrisoula was inconsolable and kept blaming Andrikos for letting Calliope go up the ladder in the first place, making the poor man feel more wretched than he already was. The shock was immense for everyone, but it was Ourania who took the news the hardest. She was totally devastated for her sister, yet tried her best not to show it; she knew she had no option but to be strong for Calliope because now it was *her* turn to support her.

Life on a small Greek island in the 1930s was not conducive to major health problems. Dr Doumas was a good doctor and took good care of his patients but he was not equipped to deal with the severity of Calliope's condition and the same went for the town's hospital, which was some twenty kilometres away from the village. With its limited resources the hospital did the best it could for Calliope, but as always relied heavily on the patient's family to help with their care. The only place Calliope would have received better medical treatment was in one of the larger hospitals on the mainland, where, if she was mobile, she could have been taken. But in her case, first in a coma and then paralysed, taking her anywhere, let alone putting her on a boat, was an impossible task.

The months that followed after Calliope left the hospital, and until a wheelchair shipped over from the mainland arrived, were the hardest for everyone. Bed-bound, Calliope felt wretched and helpless, and the logistics of moving her whenever necessary were agonizingly difficult. Yet, together with her mother, her aunt and their other sisters, Ourania did everything, and more, for Calliope. They bathed her, and put her on the commode, fed her and brushed her hair, read her books, and sang her songs. Ourania did it all willingly and lovingly, knowing without a doubt that if the roles were reversed her sister would be doing the same for her.

At first Calliope was in a state of denial; she expected that gradually her legs would recover their mobility until one day she would just get up from her wheelchair and walk again.

'I feel a tingling in my toes,' she'd tell Ourania. '*Look*, I think I can wiggle them.' But of course she couldn't.

After her initial state of despair, slowly Calliope started to come to terms with her situation, making huge efforts to deal with it in a stoic and philosophical way, as was her nature.

'If this is my fate, I must face it and continue with the life I have been granted,' she told Ourania. 'I can't do anything about my legs, but I can do something about my soul. I do not want to live in constant misery.'

But still, Ourania was distraught. She couldn't bear to think that her sister was going to be an invalid for the rest of her life. They had so many dreams, they had made so many plans together. She couldn't believe this could happen to them, because, in all earnest, Ourania felt that what had happened to her sister had also happened to her. They had shared a symbiotic relationship since early childhood and as their mother used to say, 'They're like one person those two. If one cuts herself, the other one bleeds!'

But it was not Ourania who'd been crippled; *she* had the use of both of her legs and the ability to go wherever she liked, whenever she liked, yet the idea of going any distance without her sister didn't enter her mind. It was months before she even considered going back to school, let alone thought about leaving the island to go and meet Alexis. The whole premise of their plan was that once she and Alexis were settled somewhere Calliope would join them. How could that ever happen now? How could she *ever* leave the island? Calliope couldn't even sit up without help. Their dream was in shreds.

Of course Ourania still thought of Alexis and continued to write to him, but perhaps not as often as before. She wrote and told him about the accident straight away, but that was when Calliope was still in her coma and before they knew the extent of her injuries. Once the severity of Calliope's condition became apparent, Ourania's focus shifted; for the time being her sister had become her number one priority. As much as she missed Alexis and longed to be with him, she could not imagine or contemplate leaving Calliope behind. What she desperately wished now was that Alexis had never left and that he was still there with them, lending his support.

The long absence from school had seriously hindered Ourania's entrance exams to the teachers' training academy, but under the circumstances an exemption was made and she was allowed to resume her studies with a view to sitting her exams the following year. It was nearly ten months before she actually returned to school. A few months later Calliope decided to follow, determined to continue with her education too and resume some kind of normality in her life.

Philipos, the bus driver, who loved the two sisters, had been extremely distressed to find out about Calliope's condition. He melted with sadness at the sight of the young girl in her wheelchair and he went out of his way to be helpful. The first thing he did was to take out a seat at the front of his bus to make space for Calliope and her chair; then he made a contraption to enable her to be lifted onto the bus.

After twenty years of blind obedience to time keeping, Philipos changed his timetable in each direction by twenty minutes in order to accommodate the extra time needed to get Calliope on and off the bus. In the evening, once the girls were safely dispatched and he could see they were on their way home, he would glance at the shrine on his dashboard, cross himself, and whisper a little prayer to the Holy Virgin to watch over his own girls. He knew all too well that the two sisters on the road, one in a wheelchair and the other pushing it, could easily have been his own two daughters.

In the meantime, Alexis anxiously waited to receive more news from home about Calliope, but it was two months before a letter finally arrived telling him of her condition. Ourania's initial letter to him had been full of hope and confidence that as soon as Calliope regained consciousness she was going to be fine, with just a few bruises and some broken fingers. He remembered people falling from trees during olive harvest and recalled some of his own foolish mishaps and dare-devil antics, but there had never been anything as serious as this before. Once he found out about the magnitude of Calliope's situation he became very distressed; he loved his younger cousin and couldn't begin to comprehend that she'd have to spend the rest of her life confined to a wheelchair. He felt guilty for not being with them back on the island at such a difficult time.

Ever since he'd left, Alexis had done nothing but work long and hard, with only one aim in mind – to save enough money to send for his sweetheart. Now, just as he was nearing his goal, everything seemed to have gone wrong. If it wasn't for Costandis and Uncle Georgios's support and friendship, Alexis would have been desolate.

During their time together, Alexis and Costandis had developed a real brotherly bond between them. At the end of each day the two of them would lie back on their bunks and talk until they fell asleep. Costandis was the first to take Alexis into his confidence, not long after they started working on the ship. He spoke about his life, about what made him leave his own home.

'I left for the love of a girl called Xanthi,' he confessed one night after they'd finished work and were taking a breather on deck. It was a beautiful, mild night and the two boys couldn't bring themselves to go back down into the oppressive heat of their cabin. Costandis reached in his trouser pocket for his packet of cigarettes, stretched out on his back and started to talk. 'I was fifteen when I first fell for her,' he began, 'and at first she didn't even know I existed. The roof of our building overlooked her house and one day when I was helping my mother to hang out the washing, I discovered that I could see right into her room. From that day on, most days and evenings when the washing was up, I would hide behind it and watch her. To begin with she didn't know I was there, and then one day as she stood by the open window brushing her hair she saw me! She didn't move, just carried on brushing and looking across at me. Then, before she turned to walk away, she waved.

'After that, she would come to the window and let me see her. She would usually brush her hair or just sit looking over at me and before turning away she'd always wave. Then one day, instead of waving, she blew me a kiss! That was it! I lived for the moment when I could see her. We'd sometimes pass each other in the street, or I would see her in church, but we never managed to speak, we just looked at each other. Her father was like a mad dog when it came to his only daughter. And her two brothers? Ha! They were even worse. It was a rich family, you see, and I was just a poor boy.

'This long-distance love affair continued for a quite a time. I was nearly seventeen and she was almost eighteen by the time we actually first met face to face. Xanthi's best friend would cover up for her and we started to meet secretly. It wasn't very often but we managed it once in a while and that went on for a long time too until one of her brothers found out and then all hell broke loose. They threatened to cut my legs off and *worse*, if I ever went near their sister again, and they put Xanthi under lock and key.'

Costandis took a deep breath and reached for another cigarette. He passed one to Alexis and then continued with his story. 'You see, her family had *given the word* that in two years' time Xanthi would be married to the son of a rich family, a friend of her father's. What could we do? If we wanted to be together I had to steal her, we had to run away.'

'Yeah, sounds familiar.' Alexis sighed, folding his arms behind his head as he looked up at an impossibly starry sky.

'It sounds so funny now to say *steal*!' Costandis laughed. 'I wonder if any other nation in the world, apart from the Greeks, steal each other! But it's hardly theft when the person you're going to steal wants to be taken! Anyway, can you believe what they did? *Giving the word* without even asking her! She was beside herself. In the end, we decided that instead of running away

189

with no money and nowhere to go, I would leave first and before the two years were up would send for her.'

'Yeah,' Alexis said again and flicked his cigarette overboard into the black night, 'sounds familiar.'

'So how about *you*, my friend?' Costandis asked cheerfully. 'Did you leave your home to see the world, or was it for the love of a beautiful girl too?'

Of course after his long confession, Alexis had expected Costandis's question, and he knew that it was only fair to reciprocate, but the prospect of talking about his love for Ourania made him anxious and his palms moist with nerves. He hadn't even uttered her name out loud for so long, the mere thought of saying it made his heart beat faster.

He knew he could never tell anyone that Ourania was his first cousin, the subject was taboo and he valued his friendship with Costandis too much to risk jeopardizing it. The story Alexis told was like his friend's, a common enough love story from the islands – he was not deemed suitable by Ourania's family to be her husband, so they too had no alternative but to run away in order to be together.

Apart from confiding in each other, the two friends took Uncle Georgios into their confidence too and sought advice and guidance from him. He was happy to assume a paternal role for both boys.

Their main area of concern was where they should set up home once the time was right to send for their sweethearts. They had to make a decision, they had to be organized and plan carefully. One possibility they discussed was to stay in Cardiff with Georgios, but then again they both wanted to return to Greece. During his time on the ship Alexis had proved to be something of a linguist. He'd picked up with relative ease a fair amount of English, Italian and German, making it possible to live anywhere; but the call of the homeland was beckoning them both.

Uncle Georgios was of the opinion that the northern Greek city of Thessalonica was the best place for the two young men to start their new lives. Apart from being a large port, which would enable the girls to reach it with greater ease from their particular islands, Thessalonica had always been a welcoming city to immigrants and refugees alike. As Georgios explained, it would be an easy way to start afresh, a new beginning with no questions asked.

So Alexis, with hope in his heart and unaware of the events that were developing back on the island, had written to Ourania to explain the plan. He asked her to start preparing herself for the journey that would change both of their lives forever.

Back home, Ourania was in emotional turmoil. She too had only ever wished for one thing – to spend the rest of her life with Alexis. But now, just as her wish was about to come true, she wasn't sure she wished it any longer. Confusion reigned in her head and in her heart. Alexis was the love of her life, the man she had pledged to spend her future with, but her sister was her flesh and blood, her soulmate, her best friend, and she loved her more than she could say. Going to find Alexis meant she would be following her own happiness; but how could she *ever* be happy knowing that she had abandoned Calliope? How could she leave her sister like that? It was an agonizing decision, and for the first time in her life Ourania had no one to turn to.

Calliope and Aphrodite were the only ones who knew about her secret and she was sure that if her sister knew what she was thinking, she would put up a fight and urge her to leave. As far as Calliope was concerned she wanted her sister to be happy, and the plan remained the same – Alexis was going to send for Ourania sometime soon. The only thing that had changed was that now she would not be joining them, not then, not ever.

The more Ourania turned things over in her head, the more she thought her head and heart were going to explode. Finally, one day, propelled by an overwhelming desire to talk to someone, she found herself knocking on her Thia Aphrodite's door.

Although surprised to see her there, Aphrodite welcomed her with civility. She took Ourania's hand and invited her into the house. She had forgiven both her son and her niece for what she considered their sin and felt that as long as the two were kept apart, there was nothing to fear.

'Come, sit with me,' she told Ourania and patted the embroidered cushion on the intricately carved oak-wood divan, a piece of heavy island furniture handed down by her grandmother as part of her dowry. Ourania looked visibly distressed.

'Tell me,' Aphrodite said hesitantly, guessing that her niece must have come to see her with news from Alexis. 'Have you heard from the boy? Is he all right?'

'Oh yes, *Thia*, *he* is fine,' Ourania replied and then started to cry. Although the two women avoided being alone together, Calliope's accident had brought the families closer, and Aphrodite had been spending most days in her sister's house doing whatever she could to help.

'What brings you here, Ourania *mou*?' the aunt said and reached out to take the girl's hand. She knew her niece was devoted to her sister and that she had been badly affected by her condition. 'How is Calliope today? Has something happened?' she asked gently.

Ourania did not answer. She couldn't. She sat, hands folded in front of her, weeping silently, choked by the tears that filled her huge brown eyes and fell down her cheeks and onto her lap. She continued to cry for a long time, her aunt patient by her side, until her tears stopped and her voice returned.

'No,' she finally said sharply, looking up at her aunt. 'Nothing has happened! Nothing at all!' she continued with the same forceful tone. 'Calliope is the same. But I wish something *had* happened. I wish a miracle had happened and that my sister could get up and walk again and run and dance and skip and swim like before, but no, Auntie, nothing has happened! Calliope will stay a cripple all her life and there is nothing any of us can do!'

There was anger and sadness and defiance in her words, and once she finished talking Ourania's tears returned again. Aphrodite reached across and, taking both of her niece's hands in hers, spoke gently.

'God is merciful, Ourania *mou*. This was Calliope's fate, and you must always remember that everything happens for a reason.'

'What possible reason could there be for this to happen to my sister?' she said angrily.

'It's not for us to say, Ourania *mou*,' her aunt replied softly.

'The only possible reason I can see,' Ourania continued, pulling her hands away from her aunt's, 'is to make sure Alexis and I are kept apart! I know you say that we have sinned, but if God is merciful why does he punish poor Calliope?'

'God *is* merciful, Ourania, do not lose your faith. Calliope is not being punished.'

'If this is not punishment then what is it?' Ourania said with bitterness.

'Calliope has a strong spirit and a good heart. She will become even stronger now. She will overcome this.'

'Calliope didn't need this to be strong, she is the strongest of us all!' Ourania threw back at her aunt. 'In any case, my sister won't have to overcome this alone! I will always be with her. If what you say is true, that everything happens for a reason, then maybe Alexis and I were never meant to be together.' She wiped her tears with the back of her hand and stood up to leave. Walking towards the front door Ourania suddenly hesitated and turned back. She stood tall and proud while Aphrodite continued to sit, and with a trembling voice that seemed to belong to someone else she spoke again to her aunt. 'No matter what happens, Thia Aphrodite, you must know this. I love Alexis with no shame, and with all my heart, no matter what *you*, or anyone else says, and even if we can't be together *I* will still love him for as long as I live!'

After her outburst, Ourania rushed out of her aunt's house before she broke into more tears and ran all the way to the beach to her secret hideout. For months she'd had to be strong for Calliope and had kept her sorrow hidden. Finally it welled up and could no longer be held back. Sitting alone in the cave she cried without constraint, without limits, letting her tears flow. She cried for her unfortunate sister, she cried for herself and for Alexis, and she cried for their doomed love.

Ourania sat hugging her knees in the cool darkness of the cave and let her mind form thoughts she'd never allowed herself to think before.

What if her aunt was right, she wondered with despair, and what if Calliope was being punished for her and Alexis's sin? She believed in God, but she did not *want* to believe in a God that punished love. After all, wasn't God supposed be the *personification* of love? Why could loving another person be sinful and why was physical love so terrible that someone had to be punished? Her thoughts were jumbled-up, contradictory, confused. She always prided herself at being logical, informed, not allowing primitive island superstitions to take hold of her. She scolded her mother if she gave into such meanderings, so why was she now being tormented by such irrational thoughts herself? There was no possible logic or reasoning in any of this. She loved Alexis, *that* she was sure of, and nothing would diminish that. If this was a punishing God then she did not love Him.

As she sat cocooned in the familiar twilight of the cave with Alexis's aura all around her, Ourania came to a profound conclusion. She realized that her love for

Alexis had not diminished one iota, but she also realized, with astonishment, that what *had* diminished was her desire to go and find him if that meant leaving Calliope behind. Her love for her sister was greater than her desire to seek her own happiness with Alexis. It wasn't a matter of guilt, it wasn't only a matter of duty; it was a matter of choice. It wasn't that she *should* not leave her sister, it was because she didn't *want* to leave Calliope. She was choosing to stay.

Gradually a calm washed over her. She had no idea how long she sat in the cave but when she eventually left it was with a heart full of love for the two people who meant more to her than anyone else in the world. Her torment of indecision was finally over. She was content that she had made the right decision. She hoped that Alexis would forgive her.

7

Greece, the Aegean, 1999

In less than twenty-four hours Anna had learned more about her family and her own history than she had in all her years. Her father's words were cutting deep into her soul, redefining the knowledge of who she thought *she* was and the people around her. Ourania and Alexis's story had been unimaginable. Perhaps she thought she ought to have felt affronted on her mother's behalf to learn of the love between the two cousins. A forbidden love her father secretly harboured for a woman whom Anna's mother considered a good friend. But how could she condemn them in the face of such adversity and such love?

'Oh Papa, did Mama know about Thia Ourania?' Anna asked through her tears. 'I always thought my mother was the love of your life. There was so much sadness for all of you, how did you live through it?'

'There were many times after Ourania made her

decision not to follow me that I wondered how I managed to live on,' Alexis replied, his voice breaking. 'But we do live on, Anna, life finds a way.'

'How did you manage to love my mother after your love for Ourania?' said Anna, her head a jumble of questions. 'Or ever *love* again at all?'

'Love has no limits, Anna *mou*, it's what keeps us alive. I want you to know I loved your mother deeply, and she never knew about Ourania. What would have been the point, apart from to cause pain?'

'But how could you love truthfully with such passion more than once in a lifetime, Papa? How is that possible?'

'I loved them both truly and with all my heart, but there are many truths in life, my girl, and there are many ways of loving. Life has a habit of surprising us, Anna *mou*.' Alexis's eyes, fixed in the distance, were looking into the past. 'You see it was out of our control in the end. As much as Ourania and I wanted to be together and we tried to make it happen, it wasn't meant to be then. There are some things in life that are bigger than all of us.'

Anna wondered if she could ever possess the courage like her aunt to forsake her own happiness for someone she loved. She could only ever imagine doing that for her children. The question of loyalty had been a constant companion to her ever since she arrived on the island. How could Max, after all these years, contemplate an exit from their life? And for what? Didn't family, history and loyalty count for more than an ephemeral emotion and selfish gratification? As her father had said, weren't some things in life much bigger than ourselves?

She wasn't sure if she could have been as selfless as Ourania, but she definitely knew she could never have inflicted the pain that Max had inflicted on her. Seeing her father and her aunt together now, their love still evident and enduring, fuelled her anger about Max's betrayal and disloyalty. A thought started to take hold. Had she finally stopped loving him? Had her anger taken over from love? Part of the reason for coming on the island was to give them time apart, time to think, and possibly find a way forward. But as much as she still cared for the life they had shared, their children, and their past, she found his actions unforgivable and she was now plunged into more emotional discord.

Talking with her father had been a revelation. His wisdom and depth about matters of love astounded Anna; he was the last person in the world she would have ever contemplated having a discussion with about *the many ways of loving*, but perhaps, Anna thought, Alexis was right. Who knows? Perhaps even Max had a right to fall in love with someone else. She had never of course entertained such thoughts but right now she couldn't be sure of anything.

Nicos had stirred new feelings in Anna and the

realization that she, like Max, was capable of a strong connection with someone that wasn't her spouse blurred her otherwise clear mind about such matters. Could she have done that if Max hadn't betrayed her? She didn't think so. But her total sexual surrender to Nicos, so out of character, caused her to question herself. When Max told her that he was *in love* with someone else, she was devastated, uncomprehending. *How could he be in love with a stranger?* she kept asking. But didn't she now have feelings for someone she hardly knew too? How was that possible? Though as she was now rapidly finding out, many things that were unimaginable before seemed to be possible now.

'So, Annoula *mou*.' Alexis's weary voice brought her out of her thoughts. 'Life sometimes doesn't always go as planned. Ourania's choice was final and I had to respect it.'

'What did you do then, Papa?' Anna asked, hoping Alexis wouldn't give in to his fatigue and stop talking.

'I will tell you, Annoula, I promise, but be patient. There is still much to tell, but first let me breathe and then let me rest for a while.'

Alexis rose from the table and made his way to his bed. A few minutes of rest always did him the world of good. Sleep is a sacred occupation for the Greeks, Anna mused. This was something she had learned from an early age. Siesta was considered essential, especially in the summer months after the midday meal. For Alexis it was a way of life, even in London. Anna remembered fondly how her mother would scold her and her brothers if they made too much noise when their father was taking his rest. In later years when Anna was a teenager and couldn't get enough of sleep, often sleeping past midday, her mother would be protective of her too. If friends called at the weekend Rosaria would ask them to call back. It never ceased to amaze them. 'My mother thinks I am a lazy layabout if I stay in bed later than nine, even on a Sunday,' was a common complaint.

When several of Alexis's English friends also questioned this habit of his, considering it a terrible waste of valuable time, he'd explain with a chuckle, 'It revives the body and sharpens the mind, my friends, you should try it sometime, you might enjoy its benefits!' As a child Anna too thought of it as a waste of precious playtime, but now she also relished the opportunity.

Following her father's advice, Anna took herself off to a shady part of the garden where a breeze always blew from the sea, and lay on a blanket under the lemon tree. She closed her eyes for a while and waited for Alexis to get up and continue with his story.

Storgé
(στοργή *storgé*)

means 'affection' in ancient and modern Greek. It
is natural affection, like that felt by parents for
offspring. Rarely used in ancient texts, and then
almost exclusively as a descriptor of relationships
within the family.

8

25 July 1939

My darling Lexi, light of my eyes,

I have been thinking about you every minute of the
day and night, and I have been agonizing about
writing this letter to you. First I want you to know
that my love for you is, and always will be, wider
than the ocean that separates us and vaster than the
sky that unites us. I want you to know that I will
love you forever and ever and you will stay in my
heart as long as I live. My dearest love, I know that
this letter will break your heart in two as mine
already is.

You know that being with you and spending the rest
of my life with you has been the only thing that I
have ever wished for, and I know all too well that you
have spent the last two years trying to make it

possible for us to be together. But alas, my love, Fate has played such a cruel trick on us. Your mother says it's all God's will, and that everything happens for a reason, but I do not know of any reason that my poor sister should be punished like this, or why you and I have to be separated.

The only thing I know, Lexi mou, is that as much as it pains me to be apart from you, I cannot abandon Calliope now in pursuit of my own happiness and I could not live with myself or be happy. I know she has the rest of our family who will look after her, but she and I are so close, we have taken care of each other ever since we can remember and I cannot leave her now.

Calliope knows nothing of this. She would be furious with me if she knew I have sent you this letter. She still thinks I will be joining you soon, but I cannot do it. I will have to face her and tell of my decision. I can only do what my heart tells me. You know me better than anyone and I know you will understand why I'm doing this and you will forgive me.

When you are ready, please come back to us, my love. Although I would never ask you to forget me, I couldn't bear that, we have to try and forget our passion and our desire for each other and the wish to live as man and wife, but try instead to live as cousins.

My heart is full of pain. It aches for you and me and for Calliope too, but I must choose willingly to stay by my sister's side. I will finish my studies and become the teacher I have always wanted to be. This will be my life from now on. I will try and be happy, as you must do too. Maybe your mother is right. Perhaps this is God's will.

Your beloved always,

Ourania

Alexis read and re-read the letter in disbelief. To begin with, Ourania's words were incomprehensible. They were just a jumble of letters that made no sense to him at all. The more he read, the more grief-stricken he became. Tears rose to his eyes and streaked the blue ink on the paper. How could his Ourania do this to him, to *them*? He sat on his bed dumbfounded, holding his head in despair while Costandis and Georgios were drinking coffee downstairs and listening to the wireless.

Suddenly, in a moment of blind anger, Alexis grabbed

the letter from his lap, screwed it up into a tight ball and threw it out of the window. An instant later he leapt off the bed and ran downstairs into the garden to rescue it. He smoothed it out, read it again, folded it neatly, and put it in his pocket. Then, trying to regain composure, he went into the bathroom, splashed his face with cold water, tucked his shirt in, grabbed his jacket and left the house for Agios Nicolaos. He left quietly, taking care not to alert Costandis and Georgios to his departure. He had no desire for discussion just yet. He needed to be alone with his thoughts. Besides, his two friends were still preoccupied with listening to the BBC news.

For days now Uncle Georgios had been glued to the wireless set. In the last few months the world events that were unfolding had given him a lot to worry about. Talk of a possible war with Germany was being discussed in hushed tones in the Greek community, inducing a sense of fear and uncertainty in the hearts of everyone.

In the silence of the empty church, Alexis started to calm down; he always found solace in prayer. For him it was a form of meditation and the church a place of contemplation. There, he could always put order in his thoughts. In the same way that Ourania had found her place of contemplation in their hideout on the beach, Alexis found it sitting on a wooden pew in a Greek Orthodox church in Cardiff, nearly two thousand miles away from his native home and the people he loved most in the world.

Ourania, he thought, had made her choice and he had no right to demand that she abandon it for his sake. He had no doubt that she loved him, but if she chose to renounce that love for the sake of Calliope then he must accept it. One thing was clear to Alexis: he loved Ourania with every cell of his youthful body but he loved her like a woman, and could never learn to love her, as she had asked of him to do, with a brotherly love. That would kill him. How could he return to the island and pretend otherwise? How could he *endure* living near her while she married someone else and bore someone else's children? He would rather stay away than do that. At least then his love would remain in his heart forever.

When he'd finally put his thoughts and feelings in some kind of order Alexis got up to leave. Before walking out, he stood for a few moments in front of the icons, lit a candle for Agios Nicolaos and once again asked the saint to grant him courage and strength.

Alexis blinked as he came out of the church into the bright light. It was unusually sunny for the first day of September. He didn't much like the grey northern days and felt sure he would never get used to them. He stood for a moment outside the church to light a cigarette and then started to make his way towards the harbour. The autumn sun beat down on his back and made a welcome change from the usual Welsh drizzle. It felt good, it gave him hope. He took off his jacket, slung it over his shoulders and stood looking at the ships lined up along the bay. *The Doric* gleamed in the sunlight. He stayed a while, gazing at the cranes and cargo nets that were unloading the vast vessel which had been his home for the best part of two years, and wondered what the future held for him. He and Costandis were due to leave for their return journey to Piraeus in a few days. He'd been ready to make it his last. He was looking forward to settling down, getting a job on land and starting a new life with Ourania. But now? He wondered with a heavy heart. Where should he go? What could he do? Was the sea going to be his future from now on?

Alexis had lived with such a clear vision about what he was going to do and where he was going for so long. Now that everything was blurred, he didn't like it at all. It frightened him.

When he returned to the house, he was surprised to find his two friends still huddled over the wireless in a state of distress. The ashtray on the side table was piled up high with cigarette ends and the room was thick with smoke.

Seeing Alexis, Uncle Georgios leapt off his chair, causing it to fall with a crash, and started bellowing at the top of his voice, his face red as an over-ripe tomato. Alexis, startled at this uncharacteristic outburst from his friend, took a few steps back, assuming that perhaps he was the cause of Uncle Georgios's distress.

'That bastard Adolf Hitler!' he raved. 'He's gone and done it now! He has sent troops into Poland!' Georgios was pointing at the wireless and gesticulating madly. Alexis was confused. He looked from Costandis to Georgios with alarm, trying to fathom what was going on.

'We are doomed!' Georgios carried on shouting. 'We'll be at war before the month is out, mark my words!'

'Perhaps not,' Costandis suggested, trying to keep calm. 'They might find a solution. No one *wants* a war!'

'That's what they said before.' Georgios's voice was somewhat calmer now. 'I don't trust those Germans.'

'Let's try and be hopeful, Uncle, you never know, they might be bluffing.'

Two days later, 3 September and the last Sunday before the boys were due to depart, Uncle Georgios prepared a full English breakfast for them. It was the only English culinary delight they both enjoyed, and despite feeling anxious and worried about the pending events, Georgios felt a sense of occasion which he wanted to mark with a loving gesture towards his 'surrogate' sons.

'You never know when the three of us might be able to sit down and eat like this again,' he said, piling eggs, bacon, tomatoes, mushrooms and fried bread on all their plates. 'You'll soon be gone, back to Piraeus, and who knows what will happen next?'

The three sat eating at the kitchen table with the wireless blaring at full volume in the next room. They'd been told that the Prime Minister would be making an announcement to the nation and all morning the radio presenters had been drawing the listeners' attention to his coming speech and urging people to stay tuned to their sets.

After breakfast the three friends took their Turkish coffee – a fresh supply was brought from Greece for Uncle Georgios with each voyage – to the living room. Like the rest of the British nation, they gathered around the wireless waiting for the news. Finally, at 11.15 a.m., the Prime Minister, Neville Chamberlain, spoke to the British people from the Cabinet Room of 10 Downing Street: 'This morning,' he began, 'the British Ambassador in Berlin handed the German government a final note, stating that unless we heard from them by 11 o'clock that they were prepared at once to withdraw their troops from Poland, a state of war would exist between us.' Then, unable to disguise the emotion from his voice, the British Prime Minister spoke the dreaded words that nobody wanted to hear. 'I have to tell you now that no such undertaking has been received and that, consequently, this country is at war with Germany.'

Since Uncle Georgios's intuition had been almost spot on, give or take a couple of weeks, that Sunday breakfast turned out to be the last one the three of them would be having together for a very, very long time.

9

Lesbos, 1939

In September, just a month before war was declared in Greece, Ourania travelled to the island of Lesbos, where she could attend the Academy and start her teacher's training. To her great joy she'd managed to win the scholarship she'd been dreaming of and had worked so hard to get. Calliope, too, hoped to join her the following academic year and encouraged her sister to go ahead, promising she'd soon be following. Both girls had decided that teaching was the path they would follow and together they planned eventually to open a much needed school in their village.

During that first year, life for Ourania seemed to carry on more or less the same as before. The developments of the war which were affecting the mainland and especially Athens hadn't quite reached the islands and although she was anxious about being away from home, it was decided that since the Academy was still open it was safe enough for her to remain where she was and continue with her studies. Most days the students were able to attend classes and everyone was hopeful that things would soon calm down.

When she first arrived on Lesbos, Ourania had expected to feel isolated and lonely away from her family and especially from her beloved Calliope, but the world events that were taking place created such an atmosphere of excitement and comradeship amongst the students, she didn't have much time to think about her own circumstances. She took a room in a house owned by a widow called Kyria Ismini, who was making ends meet by taking in lodgers. She was a distant relative of Ourania's Auntie Aphrodite and the house had come highly recommended as a respectable place for her to take up lodgings. The widow only ever took in girls, since her biggest regret in life was that she never had any of her own. Her husband had been killed in the 1918 war between Greece and Turkey and she'd been left alone and childless.

Although rather small, the house was pleasant, light and airy and was surrounded by a beautiful fruit orchard which made up for only having three bedrooms. Ourania would often take her books and sit under the cool shade of the trees to study.

Since there were four girls living in the house and only three bedrooms, one of which was allocated to Kyria

Ismini herself, the girls were expected to double up. Ourania, who had always shared not only her room but her bed with Calliope too, welcomed the company and was content with the arrangement. Her room-mate was a girl called Thalia, also a student at the Academy and studying mathematics.

Thalia's family home, although on the island, was in a remote village too far for her to make the daily journey into the town. Her father was a wealthy farmer and could afford the fees for his daughter's education, even if he couldn't see the point of it.

'My father thinks I will stay a spinster and that I'm throwing my youth away,' Thalia had told Ourania when they first met. 'He thinks all this education will put off any man wanting to marry me.'

'I know,' Ourania sighed, 'my mother thinks the same. She was keen at first, but then she started trying to marry me off.'

'All I can say is that although my parents are not educated and can't understand why I would want to be, they still let me do it. For that I will always be grateful.'

The other two girls lodging with Kyria Ismini were sisters from a small island nearby, doing their apprenticeship with a seamstress and hoping to open their own dressmaking shop in their village. They all liked each other well enough, especially Ourania and Thalia, who were both united by their thirst for learning and determination to be educated. The other two were shy, simple girls in awe of their brainy housemates. They spoke only when they were spoken to, finished each other's sentences and provided a constant source of amusement to Ourania and Thalia.

Kyria Ismini enjoyed having the girls around. Even if she fancied they were the daughters she never had, she demanded a strictly regimented rota in keeping the place clean, and the girls obliged without too much complaint. They were all used to pulling their weight in their own homes.

During her first year away from home Ourania's education went much further than her academic studies. If in matters of the heart she was more knowledgeable than most girls of her own age, her life experiences were limited to those of the close-knit community of her island. In contrast to her birthplace, Lesbos was one of the largest Greek islands. Kyria Ismini's house was situated a short bus ride outside Mytilini, the capital, which was a buzzing, busy port with shops, markets, restaurants and tavernas, the likes of which Ourania had never seen before. Far from being overwhelmed by the size and strangeness of the place, she had an appetite for change and was more than ready to embrace it. Although she had dreamt and longed for adventure, Ourania never thought she'd be doing it alone, always imagining that

Alexis would be by her side. But she was a resilient young woman and although her love for Alexis never faltered, she was determined to make things work and not allow herself to wallow in regret or self-pity. Besides, Calliope had taught her a lot about strength and bravery.

The feeling of solidarity and camaraderie that was prevalent amongst the student population in Mytilini had spread to the rest of the island; people, young and old, felt united and would gather day or night in bars and cafes, to listen to the wireless and discuss the war situation. This rallying together helped Ourania and acted as a buffer to any feelings of alienation she might have otherwise felt, alone in the strange city, and it enabled her to settle into her new life sooner than she imagined.

There was a large circle of friends at the Academy with whom the girls spent most of their free time. In particular, Ourania had formed a close friendship with a young man called Michalis who was one academic year ahead of her and also studying to be a teacher. If Michalis hadn't fallen head over heels in love with Ourania the minute he saw her it was doubtful that she would have noticed him. She didn't even know he existed until he pulled up a chair next to her in the students' common room and began to talk.

In appearance Michalis was the antithesis of Alexis. Whereas the latter was tall and athletic, with a head of thick black hair, Michalis was rather short, slight, bespectacled, and at twenty-two had already started to go thin on top. Alexis's brown-eyed gaze could ignite a fire in Ourania's heart, hot enough to burn a hole in her silk chemise, whereas Michalis's eyes peered at her from behind his glasses. His physical appearance had never provoked a second look from any girl, yet the instant Michalis started to talk, the moment he engaged anyone in conversation, his less-than-impressive physical attributes would fade into insignificance. His conversation was captivating and his voice resonated with passion as he spoke. Once you got to know him he appeared to be as handsome and as attractive as the best of them. At least that's what Ourania thought.

An active member of the newly formed communist resistance group at the Academy, Michalis was respected by many of his fellow students who shared the same liberal political views. Before the war, he had been, along with the rest of his family, a member of the socialist party, who opposed the dictatorial rule of Prime Minister Metaxas. Now the changed political climate that had seized Europe had given his ideals a new focus. Ourania felt secure in his company, she thought he was wise and clever and she liked nothing better than to sit and talk with him. She wasn't *in love* with Michalis, but she *liked* him more than she could say.

'We have to resist, Ourania, we have to resist with all our might,' he said to her one night as they sat under the stars in Kyria Ismini's orchard after they'd all shared some food together and everyone else had gone to bed. The home-grown vegetables that Kyria Ismini grew in her garden were essential since food had now started to be in short supply. The widow had always grown just a few tomatoes, cucumbers and herbs for her own use, but now with more mouths to feed she had to increase both her repertoire and production. The landlady was a sociable soul and always welcomed company and any friends her girls brought home with them. That evening Michalis had joined them for dinner. They had all shared a pot of *fasiolia* beans that the sisters had cooked, and after the meal they sat talking together for a while until one by one they went off to bed, leaving Michalis and Ourania, with Kyria Ismini's permission, to continue the conversation.

'We cannot allow fascism to spread its evil tentacles,' he was saying with passion. 'If he'd been allowed, Metaxas would have willingly taken us into the abyss.'

'Couldn't he see that Mussolini is a monster?' Ourania asked with horror.

'No! He's no better than him. He is a megalomaniac,

a fascist sympathizer. If it wasn't for Churchill and those of us who care, we would now be allied with the enemy! Can you imagine that, Ourania? The Greek people doomed and disgraced because of one man's madness?'

No one had ever spoken so expansively to Ourania about such things before. Politics was not a subject discussed at length in her family; her parents were simple uneducated people who didn't know much about such matters, and Michalis made her think, made her question things. He wasn't much older than her, Ourania thought, yet he seemed to know so much. Her heart welled up with a strange emotion, a fondness for this myopic, unathletic but cerebral young man who spoke beautifully, with empathy and passion and made everyone sit up and listen.

'It seems to me that the world is full of madmen,' she replied wistfully and looked up at the diamond sky. 'Why can't people just live in peace? Why so much hatred and pain?'

'You have a lot to learn, Ourania *mou*,' Michalis replied gently. 'The world is a hard place, you don't have to go further than this island, this country, to see the division and hatred between people who don't share the same views.'

But even if Ourania's knowledge of politics and the

wide world was limited, she knew more than he could imagine about intolerance, prejudice, superstition, and the human condition and its perils.

Part Three

Naples, Italy, 1944

1

The first time he saw her was from behind. She was standing with her back to him in front of a vast stone sink in the old kitchen, washing a pile of pots and pans with water heated in a kettle. She stood in a shaft of light which streamed through the high window, dust particles gyrating in a synchronized sun-dance all around her. Her hair, a mass of dark curls, was held back with a pink ribbon matching the apron she was wearing, which was wrapped tightly around her waist, tied into a big floppy bow that hung over the hollow of her back and onto her rounded buttocks. He noticed that her bare legs, the colour of ripened wheat, were covered to knee length by a floral-patterned dress and that her shoes had seen better days. He stood motionless, thinking that if he as much as blinked he would cause her to vanish and Signora Philomena would appear in the girl's place.

He stood staring at her for some moments, until, as always seems to happen, the girl became aware of being watched and turned around. It would have been hard to say which of them looked more flustered. She blushed a rosy pink to match her apron and Alexis felt beads of sweat break out on his brow.

'*Scusa, Signore,*' she stammered, casting her eyes down and starting to wipe her hands on the apron.

Alexis was lost for words. He leaned on the doorframe to steady himself. The girl who was now facing him had reminded him so much of Ourania that for a crazy second, a wild moment of lapsed reasoning and logic, he had fancied that when she turned around it was going to be *her* standing there.

She was quite lovely, this girl. Huge, brown, sorrowful eyes dominated her face. It was the kind of beauty Alexis understood, a familiar kind of beauty that spoke to him. But she was not Ourania.

He'd met many girls over the years. There were always plenty to be found when the soldiers were on leave and all willing to please. War seemed to have such a liberating effect on people and the paradox never ceased to amaze Alexis. Once in a while he'd meet a girl who stirred something in him and then he would give in, and let his youthful lust take hold of him, but always the memory of his cousin lingered. Throughout the eight years of separation from Ourania, Alexis had never met anyone who moved him as much, until right then in the old kitchen; the girl standing in front of him in her apron and old shoes made his pulse race in a way it hadn't since he had left the island.

'*Buongiorno,*' he finally said, finding the use of his

vocal cords again. 'Where is the Signora?' he continued in Italian, not knowing what else to say.

'She is feeling ill today, *signore*,' the girl replied shyly in the Neapolitan dialect. 'Signora Philomena, she is my aunt, she has sent me in her place.'

The Signora was a warm, friendly woman, who reminded Alexis of his own mother. She had been their housekeeper for a few months now; she came to the HQ every day without fail, always alone. She cooked and cleaned, and she was well liked by all the officers, even if most of them couldn't say more than *arrivederci* to her. All verbal communications were made through Alexis, as a result of his duties as the Allied Intelligence Unit's translator.

Any volunteers who possessed some kind of linguistic skill were considered a great asset to the war effort, as both Alexis and Costandis discovered soon after they enlisted. Anyone with more than a slight grasp of a foreign language was often directed into the British intelligence corps to act as a translator. Since both boys fell into the category of linguists, they were sent off for a few months of basic infantry and intelligence training, before being dispatched to their overseas posts. Alexis's most recent posting was to Naples, by way of North Africa, where he put his small understanding of Arabic to good use. Italian, he found from his time on *The Doric*, was quite easy and similar to Greek, so in the few months since he'd been in Italy he'd become almost fluent.

By the time Alexis arrived in Naples in January 1944, Italy had already signed an armistice with the Allies, yet the devastation he encountered was enormous. What the Allies had left standing, the retreating Germans had razed to the ground, leaving the city in ruins. Huge bomb craters, rubble and debris blocked the streets, with cars, trams, all kinds of vehicles left abandoned and the entire urban infrastructure demolished.

Air raids had destroyed the main water supplies, and people were forced to distil seawater for drinking and cooking – if they could find anything to cook. Neapolitans resorted to combing the countryside for anything edible and had even been forced to start eating the animals in the zoological gardens and fish from the city's tropical aquarium. An unbearable stench from the damaged sewers hovered in the air like a grim reminder of the city's general decay. It was by far the worst war experience Alexis had encountered.

Amongst the devastation a few buildings were still standing and one of those, a former *palazzo*, had been commandeered by the FSO and British Intelligence for their HQ. It was in a dilapidated state, cockroaches and mice had been permanent tenants there for years, and its past grandeur was only detectable from the marble staircase, high ceilings decorated with mouldings, huge gilded mirrors and lavish chandeliers. But compared to the rest of the city it was still a palace, and Alexis was more than relieved to be stationed there.

Theirs was a small unit with much work to be done. The Anglo-American alliance had prompted many people to start offering their services as informers, apparently out of gratitude for what they considered their liberation. It transpired that many of the volunteers had previously been working with the fascists, so all names had to be checked and vetted, a tedious task which was passed down to Alexis, who at twenty-four was the youngest in the unit. But it wasn't all dull desk work; since his main responsibility was translating between civilians and his officers, Alexis was regularly taken out on field work around the city and the neighbouring countryside and villages. If Signora Philomena reminded Alexis of his own mother, and her cooking transported him back to Aphrodite's kitchen, then the local citizens of Naples reminded him of the ones he'd left behind on the island. He felt a close affinity towards these Neapolitans who were so much like his folk back home, the people he loved and longed to be with, but had no idea when, or if, he'd ever see again.

Alexis continued standing in the old kitchen in awkward silence, trying to think of what to say next to the girl across the room.

'Oh, I see . . . your aunt,' he eventually heard himself speak. 'Did she say how long she will be away? Er, does she need a doctor?'

'I don't know, *signore*,' the girl replied, 'she was unwell in the night. We see how she is tomorrow. My name is Rosaria, *signore*,' she said again shyly and walked towards Alexis to shake his hand.

'Pleased to meet you, Rosaria, my name is Alexis,' he replied, snapping out of his predicament and taking her hand in his. He held it like a small bird, still damp from the washing up, and wished he could have kept it there forever.

He no longer wanted to know or cared how long Signora Philomena was going to be absent. He just wanted to stay holding Rosaria's hand for as long as possible because she was making his heart beat in an old forgotten rhythm he hadn't heard in years and which he was now welcoming back with joy.

2

After that first meeting Alexis couldn't get the girl out of his mind and did his utmost to be in her presence whenever possible. He seemed to have an inbuilt 'Rosaria radar' and was able to locate whichever part of the building she was working in and strike up a conversation. Rosaria on the other hand seemed to lose the power of speech in Alexis's presence and flushed rosy pink at the very sight of him.

Apparently, in typical Neapolitan style, no one at HQ had been informed about the girl replacing Signora Philomena; Rosaria just turned up and started working there. As it transpired, the Signora's condition had worsened and to Alexis's delight her niece would continue working there until her recovery.

Since the unit consisted of only twelve men, it was inevitable that friendships would develop between them, and Alexis had become particularly friendly with two English soldiers, Tim Anderson and John Simons. Just a couple of years older than himself they had become to Alexis almost what Costandis had been to him the years before the war. Once the two friends got a whiff that Alexis was sweet on the new housemaid, they never missed an opportunity to rag him about it.

'She's a beauty that one, better be quick and ask her out,' was Tim's initial advice.

'If you don't hurry up *I'll* do it,' added John. 'You know what these Italian wenches are like, anything in a uniform . . .'

'I can see she's got it bad for you, Alexis, my old mate,' Tim teased, giving Alexis a slap on the back. 'Better strike while the iron's hot.'

'Stop pussy-footing about, man, and get in there, she's pining for you, can't you see?' the ragging continued.

Alexis took his friends' affable jesting in good humour but ignored any advice they had for him. He knew all too well what their attitude towards women was like: *bed them, have your fun and then move on to the next one.* Besides, Alexis wasn't at all sure if Rosaria was sweet on him too. What he did know was that *he'd* fallen for her and that she was the only girl who interested him. But Rosaria appeared to be unlike the majority of Neapolitan girls, who, as Tim suggested, were eager to throw themselves at anything in a uniform. She kept herself to herself, got on with her work and possessed a shy dignity that seemed to keep the men at bay. Conversation with any of them had to go through Alexis, which he looked forward to more than any other duty. Those conversations had also become the highlight of Rosaria's day and the main reason she got up in the mornings. She liked Alexis more than she would ever dare to admit.

The majority of Allied soldiers she encountered frightened her, they were either alarmingly white-skinned with cold, pale eyes, or big as mountains and black as ebony, and they all made her nervous. He was different, his gentle manner made her feel safe, protected and at ease and when she was with him she could forget her troubles. Even though Rosaria was falling in love she would not, *could* not, allow herself to admit it. She knew it would only lead to disaster.

Having Rosaria around made all the difference to Alexis's frame of mind. As the months passed and the first signs of spring appeared, a new, more positive mood was beginning to take hold of the city. It was as if the entire population of Naples simultaneously inhaled as much oxygen as they could into their lungs and with a synchronized exhalation attempted to rid themselves of all the toxic waste they had been carrying inside them for so long.

Windows and doors were flung open to welcome light into the damp dark rooms, and the start of a communal spring clean began to take place. Carpets, mattresses, sheets and blankets were being hung out, exposed to the long-awaited sunshine. Rosaria too joined in this seasonal ritual, unfastening long-closed windows to give the *palazzo* a good airing.

'We are welcoming the new season,' she explained to Alexis when he asked what was going on. 'It's good luck to make a fresh start. This place hasn't been properly cleaned in years.'

Rosaria took her work seriously, arriving punctually each morning to take up her duties, starting at the top of the villa and working her way down to the old kitchen to begin the day's cooking. She was an imaginative cook and performed miracles with the food rations and meagre supplies available to her. Flour and water were her main ingredients, and pasta and pizza her main dishes. Alexis had never tasted pasta like Rosaria's. His mother and aunt made it at home too and as a little boy he often watched them rolling the pasta and laying it out to dry, but he didn't remember it ever tasting as good as Rosaria's. He didn't know if it was the tomato sauce she served on it from tomatoes grown in the yard or his constant hunger that made it taste so delicious.

The kitchen was Alexis's favourite meeting place with her, but Rosaria too looked forward to his visits and especially to the days when he was required to drive her to the market.

'How come you are such a good cook?' Alexis had asked, surprised to see she was as good as her aunt.

'Maybe because my aunt taught me. Or because I love it, but probably because I've been doing it since I was seven years old,' she replied, but volunteered no more information.

As the initial shock and chaos began to subside, the people of Naples were gradually venturing out into the squares along with a variety of vendors who were out selling their disparate selection of goods. A little local produce was starting to make its appearance, even if black market prices made it almost impossible for most people to afford it. Black marketeering was at its peak, with stalls displaying and selling anything from stolen American cigarettes to tins of food. Soldiers often turned a blind eye to these petty thefts, choosing to concentrate on bigger things, such as the shiploads of army goods that were continually going missing, mainly controlled by the Camorra, Naples' home-grown mafia. Many ships were loaded with medical provisions, penicillin being the most popular on the black market for the treatment of syphilis, which nearing the end of the war had reached crisis proportions.

But people didn't seem to care, the sun was finally out and the first warm rays caused the girls to shed their winter garments, which were often made from old curtains or blankets, exposing flesh, which they unashamedly flaunted at any soldier who happened to pass by.

Prostitution had been rife all through the war in Italy; it had become a means of survival, and the trading of sexual favours for food was a common enough occurrence. Alexis and his friends were not strangers to it and although he was disturbed when he first encountered it, he too had become immune like everyone else.

The first time he was blatantly propositioned by a woman was in broad daylight, while he sat in a cafe with Charles Irvin, his commanding officer. After a demanding morning both men were in need of a moment's peace and a strong glass of something. They had been called out very early to a nearby village to deal with an incident involving an old man and his underage granddaughter who, he claimed, had been raped repeatedly by four Allied soldiers, and had begun screaming the place down wanting to kill them all and demanding compensation. He had barricaded the soldiers in his barn and was threatening to hack them to pieces with an old meat cleaver.

As it turned out the old man had been trying to sell the girl, a small emaciated thing of no more than twelve years old, to one of the soldiers, who foolishly allowed the old man to engage him in conversation, oblivious to what he was saying. Not speaking the language the soldier hadn't a clue what the old man was suggesting until finally the message got through and everything turned ugly.

'You have no idea what these people are capable of,' Charles Irvin had told Alexis over a glass of what was supposed to be grappa but tasted more like surgical spirit. 'They'd sell their grandmother, or in this case their granddaughter, for a tin of bully beef. But what can we do, they are all so desperate?'

Charles Irvin had been in mid-sentence when Alexis saw a woman approach their table. He'd noticed her earlier standing by the entrance of the cafe. In fact Alexis had thought that something about her reminded him of his mother or his Auntie Chrisoula, as women in these parts often did. She was not young, probably in her forties, dressed in a threadbare housecoat and carrying a shopping basket as if she was going to the market. She walked purposefully across the room towards their table and stood very close; Alexis could feel her thigh pressing inappropriately against his arm. Then, looking at both of them, first at the commanding officer and then at Alexis, the woman asked very softly and politely, as if she was doing nothing more than taking their order or enquiring about the price of fish, if by any chance either of them would care to have sex with her in return for some of their food rations. The mouthful of drink that Alexis had just taken suddenly and violently became expelled from his mouth and sprayed all over the woman's arm and dress. Taking this as a reply of refusal she turned around and walked out of the cafe as quietly as she'd come in. It took Alexis a good while before he recovered his composure and was able to speak again. This time there was no need to translate to his commanding officer what had been said; apparently he, unlike Alexis, had heard it all before.

'What did I tell you?' was Charles Irvin's only comment.

After that first encounter Alexis found that such incidents were all too common. Apart from the traditional sex trade – brothels, pimps and street walkers – otherwise decent women, ordinary housewives, were forced to offer their bodies or their children's, to any willing member of the Allied forces in exchange for a few tins of food to feed their families. It was an act that repulsed and saddened him and he was sickened to see some of his fellow soldiers eagerly take advantage of the situation.

If these women, he wondered, were driven to such desperate measures, what was happening back home? How was the war affecting everyone there, how were his mother, Ourania and everyone he loved coping? Rosaria's resemblance to his cousin had reawakened so many feelings in him. Thoughts of home started to torment him and he worried afresh about what his family might be suffering at the hands of the Germans. He had had no communication with any of them for so long that even the memory of their voices was starting to fade. He hoped and prayed that the island had been relatively safe due to its remote location, but he had no way of knowing.

He was an honourable young man with traditional values and found that the hopelessness that induced these women to barter sex so coolly, as if they were selling nothing more than produce grown in their fields, was incomprehensible. He was deeply troubled by this exchange of carnal favours, and that the sexual virtue of girls, which before the war had always been so highly protected and valued, had now turned into a commodity.

In the hope that a soldier would treat them well, buy them dinner, and if really lucky give them a wedding ring, girls were lining up to offer their bodies to anything in khaki. The ring was the main objective for most young women in Naples. Alexis and his friends would repeatedly come across desperate females searching for an American or British soldier who might fall in love with them and whisk them away from the misery of their lives. Some were lucky. Italian women possessed an earthy sexuality, so different from the play-hard-to-get girls back home, that many soldiers found irresistible, and were willing to put that much-coveted ring on their finger.

Alexis's friends, Tim Anderson and John Simons, had each temporarily acquired one of these *girlfriends* but for them it was strictly to pass their time, as both lads had girls waiting back home. Tim had taken up with a woman of mature age, well into her thirties, who seemed confident that he would eventually marry her. She claimed she was a war widow, her name was Concetta and she lived in a one-room decrepit apartment in one of the narrow alleyways in the centre of town with bad plumbing and damp walls.

'Never met a woman like her!' Tim boasted to his friends with a nod and a wink. 'There's *nothing* she won't do if I ask her, and a few things that I'd never even thought of asking.'

John was currently seeing a girl called Immacolata, who lived with her mother in the outskirts of Naples and whose name belied her natural inclinations. Concetta had managed to turn her poverty-line flat into a love-nest in which Tim, John, and often other friends, would spend their time off duty smoking, drinking and making love. Alexis had been an occasional participant at these gatherings but after he met Rosaria he never set foot in Concetta's flat again.

'Alexis, daaarling, you com *sta-sera* to my ouse, I ave beautiful girl for you . . . sì?' Concetta would try and tempt Alexis whenever she saw him. 'She is a *bella*! *Una bella ragazza* for you . . . you come with Teem tonight, sì? You will lov her!'

'Come on, Alexis, my old mate,' Tim kept on too, 'if

you won't come alone then get that girl of yours and join us. It's about time you showed that poor lass a good time. Can't be much fun for her stuck in that old kitchen all the time.'

'If you don't ask, you don't get, my boy,' his friend added.

But if Alexis had any time to spare he didn't want to waste it casually on some girl that wasn't Rosaria. He had finally, after all these years, fallen in love again, struck by a thunderbolt, an Italian one this time, the likes of which he'd seen raging over the Bay of Naples during an electric storm, and hoped that Rosaria had felt its force too; but he couldn't be sure. He had an inkling that she *liked* him – he read it in her eyes and in her smile when they were alone. But that was all, she never gave him any other sign. Still, he was prepared to wait. After all, hadn't he learned from a very early age to be patient when it came to love?

When finally, one sunny day, after several months of waiting and contemplating, he decided the time was right to ask Rosaria on a date, her response took Alexis by surprise. She was stooping beside an old antique sideboard in the officers' dining room putting away some crockery, when he got a glimpse of her through the open door. A gentle breeze from the window was playfully blowing some curls hanging down her back. Bewitched as always, Alexis walked towards her.

'*Ciao*, Alexis!' she said, turning round to greet him with a smile.

The curve of her hips, the pull of her dress as the fabric stretched across the small of her back following the line of her haunches, made him stir with desire.

'*Ciao*,' he replied nervously and cleared his throat. 'Rosaria . . .' he started, 'erhm, I wanted to ask you something. Would you like to take a walk with me tonight after you finish here? Or tomorrow night, or any night. Maybe we can go for a drink? I'll walk you home afterwards.' He held his breath, waiting for her answer. She stopped what she was doing and breathed in. There was a long pause before her reply came back, and when it did, her eyes would not meet his.

'*Non posso*,' she said quietly. Alexis saw her flush crimson all the way from her ears down to the top of her arms.

'Why, Rosaria? Why can't you?' he said, incredulous at her categorical refusal. He hadn't asked for much; an innocent walk, an early evening stroll along the promenade, like other people, a simple drink in a bar, nothing more.

'My family,' she murmured, 'they would not like it.' She avoided his gaze.

'Tell your family I will take good care of you. I'm

242

with the Allied forces, we are here to protect you, remember!' he said, trying to jest and make light of his disappointment. He wasn't going to give up. Having gone this far he would not take no for an answer so easily. Her reply was unexpected but her shyness and even her reluctance came as a refreshing change to him, making him all the more eager to pursue her. The idea that her family wouldn't approve appealed to him. Perhaps, he thought, she had a decent Catholic family that held on to their integrity and values and didn't stoop to use their girl as bait as so many resorted to doing. But he knew almost nothing about them. Rosaria had given him a very sketchy picture of where she came from. All she'd told him was that she came from a village in the countryside, close to the foothills of Mount Vesuvius, too far to travel every day into Naples so she had been staying with her Auntie Philomena.

'She is not getting any better,' she'd told Alexis after working at the HQ for a few weeks. 'She's much weaker now and she needs someone to look after her.'

'Doesn't she have a family of her own?' Alexis asked.

'I am her family,' she replied, offering no extra information. Alexis asked no more; he was no stranger to secrecy. Whereas his friends were urging him to enquire further about the girl, he preferred to take his time, respecting Rosaria's right to privacy and hoping that slowly she would trust him sufficiently to divulge more.

He knew that when the time was right for her, she would open up enough to allow a clearer picture of her life to emerge. In the meantime, he had to be patient and wait. After all, *he* was not exactly giving her a complete picture of his own life, so why should he expect it from her?

3

Over the months, Alexis and Rosaria's relationship went from strength to strength and the sexual tension between them became impossible to ignore. Alexis lay in his bed every night dreaming of her and Rosaria lived for the moment she would see him again. She had also fallen hopelessly in love and cherished every second she spent with him, yet she continued to keep her true feelings hidden.

Even though his first attempt to invite her on a date had been unsuccessful, Alexis was not discouraged; he waited a few weeks and then tried again.

'Next Saturday, some of us are going on a trip to Capri,' he told her one day in one of his attempts to entice her out with him. He'd gone to the kitchen to get a glass of water and found her kneading dough to make pizza.

'We're going to be on leave so Tim Anderson, John Simons, their girls and me have decided to make a day of it and I was wondering if you'd like to come with us too?' he blurted out nervously and sat down across the table to wait for her response. She picked up a handful of flour without looking at him and threw it on the dough. A fine white cloud rose between them, making him cough.

'We'll get a boat to Capri, maybe stop in Sorrento,' he persisted. 'We'll take a picnic. It will be fun and you can tell your parents we'll be a crowd. You won't be alone *just* with me, there will be chaperones, in case they're worried about that,' he went on in earnest. 'What do you say, Rosaria, will you come?'

She continued to say nothing, lips pursed, a frown across her brow, and carried on with what she was doing.

'Say you will come, Rosaria?' he implored. 'Please say yes!'

Alexis sat on the edge of his chair waiting and watching as she punched and kneaded the dough in silence. Finally she stopped, brushed a lock of hair from her left eye with the back of her hand and stood looking at him. All he could hear was his breathing and the clock on the wall ticking. At last, after what Alexis thought was an eternity, she spoke.

'Yes,' she whispered, 'I don't care what anyone thinks any more, Alexis, I've had enough.'

It was one of those clear spring mornings and a flock of seagulls circled the boat as it glided out into the bay towards the Amalfi coastline. The city behind them was bathed in a golden light while a soft mist hovered over the harbour. The Bay of Naples ahead glistened in the early sun and high up in the distance Vesuvius loomed like a dragon, ominously belching plumes of smoke from his gaping mouth. Anyone turning round to glance at the shore could have momentarily been fooled that they were looking at the splendid Naples of long ago and not a city plunged into chaos.

But on that spring morning, in early March, the six people in the boat heading for the island of Capri were determined that for that day at least they would try and forget the horrors of war and the wretched place they'd just left behind.

Tim and John were both in a cheerful mood, laughing, joking and cavorting with their girls, while Alexis beamed with happiness to finally have Rosaria sitting so close to him. The women in their Sunday best were delighted with this unexpected treat. Concetta, extravagantly dressed for the occasion in an elaborate hat, silk stockings, ruby lips, and a moulting old fox-fur flung over one shoulder, sat half draped over Tim, smoking an American cigarette. Immacolata, as if in keeping with her name, wore a simple blue dress with a delicately embroidered collar and had arranged her hair in an intricate style, piled up high on her head and decorated with tiny, brightly coloured artificial flowers. Her whole appearance, despite her heavy make-up, made her look like one of the cheap plastic statues of the Madonna found in the street shrines situated in almost every corner of the city.

Earlier that morning when they met at the harbour, Rosaria had been cloaked in a blue shawl which covered her head and most of her torso, but once on the boat she let it fall on the bench. Now, as they sat side by side, Alexis noted she was wearing, washed and pressed for the occasion, the same floral dress she had on the first time he saw her in the old kitchen. On her feet she had a pair of shoes which in comparison to her usual footwear appeared to be brand new. Of course, on close inspection, he realized that the illusion of newness was due to their owner having taken great care of them. Polished to a high shine, the shoes were a cherry-red with a wedge heel and a thin strap that coiled around her slender ankle and fastened on the side with a silver buckle. Around her neck she wore a small silver crucifix encrusted with tiny sea pearls, much like the ones the girls wore back home to church on Sundays. It dangled just above the start of her cleavage, where the scoop of her neckline allowed an occasional glimpse.

For the first time since he met her, Rosaria wore her hair loose. It cascaded over her shoulders in an abundance of dark curls and every time she moved it released a delicate aroma of orange blossom. Alexis sat as close as he could to her, their thighs touching. After a while he reached across and took her hand in his and there, on that boat, in the middle of nowhere, Rosaria finally relented.

Sorrento gradually came into view, perched precariously on cliffs that rose defiantly from the sea. Alexis blinked in disbelief; he had never seen anything so splendid. The coastline that they were rapidly approaching was so dramatic, so mythical, it made him feel quite giddy. The waves lapped wildly at the rocks and the wind seemed to carry the song of the sirens to his ears. He too, Alexis thought, like Odysseus, had been lost for too long, had wandered for too many years with no apparent end to *his* Odyssey but with no Penelope waiting patiently for his return.

The salt in the air blurred his eyes and something like a sob rose silently from his breast to choke him. Tightening his grip on Rosaria's hand, Alexis shifted closer to her, and she, looking up at him, breathed a gentle sigh and closed her eyes, letting her head rest on his shoulder.

They disembarked noisily, the other girls shrieking at the splashing waves, and made their way up to the town for a quick look around and a stroll in the orange and lemon groves. They sat under fragrant trees laden with blossom and ate freshly picked oranges, smoked cigarettes and drank ice-cold limoncello while the heady perfume lulled them into a state of forgetfulness.

If Alexis was captivated by Sorrento, then Capri totally bewitched him. As the boat drew closer to the island he saw through the sea-mist a rock so massive, so powerful, so rugged and primitive that he almost expected to see mermaids basking on the shore. This was truly a land of gods and legends, and surely, if the call of Ithaca had not been so strong, there could have been no possible reason why Odysseus hadn't chosen to stay there forever. Rosaria too gazed at the approaching coastline with awe. She had so often stood looking across the Bay of Naples towards this legendary island, trying to imagine it. 'A wealthy man's paradise,' she was told. 'A playground for the rich,' she heard them say. She'd pictured lavish villas and exquisite shops, sophisticated socialites, beautiful ladies and dashing men sipping cocktails in elegant bars. But what she saw approaching her was nothing of the sort. She saw a deserted mountainous island, rising forcefully from the bowels of the sea, casting its shadow over the bay. Rosaria's eyes scanned the shore for the elegant ladies and smart restaurants but saw only a little harbour, unsuitably named Marina Grande.

Once on land, the party went in search of the town but found nothing but a cafe and a ticket office for the *funiculare* to transport them to the top of the mountain.

'The town is right at the top,' the station master

informed the group, 'but if any of you gentlemen feel particularly fit you can always take the steps. There are several thousand of them,' he said, laughing and winking at the girls.

The views from the *funiculare* were both magnificent and frightening and Rosaria, dizzy from the height and excitement, buried her face in Alexis's chest. Once they reached the top and stepped onto the Piazza Municipio, the town's main square, they encountered an entirely different world. Here time had stood still and everything Rosaria had heard about Capri proved to be true. Apart from some men in uniform there were no other visible signs of the war, only glamorous people, smartly dressed men with shiny brilliantined hair and ladies in flowing dresses, sitting in cafes. Rosaria blinked several times to make sure she was not dreaming.

After a glass of marsala at one of the smart cafes, the group set off to find a suitable spot for their picnic. They walked through twisting, winding streets, peered over treacherous cliffs at stunning views of emerald bays, and finally they arrived at the locked gates of a deserted villa where they could go no further. There, under the trees, they sat above the sea like gods. To the sound of birdsong and laughter, they ate white bread, such a delicacy, and tinned bully beef as if it was foie gras, and Naples was a thousand miles away.

At some point, while the others lay languidly on the

blanket engaged in their sexual games, Alexis took Rosaria's hand and led her away from them. He wanted to kiss her more than anything else in the world and if this was going to be the moment, then he wanted to have it in private. Willingly Rosaria gave him her hand and followed him down the path into a little green plateau. There, amongst the wild flowers and buzzing bees, Alexis took Rosaria's face in his hands and for the first time since Ourania, he kissed a girl with love and tenderness. Rosaria readily returned his kisses and gave herself with as much passion as he did. They lay together in the long grass holding on to each other, listening to the crashing waves below.

'I love you, Rosaria,' Alexis whispered in her ear.

Suddenly, Rosaria jumped up, and brushing down her dress made to leave. Alexis grabbed her hand and pulled her down again.

'I love you, Rosaria,' he told her again. 'Did you hear what I said?'

'Yes, Alexis, I heard you,' she replied and turned her head away from him.

'And do you love me too, Rosaria?'

'Yes, Alexis, I do. I love you,' she said breathlessly, 'but I shouldn't.'

'Why, Rosaria, because I'm not Catholic? Because I'm a soldier?'

'No, Alexis, because loving you might get you killed.'

'But I told you, Rosaria, I will honour you, your father doesn't have to worry about that.'

'It's not about honour, Alexis,' she said hesitantly. 'You don't know, you don't understand, you can't even imagine!'

'No! *You* don't understand, Rosaria,' he said and pulled her close. 'I want to marry you!'

'That's just it, Alexis.' She reached across and brushed his cheek with her fingertips. 'You *can't* marry me, Alexis! I'm already married!'

A day that had started with such exquisite promise for Alexis was turning into one of the worst in his life. Rosaria's words made his stomach churn and the light turn to darkness.

'Married . . . no!' he stammered in denial and disbelief. 'You never told me.' She stared at the ground, big fat tears rolling down her cheek. 'Your husband . . .' he asked, his head pounding as if it had been hit by a hammer, 'is he *dead*? Was he killed fighting?'

'No, Alexis,' she replied, suddenly looking up at him, eyes flashing. 'It's not like that, not like that at all! He is *not* dead, he has not been killed, but I wish to God he had!'

Confusion clouded Alexis's eyes.

4

As the tale began to unfold it became quite apparent to Alexis that the unwanted husband was not the only thing that was wrong with Rosaria's life. The girl he had fallen in love with was living a nightmare, trapped in a web that was threatening to suffocate her.

Rosaria was not yet eight years old when her father died from tuberculosis. The illness, which indiscriminately claimed the lives of so many people, was considered by the locals as something of a curse on their village and in their ignorance they believed any house inflicted by the disease was unclean and blighted. Rosaria's father was not the only one to be struck down; her little brother and two uncles were also taken, leaving the family fatherless and destitute, and the household tainted by the deadly malady. At twenty-five, Rosaria's mother Luisa was left a widow with two young daughters. Her elder sister Philomena was the only person willing or able to lend a hand.

'I remember those first years,' Rosaria told Alexis. 'No one would come near us, apart from my auntie and she had her own troubles. We had nothing. We had to make do with scraps for food, clothes from rags. I had to grow up in a big hurry, Alexis, my mama couldn't cope. I had to help her with everything, including looking after Sofia, my little sister. I missed my father and brother. We were desperate for someone to take care of us, to protect us. What we needed was a guardian angel but instead the devil himself walked into our lives.'

With two small children and herself to look after, Luisa had no option but to find a job, and the only possibility for any kind of work was in Naples. The prospect of the big city should have terrified Luisa but it thrilled her instead, so she packed a bag, handed the girls to her sister, and set off. Her good looks soon landed her a job as a waitress in a bar that meant she had to stay most nights away from home in a pitiful damp room above the bar. Being young, pretty and naive she soon started to attract the wrong sort of interest from the wrong sort of men, and one in particular. Salvatore De Sio was handsome and a charmer, sported a pencil moustache, wore a smart suit and smelled of expensive cologne.

Luisa had never been outside her village before, let alone worked in a bar or mixed with the likes of Salvatore De Sio. He bought her gifts, lavished attention on her, and turned her head. Soon she was crazy about him.

All Salvatore had to do was to whisper sweet nothings in her ear, pin a red carnation in her hair, kiss her sweetly on the lips and she willingly agreed to go and live with him. Her squalid room smelling of fried fish and sewage was no competition to the apartment that was now on offer. No sooner had she moved in with him than Salvatore insisted she gave up her job in the bar, promising that he would take care of her.

'I'm a rich man,' he boasted as they lay in bed. 'No woman of mine needs to work in a bar,' he murmured in her ear as he thrust himself inside her. 'You give me what I want and you can have anything your heart desires.'

This was a new kind of love and a new kind of sex for Luisa, whose husband had been a mild, gentle man who had never stirred such overwhelming physical sensations in her. To top it all she was being promised a life she'd only ever dreamt of. For that, she was willing to do anything.

True enough, Salvatore always had plenty of money and was happy to spend some of it on Luisa. Her village seemed to be a lifetime away. Once in a while she remembered to visit, and each time she arrived with food and clothes and stories about her new life, much to Philomena's disapproval.

'Who is this man, Luisa?' she asked her younger sister the first time she came home laden with gifts. 'What about your girls? Don't you want to be with them? They need you, I'm not their mother!'

'They love you, Philomena, you are a better mother to them than I have ever been. Please look after them for a bit longer. I'll send for them as soon as I'm settled. I'll talk to Salvatore.'

'Wake up, Luisa, stop dreaming! Why would he want your children? What makes you think a man like him, who takes in a pretty girl for fun, would want to take in her brats as well?'

'You don't understand, Philomena, he loves me, he wants me to be happy, he told me!'

'You don't know anything about life, Luisa. Don't believe everything people tell you, especially men like Salvatore De Sio.'

'I'm sure about him, Philomena, I love him and he loves me back and he's rich, and if you look after my girls I will look after you and all the family. I will bring you everything you never had before and we will all live well at last!'

'I don't know, Luisa, I have a bad feeling about this. You be careful, my girl.' But Luisa was deaf to her sister's worries and relished her new status as the mistress of a well-to-do man who apparently seemed to be as taken with her as she was with him. It took just three months before Salvatore De Sio's true character surfaced, and when it did, for Luisa there was no turning back.

After that she didn't have to work in a bar any more. He had other plans in mind and the kind of work he had lined up for her, and for many others like her, was the oldest profession of all. Prostitution, smuggling, kidnapping, blackmail and bribery were just some of the rackets Salvatore De Sio was involved in, along with the rest of his family, as one of the leading members of the Camorra.

One month of wooing and grooming was his usual style and the maximum length of time that Salvatore invested in his women, who were mostly provincial girls alone in the city. After he had broken them in they were moved out of his apartment and into one of his brothels, in the labyrinth of dark and putrid alleyways that made up the slums of Naples, and there they stayed. For Luisa, though, the story didn't end there.

Apparently Salvatore had taken a fancy to her. Apart from being a rare beauty, Luisa's blind willingness to please him and her readiness to become his sexual slave persuaded him to keep her with him three times longer than his other victims. She was pliable and easy to control and he was having fun with her.

Most of the other women would start to resist after a while, refuse his demands, scream and shout, but Luisa was ever ready and even seemed to enjoy it. A habitual drug user, Salvatore introduced her to hashish, his favourite recreational pastime after sex, thus increasing his hold on her and ensuring her submission to him. Even so, Salvatore had his limits. Three months was long enough with one girl before boredom set in and finally Luisa was sent on her way to join the rest of them. Besides, he needed her to start earning for him.

To Luisa's delight, Salvatore appeared to be quite hooked on her even if he didn't want to admit it. Once a week he would send for her to pleasure him. She discovered that this was a privilege no other girl had after leaving the apartment, and she was allowed to even spend the night with him. He apparently missed her imaginative sexual games. She was overjoyed. Every week the poor wretched thing was given new hope. Being singled out from the rest of the whores had given Luisa an elevated status which fed her deluded fantasy that one day Salvatore would take her back as his official mistress, or maybe even marry her.

The outbreak of war brought endless misery to the inhabitants of Naples, but to Salvatore De Sio it brought fortune. His business boomed and his brothels were thriving. The German occupiers were partial to local female company and they paid well. Salvatore knew how to cater for a variety of sexual tastes, and the new girl was popular amongst some of the high-ranking officers who needed special attention.

Luisa had been well and truly sucked into his dark

and dangerous world and she had now taken to it like a sea urchin to salt water. She hardly visited the village any more, although she still sent money and once in a while she would turn up laden with gifts. On one of those visits, soon after war was declared, she arrived in her furs and finery with a basket full of food, accompanied by Salvatore in his black limousine, wearing a fancy suit and smoking a fat cigar.

In an unusual gesture of generosity, more out of curiosity and the narcissistic impulse to show off, Salvatore had offered to drive Luisa to the village; by now he knew about the girls and Philomena, and how she disapproved of her sister's life.

'Let her see how well I keep you,' he told her. 'Let them all see what money can do!'

'And maybe finally my sister will stop preaching to me,' Luisa replied, hitching up her silk stockings.

When Philomena opened the door to her sister and her pimp, she had an overwhelming desire to spit on the ground and slam the door in their faces. She wanted nothing to do with either of them and if she had been alone she would have gladly refused their food parcel of sin. But food was running out in the village faster than water from a sieve and she wasn't alone, she had other mouths to feed. None of them could remember when they last saw a loaf of bread, and a bag of rice or potatoes would feed them all for weeks. How could she now refuse a basket full of tinned meats and vegetables, cakes, sweets, and delicious white bread, which she knew would keep them going for months?

'Where are the girls, Philomena?' asked Luisa as she settled herself down on the sofa in the tiny room her sister had kept to receive visitors, and which now was apparently being used for the girls' sleeping quarters. 'Where are Rosaria and Sofia? I want them to meet Salvatore!'

These were words that Philomena had hoped she would never hear, praying they'd be spared knowledge of the man she considered had been the ruin of their lives. It was bad enough that the girls should see what their mother had actually become.

'They are busy, Luisa, leave the girls alone,' she hissed at her sister.

'How can they be too busy to see their mama? Call them, Philomena, please, I want to see them.'

'They are better off *not* seeing you,' the older woman muttered under her breath.

'They are my girls and I want to see them,' the reply came back fast and sharp. Before either of them could say anything else, Rosaria walked into the room, followed by Sofia.

They hadn't seen each other in months and the change in the girls, especially in Rosaria, was acute. At eight, Sofia was still very much the little girl: lovely, with big dark eyes, and a mass of black hair. But at thirteen, Rosaria was blossoming into a little beauty. Her budding body displayed all the potentials of a gorgeous female, with an uncanny resemblance to her mother. At the sight of her, Salvatore's intake of breath was audible.

'*Ciao*, Mama,' Rosaria said quietly in a serious voice as she walked up to greet her mother.

'*Ciao, cara,*' Luisa replied, surprised at the sight of her changed girl. '*Sei molto bella, Rosa!* You're so beautiful, how you've changed! Come and give your mama a kiss.' Warily Rosaria approached her mother and reluctantly kissed her on both cheeks. From the corner of the room came a long, slow whistle of admiration from Salvatore.

'*Sì, sì, che bella ragazza!*' he exclaimed, with a glint in his eye as he shifted in his chair, puffing on his cigar and filling the room with smoke.

Philomena stood watching motionless by the door with fear in her heart.

5

The moment Salvatore De Sio laid eyes on Rosaria his evil little mind started to plan how best he could get his hands on her. As the war worsened, reports of air raids by the Allies on the village became more frequent. The invasion of Sicily by them in July 1943 followed soon after by Benito Mussolini's fall from power had opened the way to the Allied forces to invade the rest of Italy. With the situation getting more serious by the minute Salvatore took the opportunity to suggest to Luisa that she send for her daughters. But Philomena wouldn't hear of it. She was determined to keep the girls under her protection for as long as she could. She didn't trust Luisa and she certainly didn't trust *that sperm of the devil*, as she called Salvatore.

Night after night everybody in the village, including its entire population of cockroaches, vermin, lice and fleas, crammed into the dark and dingy railway tunnel that smelled of urine and unwashed bodies to take shelter. Eventually the raids became so unpredictable there was no time to even run to safety so immediate evacuation was ordered by the authorities. Mass hysteria broke out and people started to scurry like panicked ants, mainly to Naples where they imagined things were not as bad yet. Philomena was paralysed. Where should she go? She would rather have a finger chopped off than ask her sister for help, but she wasn't alone; she had the girls to consider. Luisa was apparently their only hope.

'We'll take just the girls,' Salvatore grunted when Luisa first told him about the evacuation. 'Your sister can find somewhere else to go.'

But Luisa hadn't entirely lost her bearings.

'She's my sister, I can't let her sleep in the street while they are dropping bombs!' she replied.

They were given a room in the basement of the brothel – if the hole that was made available to them could be called a room. But if nothing else, Philomena thought, for the moment at least, they were not in danger of being killed and they had enough food to eat. Nobody was starving there, crime paid well.

The first time Salvatore raped her, Rosaria was asleep. She had been suffering from a very high fever and she had been in and out of delirium for several days. It was Philomena who stayed by her side, taking care of her, washing her down, and keeping her cool. Luisa was too busy whoring to pay attention to her daughter.

That day was the first day Rosaria had been left alone. Her fever had started to subside, mainly due to the illegally obtained penicillin which Salvatore was now trading in the black market.

'The least you can do is ask your pimp to get some medicine for your daughter,' Philomena had screamed at her sister. 'The girl is burning up, she could die, and he is sitting on the medicine that would save her.'

That morning Salvatore was standing by a window puffing on his cigar and looking down at the street when he saw Philomena and Sofia leave. Neither of them had been out for days and the little girl begged her auntie to take her out for a breath of air. No sooner had they turned the corner and out of sight than he made his way down the dingy stairs to the basement.

He liked Luisa and her sexual games, and all the other females available to him, but he never said no to some young flesh when he could get it. He was not alone in his appreciation of the juvenile. He knew many, especially Germans, who were always willing to pay handsomely for the privilege of sampling unsoiled goods, and in these desperate times there seemed to be plenty of people willing to sell their children, girls or boys, for a price. But this one he decided he wanted for himself first. The other one, the little one, he'd be happy to pass on to whoever was willing to pay the most. But Rosaria was going to be his gift to himself for all the hard work he'd been putting in lately. He would sample her first before passing her on.

She was sound asleep, her forehead damp, her cheeks flushed from the high temperature. He didn't even wake her. He silently unbuttoned his fly, took out his member, and within seconds he was on top of her, lifting her nightdress and groping her body, frail and thinner than before because of the illness. She woke up screaming as he forced himself inside her.

The more Rosaria told Alexis, the more he despaired. He thought that nothing had been worse than the things he'd witnessed and lived through when he first arrived in a war-torn Naples, but what he was now hearing from Rosaria made his skin crawl. At the beginning when the war first broke out, Alexis knew people were fighting to defend themselves, to avoid being killed. At least then, when the fight was for liberty in order to defeat an enemy, it was for the common good and there was a kind of dignity about it. But after years of war, when the fight to stay alive took over, some with no common goal any more other than their own self-preservation were capable of terrible, dreadful things. When he first arrived he saw desperate people willing to sell their souls, their children or their mothers, for a crust of stale bread; as much as Alexis deplored this depravity he knew it was part of the grim necessity for survival. But what Salvatore De Sio was involved in was beyond his comprehension.

After that first time Salvatore told Rosaria he would kill her if she told anyone. He would sell Sofia to the first man who wanted to have sex with her, he added, and throw the rest of them out into the streets so they'd all die because of her. He liked that, he enjoyed the young girl's fear of him and he liked the power he had over her.

Rosaria prayed every night for the war to end, or for their village to become safe again so they could return, but far from ending, the war continued with a vengeance, and with new developments all the time. For over a year Rosaria dared not say anything. Philomena suspected something was going on but Salvatore was devious; as much as she tried, she never managed to catch him in action. With dread in her heart she watched her niece change into a moody, nervous, withdrawn creature. She wanted nothing better than to find somewhere else to take the girls, she even begged Luisa to help them, but as far as Luisa was concerned she had done her bit to help her family. Salvatore was her king who meant more to her than her own daughters. She was quite willing to give them up to keep her lover happy. She even turned a blind eye when she found out that little Sofia was promised to a German officer with a taste for the prepubescent.

Then Alfonso arrived on the scene.

Alfonso De Sio was Salvatore's younger brother, who had come home for a visit after travelling around the region taking care of family business. As soon as he saw Rosaria he was instantly in love, making him want for himself the young girl in the basement who his big brother had been bragging about. Her quiet fragile beauty, her tender years, and his brother's apparent enthusiasm, ignited his lust for her. But it wasn't just the sexual conquest that made Alfonso want to claim Rosaria as his. The obsessive competitiveness and sibling rivalry he always felt for his older brother was an even bigger motivator.

From an early age, whatever Salvatore had, Alfonso had to have too. If Salvatore thought Rosaria was so marvellous and declared ownership of her, then Alfonso had to take her away from him. She had to be his. His alone, and no one else's, especially Salvatore's. What Alfonso lacked in years as the youngest member of the De Sio clan he more than made up for in pathological temper. He was the only person who frightened Salvatore. Alfonso warned his brother to keep away from Rosaria and told him that if he ever laid as much as a finger on her again he would kill him. Of course Rosaria was never consulted; Alfonso wanted her and that was all that mattered, and what's more, in order to ensure that his brother kept well away from her, he was going to marry her! And so it came about that Rosaria, fourteen and a half years old, became Alfonso De Sio's wife, and a member of one of the most notorious families in the whole of Naples.

Given she had no option, other than to remain at the mercy of Salvatore De Sio, Rosaria realized that becoming Alfonso's wife was preferable to being the older brother's plaything and whore. Alfonso spent much of his time travelling; he wouldn't be there often. Moreover Rosaria was able, through pleading with Alfonso, to save her little sister, at least for the time being, from a life of childhood prostitution.

He married her in a rush before he had to leave town again, in the church of Santo Agnello, which was famed for the many miracles that had taken place there. Apparently it was this very church that the king and his court used to visit annually to watch the royal barber shave the hair that had miraculously grown over the previous twelve months on the ivory head of Christ. If it was good enough for the king then the church was good enough for the De Sio family. The ceremony was attended by Alfonso's formidable mother, father, two unmarried sisters, Salvatore, Luisa and a miserable Philomena with Sofia. Rosaria, wearing a white lace dress provided by the two sisters, stood wretched next to the groom, who held on to her hand with more force than was necessary.

As soon as he married her, Alfonso moved his bride out of the brothel's basement and into a small apartment by the port. Sofia and her Auntie Philomena would move in with her as her chaperones. Alfonso was satisfied with this arrangement; he would have access to Rosaria whenever he was in town and the rest of the time he would have his freedom. Besides, his main objective of taking Rosaria away from his brother had been achieved.

Poor Philomena felt helpless and guilty for not managing to protect her girls better. Every day she lamented the fate that had been bestowed on her family. Luisa was lost to her, but at least the girls were still all right, and with her. All she could do now was to keep them close and pray to the Madonna to spare them from further hardships.

After what they'd been through, living on their own in the apartment was a huge relief, but even if Alfonso was willing to provide a roof over their heads and contribute to Rosaria's keep, his generosity didn't stretch to the rest of them. Rosaria shared everything with her aunt and her sister but there were days when they barely had enough to eat.

'We don't want the De Sios' charity,' Philomena would tell Rosaria. 'I'll soon find work, I'm more than capable of earning our keep. I wish we didn't have to accept their dirty money at all.' But work was scarce, and coming across a decent, honest job was nothing less than a miracle, which is what the Madonna provided when after months of searching, Philomena finally found work at the Allied HQ.

'You keep your ears and eyes open,' Alfonso told Philomena when he first found out about her new job. 'Good to have inside information. Any shipments, any news, about anything, you be sure to report back to me.' Alfonso was more than pleased to have what he called a *spy* inside the Allied Headquarters.

6

Greece, the Aegean, 1999

Anna sat gasping for air and shedding tears of grief and sorrow for all those who came before her. An amphoraful of unimaginable family secrets continued to spill out with such force she thought she would drown in them. In a state of shock she remained speechless long after Alexis finally stopped talking.

'Why did neither of you ever tell us any of this, Papa?' she asked once her power of speech returned.

'Your mother was deeply ashamed, Anna, she swore me to secrecy. I could never break her trust.'

Wiping away the tears with the edge of her shawl, and trying to regulate her breathing, she reached across and placed her hand over his. 'At least about the hardships of the war, Papa, you could have told us that much.'

'Where do you start, Anna *mou*?' Alexis closed his eyes. 'Where do you begin? When your mother was alive there was no way I could ever have spoken about any of it.'

'And what about Thia Ourania?' Anna asked, troubled by conflicting emotions again. Who was more betrayed, she pondered, her mother or her aunt? Did her father spend a lifetime loving two women equally in an impossible love triangle? How was that possible? Her mother apparently didn't know about Ourania but how did her aunt feel about her mother? Ourania and Rosaria had become good friends over the years, how did her aunt cope with that? Anna's loyalties were divided and in danger of projecting her own feelings of betrayal onto the three.

'Who did you love more?' she finally asked, unsure if she wanted to hear the answer.

'There was never a question of more, Anna. No comparisons,' Alexis replied without hesitation. 'I loved your mother unconditionally, but I never forgot Ourania or forsook my love for her either, how could I?'

'But you lived with my mother all your life, she had your children. Didn't it make a difference?' Anna insisted.

'You see, Anna, it's like this; I love you and your brothers in the same way. There's no distinction, it's the same. Love is love, my girl!' Alexis took a deep breath and held it in for a long while before exhaling. 'You see, Annoula *mou*, if you have real *agápe* in your heart it never leaves you. Life is not black or white. Life is not straightforward.'

Holding her head in her hands, haunted by images of her poor mother, Anna continued to weep.

'You see, Anna,' Alexis carried on, 'you see how hard it is to hear it all? How could I have told you before?'

'Oh Papa, my poor mother,' she said through her sobs. Anna had idealized her parents' love and marriage. What she knew, what she had been told, was that their great passion withstood all obstacles, especially that of her Italian grandparents' opposition to the love-match. How could she ever have imagined that her own grandmother was a heartless whore willing to sell her own daughters? The little girl in Anna was crushed, things she believed to be true till then, shattered.

They sat in silence for a long time. Alexis lost in the past, Anna trying to find composure and put some order to her thoughts. She was now almost ashamed to have even thought of equating what she was going through to what her parents had endured. The similarities were so tenuous; the most you could have said was that there was a certain 'love triangle'. If those people in her bloodline had managed to withstand such adversities, shouldn't she be able to cope with what, in the scheme of things, seemed like a minor upheaval? Shouldn't she be letting go of the anger? She considered her own marriage again. Until some months ago, she had to acknowledge it had been a solid one, her life a charmed one.

Yes, Max could be intellectually arrogant at times but she also had to accept that she'd let him get away with it.

'Mum, don't put up with it!' Chloe had said once or twice when she deemed that her father was being pompous. 'He doesn't have the key to all knowledge.'

'Oh it's OK, you know what he's like,' Anna would excuse him. 'He has his students bowing to him so he expects us to do the same. He doesn't mean anything by it.' So Anna had to admit she enabled Max to be that way. But in the main, he was loving, caring, fun, a good father and up until now a good husband. There had been such happy days between them, when did it all go so wrong, she wondered? His betrayal had cut her deep, but his utter disregard for her feelings hurt the most.

Not that long ago, Anna and a few friends, on a girls' night out, had had one of their usual debates on the topic of infidelity.

'I guess, if it happens you'd have to sit down, and together examine what caused it,' Anna had said earnestly and true to her beliefs.

'If I found out that Jack had an affair I'd cut his dick off,' Angela, a divorce lawyer, declared, sending them all off into wine-induced giggles, '. . . and throw it out of the window!'

'I don't know, girls,' Sam, Anna's closest friend and fellow artist, replied, 'what if it was one of us. We assume it's only men who have affairs, but women do too . . .'

'I know I wouldn't,' Anna said with conviction. 'I love Max too much to betray him.'

'Why is it a betrayal if it's just a fling, just sex—' Sophia, Anna's sister-in-law, her brother's wife, added and stopped in mid-sentence. 'I guess it never is with us girls, is it?'

'Yeah, if we have sex, we get involved, fall in love and it all ends in tears, whereas with men it's mainly about the sex, right?' another friend added, and so the discussion continued.

So when Max told Anna of his affair, it was his ambivalence about his love for her and their marriage that shook her and her principles. She was sure that if he had been regretful of his actions and had asked for forgiveness, willing to have a discussion, she could have put her beliefs into practice. His indifference was intolerable.

'You are right, Papa,' she heard herself say after a long while, 'I guess life isn't that simple.'

'Even when you think you've got it under control life has a habit of surprising you,' Alexis replied, breaking his silence too.

'Please carry on, Papa, I need to know more,' Anna

said, while understanding that perhaps she should stop pushing him so hard.

'Patience, Anna *mou*, I'm not young any more, my breath is shorter than it used to be.' He reached across to pat the back of her hand.

'I know, Papa. I'm sorry,' she replied, feeling guilty but still carrying on. 'What happened during the war on the island? Were you in contact with any of them?'

'Oh my girl, you can't imagine . . .' Alexis let out a big sigh, the painful memories visible on his face. 'For a very long time I had no news at all and would go out of my mind with worry. Towards the end of the war, once in a while I'd receive a letter from my mother – your grandmother – which would eventually find its way to me and then I would learn some news of the family . . . and Ourania.'

7

In the meantime, back in Greece, 1944

'When the war is over I would like to come and help you set up your village school,' Michalis had said to Ourania when she first told him of her dream. 'Of course, that is to say,' he added hurriedly, 'if you and Calliope would wish me to.'

'I can't think of a better offer,' Ourania replied with genuine enthusiasm.

Her relationship with Michalis had become very important to her and the two of them spent most of their spare time together. When he wasn't visiting her at Kyria Ismini's house, they were taking long walks on the beach, or sitting for hours in cafes exchanging views and making plans. Michalis made no secret of his love for Ourania, and soon, much to her surprise, she found that she too was starting to feel more than just pure friendship for him. Although her feelings never approached wholehearted commitment as they had for Alexis, she was nevertheless very attached to Michalis.

Ourania was certain that Calliope would like him as much as she did and would welcome his help and knowledge; she was sure the three of them would make a great team. She had already spoken of Michalis in her letters, and Calliope was eager to meet the young man who had finally captured her sister's interest.

But the war was far from over, and it was obvious to both of them that any plans or dreams they had would have to be put on hold; the army needed all the able-bodied young men it could get, and soon Michalis, along with most of his friends, had to join up.

'Let us hope that we will be together again before too long,' he'd told Ourania when he came to visit her the night before he left. 'Then our country will be free, and democracy will rule again.'

It was a clear night and the moon was high in the sky, illuminating their faces. They'd strolled into the garden and were standing under a lemon tree laden with blossom. Earlier, they'd all eaten a farewell dinner cooked by Kyria Ismini herself, who, sad about Michalis's departure, wanted to create a feeling of occasion for their last meal together. For this, she was even prepared to kill her favourite hen and set the table with her best linen and bone china, both part of her wedding trousseau. When the dinner was over she ceremoniously produced a bottle of brandy which she'd kept for special occasions and asked Michalis to open it.

'Tonight calls for a toast!' she'd said as she handed the glasses around. 'Tomorrow, dear Michalis, who I have come to love as my own son, will leave us to go and fight, putting his life in danger for our sakes, so we must drink to his safety and send him on his way with our love.'

They all agreed, and raised their glasses to Michalis and wished him a speedy return. Then, as it always happened, one by one the girls and finally Kyria Ismini went to bed leaving the couple alone.

'Will you wait for me, Ourania?' he asked slipping an arm around her waist to pull her closer.

'Of course I will,' she said softly, brushing his cheek with the back of her hand.

'I will hurry and come back to you. I will come to the island and ask your father to let you marry me. Will you speak to your family about me, Ourania? Will you have me? *Could* you love me and will you be my wife when the war is over?'

He brought her hand to his lips and kissed it.

Unexpected tears welled up in her eyes and the storm that his questions stirred in her took her by surprise. A bittersweet emotion rose up from deep inside and a single word, a name, came to her lips. She swallowed hard to push it back but the word stayed hovering on her lips, demanding to be spoken. *Lexi!* Desolation and sadness overwhelmed her. For long moments she hesitated and pulled away from him. Michalis, wretched, stood waiting, his face pale in the moonlight; rejection seemed inevitable. After a pause that seemed endless Ourania brushed away her tears, took a deep breath and regained her composure, reaching for his hand.

'Yes, Michalis. I will,' she said gently. 'I will speak to my father and I will be your wife when the war is over, and I *will* love you, I promise.'

Without Michalis, Ourania felt vulnerable and nervous. The news from Athens was starting to be troublesome and every day they heard new bulletins on the wireless; the German invasion of the capital meant that it wouldn't be long before their presence would be felt on Lesbos too. Rumours were everywhere and Ourania knew she couldn't remain there any longer. She had no option but to return home to the fold of her family and wait for events to stabilize. Thalia too was going back to her village where her parents were anxious for her, and the sisters also were returning home; Kyria Ismini would be left alone.

'I wish I could take her with me,' Ourania said when she realized they were all leaving at the same time. 'What will become of her here all alone?'

'I'll ask my father to bring me into town to visit her sometimes,' Thalia reassured her, 'and she can always come and stay with us up in the village if things get really bad.'

Kyria Ismini, the eternal optimist, was confident that things would soon stabilize.

'What we have now is just a dark cloud and it will pass,' she kept telling her girls. 'We will have blue skies again soon and you will all be back to me to continue with your studies; you'll see.'

Of course Kyria Ismini couldn't have been more wrong.

When Ourania first arrived back home little had changed. Everything seemed the same; the effects of the war hadn't yet reached the outlying islands and life continued almost as before. Calliope was over the moon to be reunited with her sister and everyone, including her Aunt Aphrodite, welcomed her back with open arms.

'I'm so glad you are back home, Ourania *mou*.' Calliope embraced her sister. 'I have been so worried for you, we all have. You will be safe here with us now.'

But the war left nothing untouched and their respite was short.

As if in a dream Ourania heard the sound of motorbikes outside her window, followed by the shrill cries of Kyria Maritsa, the next-door neighbour.

'*The Germans are here! The Germans are here!*' she was screaming at the top of her lungs. Ourania sat bolt upright and looked at the clock on the wall – 5 a.m.; through the shutters she could see that day was just breaking. Shaking Calliope awake, she climbed out of bed and walked to the window. Through the slats she saw them, two by two, sometimes three, sitting together on the same motorcycle. They arrived with great speed in clouds of dust, halting noisily in the village square. At first there were half a dozen bikes. Then came the army trucks. Soon the square was almost full of Germans, dusty and tired-looking.

'Calliope! Calliope! *Panayitsa mou!* Mother of God,' she called to her sister who was struggling to shift her weight to the edge of the bed. 'They are here, and so many of them!'

'Who? Who's here? What's happening?' Calliope cried, still heavy with sleep. 'Help me, Ourania *mou*, help me get out of bed.'

Once they'd arrived, the first thing the Germans did was to take over the town hall as their headquarters and barracks for some of the soldiers. The rest, including many of the officers, were to requisition local houses. The undesirable task of informing villagers that they were obliged to play host to the enemy fell on the Mayor, who reluctantly went knocking from door to door, spreading the bad tidings. Ourania's father was told that an officer and his batman would be billeted with the family. They required separate rooms plus the use of the kitchen, bath house and latrine.

'Bastards!' Andrikos raved when the stressed and embarrassed Mayor delivered the news. 'I have a houseful of daughters! What am I expected to do with them?'

'I don't know why the evil sons of bitches didn't choose to move into my house,' his brother Costandis cursed when he found out. 'It's just me and Aphrodite living there. Yours is full to the brim.'

'I think they got a whiff of female scent,' Andrikos replied and spat on the ground.

'There is only one thing to be done!' Costandis thumped his fist on the table. 'The girls have to move in with us!'

That night, before the Germans arrived, four of the five Levanti girls moved into their aunt and uncle's house under cover of darkness. Asimina, the middle sister, who had given up waiting for Ourania to make her mind up about marriage, had accepted the previous year a *proxenia* and was now living with her husband's family.

Andrikos watched helplessly as their house was taken hostage by the two Germans who thundered about in their army boots, greeting each other with their hateful *Heil Hitler*, cooking their foul-smelling German sausages in his kitchen and shamelessly stripping down to their underpants when the sun was shining to wash themselves under the hose pipe in the back yard instead of using the bath house.

'They are like animals!' Chrisoula cried, horrified the first time she saw them. 'They have no shame or modesty.'

'I cannot tolerate this behaviour,' Andrikos hissed under his breath, red in the face. 'Can you imagine if the girls were here? Oh, the indignity!'

In an attempt to avoid too much contact with the Germans, the couple soon retreated to just one room on the top floor of the house, surrendering the rest of their home to the enemy.

The effect of the German occupation hit the island like a tsunami. Trade stopped abruptly, electricity was cut, censorship of the press was imposed and food rationing began. The new regime made itself felt instantly and the whole island was in a state of shock. Up until the Germans arrived, Costandis and Andrikos and the rest of the fishermen were more or less able to continue with their trade, but now it was proving very difficult. The Germans requisitioned food and provisions from everyone who had it or was producing it. Informers who were willing to rat on their compatriots for privileges and enemy money would pass information and point the Germans to the appropriate households. Soldiers would turn up on their bikes to search around and having established what was available would return in trucks and load them up with food and livestock.

The Levanti family had always grown their own fruit and vegetables, produced their own olive oil and wine and kept a few goats, chickens and rabbits. With the fishing, they had enough food for themselves and even shared some of it with other families, until the Germans started seizing everything. The only way to survive this abuse and fend off starvation was to find clever ways to conceal a certain amount of provisions for themselves. The livestock had been taken, but there was still all the produce from the garden and orchard and the girls became creative at hiding it.

They would keep food anywhere except the kitchen or the larder. They hid eggs and bread in a basket amongst their cotton reels and yarns for embroidery, milk and cheese in the washroom under piles of laundry, and vegetables in wash bowls in the bath house. They were clever too at distracting the blue-eyed, fair-skinned youths who were sent to carry out inspections. As much as the girls detested them, survival demanded that they do whatever was needed in order to divert their attention. The sisters were all pretty, and with four of them in the house it didn't take much to create confusion and put the soldiers off their task.

The only animal the Germans failed to take after their first search was a little brown hen which had developed an unusual attachment to Calliope, who had looked after her since she was a small chick with a broken leg.

'Most people have a cat for a pet,' Eugenia the youngest sister teased, 'or a dog, or a nice yellow canary in a cage that sings. *You* have to have a chicken for a pet!'

But when the unusual pet grew into a fat little brown hen with an impressive capacity for producing eggs, no one laughed any more. On the contrary, they all did their utmost to look after her and keep her hidden from German eyes. For her part, Kotoula, as Calliope called her, did her best to keep herself a secret too, as if she knew what was happening. The moment the army truck screeched to a halt outside the house, the hen would let Calliope pick her up and place her in a basket which hung from the arm of her wheelchair, topped with knitting yarns and needles. There she stayed, silent as a mouse, until the coast was clear. No soldier ever suspected anything and they all gave a wide berth to the strange crippled girl in the wheelchair.

In her disabled state, Calliope would have normally been at risk from Nazi policy, which had no tolerance of the ill, insane or crippled, but due to an impossibly lucky break she was saved. One of the German soldiers who'd been assigned to inspect the Levanti family had a sister who after a recent car accident had also been confined to a wheelchair back home; the sight of Calliope induced in the soldier confusion and uncharacteristic feelings of sympathy towards the Greek girl, so she was left alone.

During the German occupation education on the island was severally disrupted and most schools in the town and villages closed down due to lack of teachers. The young male teacher in charge of the village's elementary school had signed up and left the island, and although the high school in the town was still open, few teachers were left to take classes. Transport was minimal and no one felt safe to travel, especially the children. Even Philipos had now stopped his daily pick-ups in The Eagle; the village felt very isolated.

It was then that Calliope and Ourania came up with the idea of opening the village school again and volunteered to teach the children. The scheme was greeted with enthusiasm and pupils flocked back. Older children, now unable to make the journey into the town, also wanted tuition. Suddenly Ourania and Calliope found themselves very busy indeed.

Traditionally the children were used to being taught

sitting all together in one room, in rows of six, each row corresponding to a different age group. Each morning the teacher would start with year one, age six, and work his way up the age scale to age twelve. He would dedicate a period of time to each group and then once he had given them a task to perform he would move on to the next row, and so on. By the end of the day the teacher would have given some, but not much, attention to all six years. A laborious and time-consuming method of teaching.

With the older children keen to attend school too, Ourania and Calliope were faced with a challenge. They had to devise a new method of teaching to accommodate all the different ages. Instead of teaching all six classes at the same time as before, they decided to divide the years into three groups of two classes. Years one and two on Mondays, years three and four on Tuesdays, and years five and six on Wednesdays. The remaining two days of the week would be spent with the older children. Since there were two of them to teach, Calliope would take one group and Ourania the other, thus spending a whole day each week with each year.

The scheme was a success. The children were pleased to have an entire day of learning dedicated to them when they could ask questions and be given special attention, as well as having free time too. School had never been so much fun for any of them. The plan was effective; the girls worked very hard and managed to turn their own private dream into something that helped the whole community.

8

Naples

What Rosaria told Alexis didn't make him love her any less; her vulnerability made him love her more and long to protect her. Every time he saw her now he just wanted to scoop her up in his arms and kiss her troubles away. He wanted to help her, take her far away from Naples and the awfulness of her life. But how could he? Now, each night, instead of lying in his bed imagining he was making love to her, he lay awake trying to devise ways to run away with her. He wanted some advice and longed to talk to his pals Tim Anderson and John Simons to find out what they thought of the situation, but Rosaria had begged him not to.

'People are not always kind, Alexis,' she told him, 'they pass judgement. I'm not a whore, but I am the daughter of one.'

'The sins of your mother are not your sins, Rosaria!'

Alexis protested. 'You have done nothing to deserve your life. I love you, Rosaria, and I want to help you.'

'I love you too, Alexis, but you can't help me. When the war is over you will go back to your country and I shall stay here.'

'I want you to come with me! I want you to leave that monster,' he said and felt the blood rush to his head.

'This is a Catholic country, Alexis. Whether we like it or not, there is no divorce and even if there was, I'm married to a vicious criminal and I can never get away from him. Don't you see, it's hopeless.'

'Then I will stay in Italy and we will run away together, hide somewhere in the north, change our names,' he said, determined not to give up.

'There is no way out. He'll find us. Besides, I can't leave Sophia; my auntie is still sick, who is going to protect my sister if something happens to her? How can I abandon them both?'

Almost a year had passed since Alexis first arrived in Naples; a year full of life-changing events for him. He'd seen unimaginable human suffering and hardship, he'd encountered situations he couldn't have believed, met new people, made good friends, and finally after so many years Alexis had found love again. That fateful day in Cardiff in Uncle Georgios's kitchen, when the three friends first heard the declaration of war, was almost a distant memory now. In Alexis's mind decades could have easily passed since then, and the day he'd left Ourania might have been a lifetime ago. But even if everything he'd gone through since then had left its mark on him, that innocent young man of long ago, full of passion, love and conviction was still somewhere in there. When Alexis stopped and searched, he knew he was still that same person. That same young man who never wished for more than peace of mind and to be with the girl he loved.

After all the years of misery, finally the war appeared to be coming to an end and the peace Alexis so desired was at last on the horizon. A sense of hopeful anticipation was taking hold, yet contrary to everyone else he was gripped by fear of what the end of the war would mean for him and Rosaria. Things were changing very rapidly at the HQ and every day some new situation was thrown at them. The first thing to happen, much to Alexis's distress, was the announcement that his friend John Simons had been instructed to prepare for departure. He had no idea where he was being posted or why, but they were all warned that similar orders could be issued to any of them at any given time. Alexis was in a panic; he wasn't ready to leave Naples just yet. He couldn't leave Rosaria, not like this, not before a resolution or some plan was in place for their future together.

Despite Rosaria's request not to speak to anyone

about their situation, Alexis made up his mind to seek advice from his friend before he left, since he considered him the most equipped with the relevant experience and knowledge about life and matters of the heart.

'That's a bit of a jam you're both in, Alexis, my old chum,' John said after hearing the whole story, or rather *most* of the sorry tale of Rosaria's life. For some reason Alexis had omitted to mention that Rosaria was actually married to Alfonso De Sio, instead implying that she was his common-law wife. Why had he withheld that information from his friend? He rather suspected it was because he couldn't bring himself to utter the words *married* and *Alfonso* in reference to Rosaria without developing an acute pain in his gut.

'These Camorra fellows are pretty vicious,' John continued, 'you don't want to be messing around with them. What about the rest of the family, do they have anything to do with her?'

'Apparently not. They've all been warned off, especially Salvatore, Alfonso's elder brother, and she never has anything to do with her mother any more either. She now lives with her aunt and her sister.'

'Listen, Alexis,' John said, lowering his voice, 'it looks as if we'll all be out of here soon; things are changing very quickly, so there might be a way out for you.'

'But that's just *it*,' Alexis interrupted, 'I don't want to be out of here, not without Rosaria!'

'I know, my friend, this is what I'm trying to tell you. Hear me out. I know you don't want to leave your girl behind, which is why I think you must talk to the Colonel. He's a decent man and he will understand the situation. I'm sure he'd be able to help you; both of you.'

'What can he do?' Alexis replied, shaking his head.

'You'd be surprised; there *are* ways round this. One of them is for you to ask permission to marry Rosaria. You just told me this Alfonso is hardly ever in Naples, didn't you? That means he doesn't have his beady eye on her all the time. Presumably her aunt is on her side and would want to help her escape?'

Alexis's head started to ache. John's words stayed suspended in the ether and danced tantalizingly around him.

'Your main problem is dodging the boyfriend,' John said, 'and the wrath of the Camorra. I agree it's not a small problem but I'm sure there is a way round it.' A smile played on John's lips this time. 'You wouldn't be the first soldier to go home with an Italian bride!'

Marry her, and take her home! Alexis's head was both aching and buzzing now. What a fantasy! For a few minutes he allowed himself to indulge in the pleasure of it. But how could he, and where would he take her? *Home*. The very word stabbed at him accusingly. Where was that? Even if it was possible to marry Rosaria, where would he take her that he could call home? The affirmation that he had no home to go to filled him with despair. The island was his home but he could *never* go back there, no matter how much he longed to return. He loved Rosaria and wanted to protect her but Ourania had never left his heart either, and the pain of her loss lingered on. In one of his mother's letters he'd learned that Ourania was engaged to a young man she'd met at the Academy. For all he knew, by now she could be married to him and have his child. No, he couldn't go back. The nearest such place he could call home was Uncle Georgios's house, and the city of Cardiff.

'So, Alexis, my friend,' John continued, breaking into his fantasy, 'how about talking to the Colonel? I'm sure he'll be willing to help you find a way out.'

The conversation with John Simons made Alexis think. What if he kept silent about Rosaria's marriage; could he then marry her himself and take her to England where no one could find out about them? He hadn't concealed from John that Rosaria was married to Alfonso in order to mislead him, but because he'd been living with the denial of it ever since he found out and couldn't bring himself to speak of it; he'd never imagined that his friend would think marriage such a good idea. John wasn't one for that sort of thing, Alexis knew that, he was happy to leave without a second thought for Concetta. So, what if he told the

Colonel the same story he'd told John, and what if his superior officer approved the marriage? Could he pull it off? Could he actually marry Rosaria and be given permission to take her back with him? And would Rosaria agree to such a thing? Alexis knew well enough that even if she did agree to the deception, she would never contemplate leaving her sister behind, so could he perhaps organize a passage to England for Sofia and even Philomena too? The little girl was like a daughter to Rosaria, and he was extremely fond of her, and their aunt was the only mother the girls had. Their situation was so dire Alexis hoped that once he explained the circumstances, the Colonel would show compassion. The more he thought about it, the more he thought he had a chance of making it all happen. But first he had to ask for permission to marry her. It would be illegal, it would be fraudulent, a sacrilege in the eyes of the Church, it would make Rosaria a bigamist, but it would be glorious, and the only possible way out for them.

He had no option but to give it a try. He made up his mind to talk to his superior officer, but not before presenting the plan to Rosaria and Philomena. He had no idea what the two women would think. He hoped Rosaria would agree, but he wasn't sure about Philomena. Even if Rosaria found the idea acceptable, there was no way the plan could work without the aunt's consent and help, and he feared that she might object on religious grounds.

The two women sat motionless, listening while he talked. Neither of them said a word until he finished and even then they both continued to sit in complete silence. The only sound Alexis was aware of, for what seemed to him like hours, was the thumping of his heart. The early autumn sun made pretty patterns through the lace curtains on the old marble floor scrubbed and polished by the women. The room smelled vaguely of disinfectant. He'd spent a sleepless night imagining their reaction, fearing the worst; the minute he could get away he'd rushed to the apartment to find them.

Suddenly, Philomena leapt out of her chair like a mad woman, knocking over a footstool in the process, and ran towards Alexis. Arms outstretched, she threw them around his neck, pulling him to her while Rosaria followed behind her. Both women in tears stood clinging on to Alexis for dear life.

'Bless you, my son! Bless you!' Philomena cried, tightening her embrace.

'I . . . I . . . was so nervous,' Alexis stammered, and hugged them back. 'I was worried . . . that . . . that you would think it was a bad idea . . . because of the Church.'

'The *Church*!' Philomena shouted, stepping back to

look at him. 'What do we care about the Church! Do you think it ever cared about us?'

'I didn't know,' Alexis replied, still in some state of shock.

'I would follow you anywhere, Alexis,' Rosaria said through her tears, 'married or not!'

'I don't know who sent you to us, my son,' Philomena continued, 'but whoever did, I will be thankful to them for as long as I live.'

'You are the best thing that has ever happened to me, to all of us, Alexis,' Rosaria said, tightening her grip on him. 'I would gladly lie, cheat, or even kill to be with you.'

Alexis's heart soared with relief.

'Thank you, my son, thank you,' Philomena said again, finally letting go of him.

'Do you really believe you can arrange for us *all* to come to England?' Rosaria asked, looking up at him.

'I don't know, but I will do everything I can,' he replied with conviction.

'Can you imagine, Auntie? Can you even think of it? The three of us with Alexis in England, together away from here!'

'I'm so grateful to you, my son,' Philomena said and kissed his hand. 'I will die a happy woman knowing my girls are being looked after by you.'

'You are not going to die!' Rosaria said, turning around to look at her aunt. 'You are going to England!'

'Yes, it's true,' Philomena replied with a smile. 'You're right, *cara mia*, I'm not going to die; I'm much better now. Don't worry, I'm not going to die, not yet anyway, but I'm not going to England either. I thank you for even thinking about me, but I must stay.'

'Why?' Alexis and Rosaria said in unison.

'First of all I can't believe for a moment that you will get permission for all of us to come with you, my son, but even if you did I must stay.' And wiping her eyes with a big white handkerchief she turned to Rosaria. 'What about your uncle, *tesoro*? What if he is still alive?'

There had been no word from Philomena's husband, not since they left the village for Naples, and although it was not confirmed, everyone, apart from her, presumed him killed in action.

'I will go to the north where his family lives; if he is alive they will help me find him. I can't leave, *cara* . . .' she continued. 'Besides, I want to stay, I still have much to do.'

'You can't stay here!' Rosaria burst out.

'Who said I'm going to stay *here*? I shall go to Bologna where your uncle's sister lives. She'll take me in, I know, she is a good woman.'

'What about Alfonso and Salvatore and the rest of them?'

'I'm not frightened of those sons of the devil! Without you two girls to worry about I can more than handle them. Don't you worry about me, *cara mia*. Besides, the minute you all leave I will disappear too.'

Philomena was adamant that she would not go with them, but she was even more adamant that Alexis should go ahead with his plan.

'I have to stay,' her aunt told Rosaria. 'But you and Sofia, you both deserve a life away from this godforsaken place.'

Alexis thought hard about what he would say to his commanding officer. He had to be strong, he had to have faith and believe that although what he was doing was wrong, it was also right, and the *only* thing to do.

Shortly before his appointment with the Colonel, excited and nervous at the prospect of the meeting, Alexis went to visit Rosaria and Philomena. Both were in a terrible state of distress. Little Sofia had been taken ill. What had at first appeared to be the same virus that a few months previously had attacked Philomena had now turned into something extremely nasty.

'She is delirious,' Rosaria said, running into Alexis's

arms as soon as she saw him. 'She is burning up and we don't know what to do with her.'

'Why didn't you send for me?' he asked, rushing to see the girl.

'We didn't want to bother you. We thought she would get better soon.'

But young Sofia had a delicate constitution and was prone to poor health, and her condition rapidly deteriorated.

Alexis rallied round, anxious to help. But as bad luck would have it, Sofia's illness coincided with Alfonso's visit to Naples so he had no option but to keep well away from them. All Alexis could do was hope to God that Alfonso would do the decent thing and provide the much-needed penicillin that he and the rest of his family were still trading on the black market.

To everyone's relief, Alfonso did provide the penicillin, but what none of them realized was that the drug was worse than useless due to the Camorra's habit of diluting it in order to sell more. The weak penicillin had no effect and Sofia's condition, instead of improving, went from bad to worse. By the time Alfonso left and Alexis was able to get back to them, the girl was already in the grips of typhus. There was nothing he or anyone could do for her.

They buried her fragile little body in the village cemetery, next to her father, brother and two uncles. Philomena and Rosaria stood clinging to each other in grief and disbelief along with Alexis and a few people who still lived there. Luisa was absent, which was probably just as well, because her sister and her daughter would not have been responsible for their actions if they'd seen her.

In the four years since she'd left the village, Rosaria had dreamt endlessly of the time she would return, but she had never imagined she would be coming back with her baby sister in a coffin. Nothing was as she had left it. Their house was a pile of rubble, and the village square a bomb site. The village, by then, had been ripped apart not only by the war, but also by the eruption of Mount Vesuvius the previous year which had completed its destruction. There was nothing to keep Rosaria or Philomena there any more; their dream of ever returning had been destroyed.

The loss of Sofia was a heavy blow, one she had never anticipated. Her grief was boundless. She had feared for her sister's safety and virginity, but not for her life. That was not how she'd hoped their sad little story would end. The two sisters had been through hell, and then, Alexis came along to give them hope, and a vision for a future.

Philomena was no less grief-stricken by little Sofia's death, but she was determined to keep her focus and concentrate on Rosaria. She had lost one girl in circumstances beyond her control but the other had a chance, and she was going to try and save her no matter what it took. In her grief Rosaria was beginning to doubt Alexis's plan. Philomena had to keep a cool head for both of them. It was now or never. Alexis had to put his plan into action and marry Rosaria as soon as possible. The fraudulent marriage was her passport to freedom, and her only chance of happiness.

'Listen to me, Rosaria,' Philomena told her niece when she started to voice a reluctance about leaving. 'Sofia has been taken away from us before her time, we can't do anything about it apart from mourn her; but we can do something about *you*! You love Alexis and he loves you. You have *nothing* to stay for in this hell hole any more. Don't throw away your one chance of happiness, *tesoro*, it would be a crime, and if you stay, that would kill me.'

Part Four

Love on a Greek island, 1945

1

Ourania liked to be up with the dawn; she always wanted to make an early start for school. Besides, she had much to do before leaving the house. The two sisters kept the school going, despite all the obstacles. Apart from Calliope and Aunt Aphrodite, the rest of the house was still fast asleep and silent.

Ourania always helped Calliope get washed and dressed first, before attending to her own ablutions, while her aunt made coffee and laid out some bread and olives for the three of them. She too liked to start her day before everyone else was up.

Spring came early that year. By May the countryside was a carpet of wild flowers, and yellow daisies lined the ditch along the dirt road to school. Sometimes Ourania loved to take the shortcut through the fields. It was harder pushing Calliope's chair over the rough path but she didn't mind, it was so lovely, and she could pick some flowers on the way, which she liked to keep in a jar on her desk in the schoolhouse. Anemones were her favourite. If she was lucky there'd still be some left, and if they were very lucky they wouldn't meet any Germans along the way.

That morning was like any other; the two sisters and their aunt had breakfast as usual, while outside a pair of swallows darted in and out of the nest under the kitchen window. Dawn was coming much earlier now and the sun in the east had made the milky sky blush a rosy pink. Nothing seemed to stir outside, not even the early morning breeze.

The sound reached Ourania's ears when she stepped into the yard to feed Kotoula. It came from some distance away, muted and muffled at first, and she thought she must have imagined it. But in no time at all it became louder and louder, picking up momentum and echoing across the village. Ourania stood rooted to the spot, listening but not believing. It had been years since she, or anyone else, had heard it. The bells of the old church Agias Ekaterinis on the other side of the village were once again ringing loud and clear, with all their might and strength. They pealed with joy and jubilation as if the Resurrection of the Lord was being announced, as if the victory of life over death was being heralded. The last time anyone heard them resonate like that in the village was on the Easter Sunday before the Germans arrived. But Easter had already come and gone, and the village church bells hadn't sounded like that, not for three years.

Flustered, Ourania dropped the chicken feed and ran back into the kitchen to find Aphrodite and Calliope also in a state of shock.

'You know what this means?' Aphrodite gasped.

'I don't dare think of it!' Ourania replied, blood draining from her cheeks.

'They are leaving! Finally, they must be going!' Calliope shouted and tried to get out of her wheelchair. 'Oh, how I wish I could jump for joy,' she said, falling back, just as the excitable screams of Kyria Maritsa from down the street ricocheted through the air.

'The Germans have gone! The Germans have gone!' she screamed, as she ran into the street.

It was true. The occupiers had finally left as abruptly as they had arrived. They disappeared in the night, taking their motorbikes, trucks and guns, leaving behind only debris and mess. It took everyone weeks of scrubbing to eradicate what Andrikos called *that filthy German stench* from their house, but the exodus was marked with the biggest celebration the island had ever seen. Every village and every town rejoiced in the way they used to do at weddings and feasts in the days before the war. Even if food was still in short supply, large quantities of homemade alcohol more than made up for it, and for three days and nights, the whole island pulsated with dancing and singing and undulated with the blue and white Greek flags that hung from every balcony, every window, every telegraph pole and tree on the island.

Over the next few months things gradually started to normalize again. The men returned to their fishing and the women tried to make their homes their own once more. Everyone lamented the lost lives and aftermath of war but were happy and relieved to welcome back those who survived it. Among the lucky ones was the young teacher eager to take up his post at the village school again.

The Academy in Lesbos had also resumed normal function and Ourania started to prepare for her return. This time her excitement was doubled; Calliope would be coming with her, and Michalis, who was back from the front, would be returning to his studies too. The two sisters were full of anticipation, a new chapter in their life was about to begin. Once they received their diploma, their dream for a new school to accommodate the older children in the village would be within reach.

'I'm so happy you will finally meet Michalis,' Ourania told Calliope as they packed their trunk in preparation for their journey to Lesbos. 'I wonder what effect the war has had on him? I wonder if it's changed him at all?'

'The war has changed us all, Ourania *mou*,' Calliope

replied. 'It would be a miracle if he hasn't been affected too.'

Through the years of separation Ourania and Michalis had managed to keep in touch by writing to each other. His letters, even if they were few and far between, always reached her. She wrote to him regularly and conscientiously, even if there was no guarantee he'd receive any of her letters.

Each time Ourania went to the post office to collect a letter from Michalis, she felt a tightening in her heart. The memory of Alexis and those letters of long ago reproached her, and made her ache for him. Not that she didn't care for Michalis, or that she was not glad to receive his news. On the contrary, she cared deeply for him and was genuinely looking forward to the day they would be together again. But by now Ourania had become resigned to the fact that no matter how many years had passed, or were still to come, Alexis would always be the love of her life.

Preparations were underway for the girls' imminent departure to Lesbos and unlike the last time, Chrisoula was not making herself sick with worry about sending her daughters away.

'Ourania is such a good girl,' she told her husband, trying her best to keep calm, 'I know she will take care of her sister.'

Calliope, full of anticipation, couldn't wait for her new adventure.

'You will love everyone,' Ourania told her. 'Kyria Ismini is just like mother, a bit of a task master but a very good cook and she means well. And Thalia, oh! She's wonderful! You'll love her too, and the other girls, they are such fun, and all my friends at the Academy . . .' Ourania's cheeks were flushed with excitement.

'And?' Calliope said, giving her sister a playful nudge, '. . . haven't you forgotten someone? How about Michalis, isn't he wonderful too?'

'Of course, Calliope *mou*, Michalis too! I'm so looking forward to introducing you to him. He is fiercely intelligent! When he talks you can't help but listen. You will have never heard anyone speak with such passion about the things he believes in, but not only that, he's a gentle soul too. You'll see, you'll really like him and we'll all get on famously together.'

A few days before the girls were due to leave, Andrikos and Chrisoula decided they wanted to send their daughters off with a festive farewell. Family and friends would all be invited. It would be the first proper family celebration and gathering since the war began.

Costandis and Andrikos had made a good catch that day. Usually on such occasions it was customary to roast a whole lamb or goat on a spit, but with livestock still in short supply, their feast that day was going to be an offering from the sea. Most of the women were busy preparing the rich and varied selection of fish that was brought into the house by the men, while Ourania was outside in charge of the tables. In the kitchen the fish was laid out on slabs of ice, while Chrisoula was busy giving instructions on how each dish was going to be cooked. There was octopus and red mullet, calamari and sardines, all so fresh; the whole kitchen smelled of the Aegean.

Outside, trestle tables were lined up under the lemon and mandarin trees in a row that stretched across the entire length of the back yard.

There would be thirty guests in all, and Ourania was busy working out the seating arrangements, making sure there were enough chairs to accommodate everyone. She was deep in contemplation, counting out knives, forks and plates, when all of a sudden, someone sneaked up from behind and, catching her unaware, covered her eyes with their hands. Startled, she screamed and dropped the handful of cutlery she was holding, scattering it all over the dusty ground.

'Stop that, Stratos!' she snapped, trying to pull his hands away, thinking it was one of the younger cousins playing around. 'I don't have time for games now.'

'You guessed incorrectly!' a man's voice breathed in her ear, and swiftly swung her around to face him. Flustered, Ourania stumbled, and then regaining her balance she stared in disbelief at the man standing just inches away, his hands around her waist.

She almost didn't recognize him. Dressed in civilian clothes, and looking smarter than ever, positively handsome in a dark blue suit, white shirt and tie, and a huge smile across his beaming face, stood Michalis.

'A nice surprise?' he asked, taking hold of her hands and stepping back a little to look at her. Suddenly he looked nervous. 'Did I scare you?' he asked, searching her face for clues.

'Oh no! No, Michalis!' she cried out and fell into his arms, 'It's a beautiful surprise! When did you come . . . how . . . why?' she blurted out and then stopped in case he imagined she was less than delighted to see him. 'I mean, I'm glad you are here, but in three days I would have been with you, in Lesbos.'

'I know, Ourania *mou*, I know, but I couldn't wait any longer,' he said, lifting her hands to his lips and kissing them. 'Three years is long enough. Besides, I *had* to come. I've come to ask your parents if they would let you be my wife . . . will you still have me, Ourania? Will you still be my bride?'

So, on a warm September day when the grapes hung heavy on the vine and the wheat in the fields was as yellow as the midsummer sun, Andrikos and Chrisoula agreed to give their eldest daughter to Michalis, who in return promised to love, cherish and take good care of her for as long as he lived. With no time to lose, the priest was summoned to the house to conduct the official religious ceremony that sanctified the couple's union in the eyes of God. Michalis had brought with him two gold bands, the *aravones*, which had to be blessed by the priest and placed on the third finger of their left hands to signify a promise of matrimony and their commitment to each other and their families. The *aravones* would stay there until the wedding ceremony when they'd be removed, blessed again, and placed this time on the same finger of the right hand, where they would be expected to stay for ever. Many tears of joy were shed for the couple's happiness, especially by Andrikos and Chrisoula who had given up hope that their eldest daughter would ever agree to marriage. Aphrodite too shed tears of joy and gratitude. The burden of the secret she had been carrying for so long was a heavy one and she had feared that Ourania's love for Alexis would prevent her from ever finding a match or happiness in her life.

Over the years Aphrodite thought a great deal about the love between her son and her niece. Although she could never condone it, she was filled with sorrow for the young couple's fate. The accident of their birth was not their fault, yet it tore them apart and separated her from her only child. She missed Alexis more than she could ever speak of, and not a day went by that she didn't pray for his safety, or light a candle in his name. Through his letters she knew that her son had been a lost soul and unhappy for years, so when he wrote to tell her that he had finally found love again and was going to marry Rosaria, she thanked God and wished the same for her niece. Now that finally Ourania too had found love, all she asked from the *Panayia* was that some day Alexis would be returned to her.

So on that day, what had begun as a farewell gathering for thirty people in the back yard, turned into the betrothal celebration of Michalis and Ourania, held in the village square, and all were invited. After the blessing, tables and chairs were quickly arranged in the square to accommodate everybody, and each household, along with the baker, the butcher and the greengrocer, rushed away to prepare whatever they could find in way of contribution to the feast. Once again, for the second time in six months, the village was going to enjoy the kind of festivity they had missed during the years of German occupation and they celebrated with food, drink, song and dance well into the warm autumn night.

Philía
(φιλία philía)

is 'mental' love. It means affectionate regard or
friendship in both ancient and modern Greek.
This type of love has give and take. It is a
dispassionate virtuous love, a concept developed
by Aristotle. It includes loyalty to friends, family
and community, and requires virtue, equality and
familiarity.

2

Kyria Ismini was overjoyed to have a full house again and be reunited with her girls. Ourania's friend Thalia had also returned to her studies at the Academy, although the other two lodgers remained at home. Three years was long enough for them to practise the dressmaking skills they'd picked up, and they had accumulated enough customers on their island to keep them going without having to continue further with their apprenticeship. This meant that one of the bedrooms was now free, and after some discussion it was agreed that due to Ourania's new status as a betrothed woman, she should be the one to occupy it. Kyria Ismini, Calliope and Thalia all agreed that Ourania now needed access to some privacy. A place that she and Michalis could go to to be alone; but Ourania was adamant that she should continue sleeping with her sister.

'What if you wake up in the night and need help to get out of bed?' she told Calliope while all three women were trying to convince her that this was the right thing to do.

318

'I'm more than capable of helping her,' protested Thalia.

'You have to have a place where you and Michalis can spend some time together without all of us breathing down your necks,' Calliope insisted.

'You are a couple now,' Kyria Ismini said, patting her left hand and her *aravona*. 'You have to get to know each other in more ways than one. You will be married soon. An engagement is like a trial marriage. When I got engaged to Demetris he moved into my parents' house until were married.'

'We're not getting married just yet!' Ourania objected. 'Besides, if we want to be together we can go in the garden, the orchard is big enough, we managed fine before the war.'

'It's not the same,' Kyria Ismini argued. 'Before the war you weren't engaged; now you are allowed . . . expected, to spend some time alone.'

'I can be alone with Michalis anywhere,' she persisted. 'That doesn't mean I have to sleep alone, too!'

According to local custom, once a couple was engaged they were permitted to indulge in a certain amount of carnal relations. Intercourse, however, was strictly reserved for the wedding night, although cases of 'premature births' were fairly frequent among newly-weds in those days. The reason for these *seven-monthlies*, as the babies were euphemistically called, was blamed on the delicate state of the bride's health or other external factors such as hard work or excessive heat, cold, or spicy food.

In the end it was decided that the three girls would all sleep in the same room but keep the other one as their communal parlour where they could go to study, or contemplate, or where Ourania and Michalis could go if they wanted some privacy. Kyria Ismini gave them whatever spare furniture she had: an old sofa and some chairs, which the girls covered in brightly coloured rugs and cushions turning the room into a cosy, cheerful, sunny place. For the first time since they met, Ourania and Michalis had somewhere they could actually sit on their own with the door shut. Michalis was over the moon. He felt at liberty to hold his sweetheart in his arms and kiss her without fear of being misconstrued. Ourania too was very pleased with the arrangement. Even if nothing compared to the thrill she felt from Alexis's touch, she cherished Michalis's love and enjoyed his kisses and caresses.

Ourania was as happy with Michalis as she would ever be with any man who wasn't Alexis; she had concluded that a long time ago. If she couldn't have Alexis, then Michalis was the right man for her; he was decent and kind, he loved her and she loved him back, and when their studies were complete they would return to the island together and set up their school. The sisters' dream had now become his too.

A number of the students they knew before the war had also returned to the Academy and they were able to pick up their friendships from where they had left off. But the reunions were not always joyful; several of the young men had not been as lucky as Michalis. One friend had lost an arm, another his left eye, and two young men in Ourania's year never made it back. They'd been killed in action. One way or another they'd all been tested, but not crushed; their young spirits continued to look ahead.

Calliope flourished in Mytilini; the student life seemed to suit her well, and her feisty spirit won her much popularity. Life at the Academy was good, and Kyria Ismini's house was a home from home. The land-lady soon returned to her role as mother hen, happy to have her girls back, and delighted to have a man about the place. Although Michalis never moved in, he spent most of his free time at the house and took his meals with them.

'I used to say that I only ever wanted daughters,' Kyria Ismini told the girls. 'But if I'd had a son like Michalis I would never have said that.'

The scars of war were starting to heal slowly and the first academic year passed with little worries. Food was still scarce but they'd all learned to do with much less and the produce from Kyria Ismini's garden continued to provide them with many essentials. For the summer break Ourania and Calliope went home to the island, and Michalis joined them for a few weeks.

'I think you should get married,' Chrisoula told her daughter when she first arrived. 'I don't see the point of waiting, we can do it this summer. It will be more decent if you were blessed and finally married; people are starting to talk.'

Ourania was incensed.

'When have you ever known me to care about what people say?' she told her mother, trying to keep her anger at bay.

'This way you can live as man and wife,' her mother continued. 'Don't you think that would be best?'

'What I think would be best,' Ourania bellowed, 'is for everyone to mind their own business! Michalis and I will get married when we are good and ready and that will be when we finish our studies.'

Chrisoula didn't raise the subject again; she knew not to argue with her eldest daughter.

That summer Ourania spent a great deal of time showing Michalis around her island. They explored the countryside on bicycles, they visited the town, they went grape picking, and hiking, they swam in the lagoon and watched the August full moon rise from the sea. She wanted to show Michalis everything that she loved, apart of course from the secret places that belonged only to her and Alexis. They were not for sharing.

'I love your home, Ourania *mou*, and I will be really happy living here with you,' he told her as they sat on the rocks watching the sun set.

'I too will be happy, Michalis,' she said and reached for his hand. 'We can do great things together, I know it. You, me and Calliope, we will be a great team.'

The next day she took him to see the old schoolhouse, and the plot of land next to it that belonged to her grandfather and for which he had given his permission to build the new school.

'It will be our legacy,' she said excitedly. 'We can start planning straight away. By the time we finish our studies, the building will be complete.'

That summer was blissful; at last the war was behind them and they could now start making plans and look to their future. But by the time they had returned to Lesbos for the new academic year, and before they or anyone else in Greece had time to enjoy peace like the rest of the world, the country was plunged into the misery of another conflict, this time a bitter civil war. No sooner had the Greeks laid down their arms against the Nazis than they picked them up again to fight each other.

Ourania knew that Michalis had strong political

principles and she respected his opinion, sharing his views about what they considered the oppression and colonization of their country by the western powers. But when he told her that he wanted to join the partisans in the struggle against fascism, which had taken hold of Greece at the end of the Second World War, it was with a heavy heart she accepted his decision.

'It's just one more thing we have to do for our country, for our liberty,' he said, holding her tight in his arms. 'We have come this far, we fought so hard, we must complete the task.'

She said nothing; she knew she couldn't prevent him from going. The country was divided now between those who wanted an independent socialist state and those who embraced western capitalist values. A full-scale guerrilla war had already begun, and within weeks Michalis, along with many of his friends, had joined ELAS, the Greek Communist Partisan Army, and all of them were willing to start fighting again for their beliefs.

All through the civil war Ourania remained with Calliope on Lesbos until the end of their studies. The struggle lasted three long years, during which the only news she ever received from Michalis came through messages passed secretly to her from other members of ELAS. At the beginning, once in a while, a hurriedly written note would be smuggled to her, but eventually they too stopped and the only news she got was word that Michalis was still alive.

She waited patiently; Ourania had learned to be stoic about life and what it threw at her.

The fighting took place primarily on the mainland and in the mountainous interior of the country, leaving most of the smaller islands relatively unaffected. In Lesbos things remained reasonably calm, and the Academy continued more or less normally. Finally Ourania graduated, gaining her diploma with distinction, but since she was a year ahead of Calliope she stayed with her until she completed her studies too, by which time the struggle had also come to an end.

The girls returned home and proudly unrolled their diplomas to show off their qualifications. No one in the family had ever attained such level of education before, and Chrisoula and Andrikos were as proud as they could be of their daughters' achievements.

'You see! In the end it paid off,' Chrisoula told her husband. 'I knew those two could do it! I wish I had their opportunities . . . or their brains!'

'Times were different then,' Andrikos replied.

'My father didn't even want me to go to the elementary school,' Chrisoula said and let out a sigh.

The priest and the teacher had always been the most respected and educated people in the island's community and to have not just one but two of them in one family was an inestimable honour. By the time the sisters returned to the island the new school was almost finished. In no time they could start making arrangements for the lessons to commence. But Ourania would not hear of it until Michalis returned too.

'We said we would do this together,' she told Calliope. 'I must honour that agreement, we can't begin without him, it would not be right.' Of course Calliope agreed.

When the hostilities ended and it was clear that the communists were defeated, many of the remaining fighters fled the country into neighbouring Albania; Ourania was confident that the reason Michalis had not yet returned was that he too had gone there. She was certain that he would eventually come back unexpectedly to surprise her as before. But a year went by with no sign or word from him. Finally, one day, instead of Michalis, a friend from the Academy, a member of ELAS, turned up to see her.

'Andreas!' Ourania cried out at the sight of him, her face turning deathly pale. It took her a good while before she could bring herself to ask what brought him to the island. She made him coffee and they both sat silently on the sofa not daring to speak.

'We were together when he was wounded,' Andreas said at last, his voice trembling with emotion. 'He made me promise that if he didn't make it, I should come and find you and give you the news myself.'

Michalis's death hit Ourania hard. She mourned publicly and privately for him, everyone did. His goodness and generosity of spirit had touched all those who knew him. But gradually, even in grief, Ourania picked herself up, and recovered her will to continue. She threw herself with fervour into the task of getting the school project underway. Her passion for teaching and education was going to be her life from now on and she owed it to Michalis to make of it the best job she could.

Over the years Calliope and Ourania created miracles in the small village school. They were known to everyone and loved by many of their pupils. They evoked respect and admiration, if perhaps a little pity too, for everyone thought it unfair that destiny had not smiled favourably at the marvellous Levanti sisters. But Calliope and Ourania were content with their life and considered themselves privileged in the work they were doing and lucky to have each other; they took what had been granted to them with grace, and thanked God for it.

3

Greece, the Aegean, 1999

This time it was her aunt who did most of the talking. Once again Anna listened and wondered how she could have got to the age she was, with no idea about who the closest people in her life really were, or what they had gone through.

It's often the case, she thought, that we tend to project what we want to see in people or what we perceive as being the truth about who they are. For her, all through her life her father was the adoring dad who married the woman of his dreams and took care of everyone; her mother was the lucky girl who was swept off her feet by the gallant soldier she fell in love with to live happily ever after, spreading love to her children. And Anna had assumed her Thia Ourania was the caring tragic maiden aunt who had never been loved or ever experienced a great passion. How wrong could she have been!

'Did you know him, Papa?' she asked, looking at her father through her tears. 'Did you ever know Michalis?'

'No, Anna *mou*, I didn't, but I knew all about him. Ourania told me.'

'When did the two of you see each other again?' she asked, wiping her eyes.

'If I have any regrets in my life,' Alexis said and looked away from both of them, 'they are that I didn't come back to the island earlier. I just couldn't, you see. I couldn't do it.'

Knowing how he had felt when he had found out Ourania was going to marry Michalis, Alexis didn't want to see her with him and had assumed she would feel the same if he came back to the island with Rosaria.

'I didn't know how Ourania would feel and I couldn't risk putting her, or me, through the pain of that. I wanted Ourania to be content, but I couldn't bear to see her with another man; I know I had no right, and I felt I was a hypocrite. I kept trying to reason with myself: if I was with Rosaria and happy, why couldn't Ourania be married? But it was no good. I couldn't help it. Then, when I found out that Michalis was killed, I didn't want to flaunt my happiness, I didn't want to hurt her.'

'But you see, Anna,' Ourania interrupted, 'what Alexis didn't realize was that my feelings were different to his. Somehow, all I ever wanted was for him to be all right. He was the one who had to leave, I was the one who didn't follow him, and he was the one who spent all those years wandering alone. Of course I still loved him, I always did, but I accepted our fate.'

When Alexis eventually returned to the island it was for his mother's funeral, when he already had three young sons and Anna was on the way.

'I never even said goodbye to her,' he said, his voice breaking up with emotion. 'She died without my seeing her again, not once in all those years.' Tears were now rolling down his cheeks. This was only the second time in her life Anna had ever seen her father cry; the first was when her mother died, and the sight of him made her weep.

'Oh Lexi,' Ourania whispered, and reaching across she cupped his face with her hand and gently wiped away a tear. At that moment Alexis turned his face towards her with a look that Anna had never seen before. Was it the sound of his childhood name resonating like a forgotten melody in his ears that provoked it, or was it the touch of Ourania's hand on his face? She couldn't tell, but all Anna knew was that she had never seen her father look more content or more at peace than he did then.

'She knew you loved her and she never judged you,' his cousin told him. 'She knew you had to leave, and that you'd been through a lot. She understood.'

Anna's grandmother died a few months before she was born. When Alexis got the news that his mother was gravely ill he went back to the island by himself, encouraged by his pregnant wife, who stayed behind with her three boys. The journey was long, and the boatride from Piraeus treacherous. Reaching those islands during winter could be very hazardous and by the time he arrived his mother had died. It took everyone, and especially Ourania, to help him get through his grief. Finally, after so many years, Alexis was able lay his ghost to rest and discover that his fears about returning home had been unfounded.

Ourania, remarkable woman that she was, showed no hard feelings or reservations about his life or his happiness, only contentment to see him again. Their connection went further back than their desire for each other; the familial love they had felt since birth had never vanished. They were able to pick up from where they'd left off, filling in the missing parts of the picture that had been their life since separation. When he left, Ourania urged Alexis to return to the island again and bring his family along.

'When I first met you, Annoula *mou*, you were not even two years old,' Ourania said, reaching for her niece's hand. 'I loved you from the moment I laid eyes on you! You were just like your father. The same fiery eyes, the same smile . . . I felt you could have been the child I never had.'

'Did you like my mother?' Anna asked, trying to imagine how she might have felt, how it might have been for her when she first met Rosaria.

'I did Anna, I liked her very much. She had suffered enough through her life. We all did, but she suffered more, yet she had courage and integrity. She loved the island. Remember how she learned to speak Greek?' Ourania gave a little laugh. 'She learned it so well with hardly an accent! She became one of us.'

Once again Anna considered the fact that Ourania knew all about Rosaria's life from Alexis, but Rosaria knew nothing of the love between her husband and his cousin. Their secret continued all through their lives, unspoken, untouched.

'Was it right to keep my mother in the dark?' Anna asked. 'Wasn't it a kind of betrayal?'

'Oh Annoula *mou*!' her aunt said, moving a little closer to her. 'What is right, and what is not? Who is the judge of that? Your mother didn't need to know about me and Alexis. He loved her, we all did, that's all that mattered, so what good would it have done? Nobody knew. The only two people who ever knew about us had already left us by the time Rosaria came here.'

Anna nodded in agreement; her aunt was absolutely

right. No good would have ever come out of that knowledge, only more pain.

'I wish I had met Calliope,' Anna told her aunt, holding tightly on to her hand. 'She sounds like an extraordinarily brave woman.'

By the time Alexis and his family started coming to the island for their summer holidays, Calliope had died, and not long after her, Anna's grandfather too. Calliope's health had never fully recovered after her fall, and an epidemic of influenza on the island finally proved fatal.

'She would have loved you, Anna *mou*,' Ourania said, smiling with the memory of her sister. 'She would have appreciated your work too. She was a keen artist, you know, but never did anything with her talent. We were always too busy with the school, you see. But she loved to paint with the children. I've always been sure that's where your gift comes from.'

'So you see, Anna,' Alexis said, looking at his daughter and reaching to take her hand. 'I have finally come home. This is where I belong now. Ourania and I can finally be together. There are no regrets from either of us but I have returned to where I belong and here I will stay now.'

'Oh Papa!' Anna let out a sob. She couldn't find any other words to say.

'No one can keep us apart now, Annoula *mou*, we

have waited long enough for this time,' Ourania added. 'We are old and we only have a few years left, if God is willing, so we are allowed to spend as much time together as we want. I have my house, Alexis has his, and being together is only natural. No one can think it strange, and if they do, we don't care, we never did!'

That night, after they'd done talking, and finished their third bottle of wine, Ourania spent the night in the house with Alexis for the first time. Arms around each other, they took themselves off to bed. Anna had no way of knowing if that was the first time since she'd been on the island that the two of them had lain in bed together. They'd had plenty of opportunities to do that if they wished, since she was hardly ever there, but Anna didn't care. Far from feeling scandalized or shocked, her eyes watered with delight for the two octogenarian lovers. Was it all too late for them now, she pondered, or is it always better late than never? Back in her room and on her bed, Anna concluded that late is definitely better than never, even if the beauty of youth and the vitality of younger flesh had both long vanished. It seems the spirit remains the same. It lives on and it carries us through to passion. Anna knew about that all too well. She was no young thing either, but hadn't passion just taken her by surprise and carried her where she hadn't been for a very long time?

She lay beside the open window, the hot summer air

that blew in was keeping her awake. The moon, almost full again, was playing a tantalizing game of hide and seek with the clouds and promising his sensual delights.

The heat was intense but she relished the physical pleasure of having a hot body; the heat wasn't the only thing that was depriving her of sleep that night. Her head was swimming with the revelations of the last few days and all that had happened during the summer. Yet again Anna found herself astonished at her own actions; she had never imagined having an affair, but then nor had she ever imagined the sequence of events that had led her to the island. Looking at her perceived problems now, they appeared so trivial. The fates, unlike her parents, had smiled at her life from the start, filling it with love and good fortune; she'd been blessed. Her recent marital crisis seemed almost insignificant. Yes, it had shaken her equilibrium but only because it was the first major upheaval in her otherwise content and easy life.

She lay there going over everything with a new perspective; her crisis was not unique. It happened often enough, even if she didn't believe it could happen to her and Max. But it had. A betrayal had its consequences, she knew that, and Max had caused an avalanche. Reconstruction and forgiveness would take its time.

There were times during the summer that, through her anger, Anna had thought she had completely stopped loving Max. But perhaps, she now considered, she had stopped loving him as she used to; perhaps her love had been altered. Love doesn't vanish in a few months. After all wasn't she the one who talked about the many ways a person could love? Didn't she also just learn that from her father? *Agápe* is vast, real love is enduring.

Her mind was a jungle of memories that turned to happier times, life before Max's illness and to what she called his *loss of reason*. They had been a good couple in so many ways. The same values, the same goals. Their London life before children was exciting; they both loved their work, had a great circle of friends, and supportive families. Summers spent on the island together had been glorious. Before Alex and Chloe the two of them had spent days of splendour, romance and passion there. Anna looked up to Max, admired and respected him for his brains, knowledge and his good looks. They would spend days basking in the sun and balmy moonless nights, encouraged by Anna, swimming naked in the warm Aegean. Max fell in love with Anna's *otherness*, her free spirit and her love of sensual pleasure. His touch thrilled her and she liked nothing more than to lie in his arms.

Max embraced her culture and made efforts to learn Greek, even if he hadn't been too successful at first. Later, when both of the children had started speaking the language, he became determined to improve his linguistic skills and join in.

'I want to know that you guys are not talking about me,' he joked. 'I also really want to be able to have a basic conversation with your Auntie Ourania,' he had said the first time they visited the island. Much to Anna's pleasure, her beloved Thia Ourania was the relative Max liked the most. She fascinated him. 'She is an enigma,' he had commented when he met her. 'And a contradiction too!' he joked. 'Surely she is unique in these parts. She is content to be alone, to live a life of solitude, yet she is a Greek!' Max never ceased to be amazed by the lack of privacy on the island. 'It's all so tribal,' he would laugh. 'Unless you are a crowd you don't exist.' Later on, in years to come, he would appreciate these cultural differences and much preferred them to the stiff-upper-lip and social shortcomings of his own English family. So, yes! Their roots went deep, Anna thought. What they'd built together over the years had strong foundations; shouldn't they now be able to withstand a slight tremor?

The last few days had been intense. It would take her time to get over everything she'd learned, including that her beloved father would no longer be living close to her. The feeling was bittersweet. She had gone from having two loving parents always available to her, to having no parents. But, of course, she consoled herself, Alexis would still be available and so would the island and her aunt. A new chapter was about to begin for all of them.

4

The ride up to Elia was as lovely as ever but for the first time since Anna had been making it her heart was pounding not only through the anticipation of seeing Nicos but about what she would say to him.

Earlier that morning the insistent ring of the telephone dragged her out of a deep sleep in which she was dreaming, for the first time since her arrival in Greece, of London and Max. The children often visited her in her sleep but Max and London had apparently been banished till now. Anna ignored the phone, hoping that her father or aunt would deal with it, but when it became clear that either they had already gone out or they were also choosing to let it ring, she jumped out of bed and ran to answer it.

'Hey, Mum! *Yia sou!*' The cherished voice of her youngest offspring shouted down the line. 'What's going on with you lot there? Why don't you turn your mobile on sometime!'

'Alex!' she screamed, and a wave of maternal love choked her. 'Where are you?'

'I'm in Athens, with Dad, we're coming to see you.'

'What! When?' Anna screamed again.

'In a couple of days. We've been trying to call you since before we left London. What's with the phones there?'

'Just the two of you?' she asked, ignoring his question. 'Where's Chloe?'

'She's still camping. She might come later, I'll tell you about it when we see you. Anyway, here's Dad, he wants to say hello.'

'Hi, Anna!' he said, a slight tremor in his voice. 'How are you?'

'I'm fine, Max,' she replied and didn't know what to say next.

'We are catching the boat from Piraeus on Thursday,' he said, ending the silence. 'Should be with you by late afternoon.' He hesitated. 'Is that OK with you, Anna?'

Seeing her family never failed to delight her, she could never get enough of either of her children and the same usually applied to Max. But with good reason, since Anna arrived on the island there was nothing she desired less than seeing her husband. Yet after his phone call a couple of days ago, and her nocturnal thoughts of a happier past, she now felt different. She felt it was time for some decisions, and apparently so did Max. Gone was the alienating steely edge in his voice of late; once again it was soft and gentle in Anna's ears, and despite herself she was comforted by its sound. At times of stress Max's voice would wrap itself around her like a warm blanket.

When she hung up she didn't dash out of the house like a woman possessed, as she had before. Instead Anna went into the kitchen and calmly made herself some coffee, took it into the garden and sat in the shade to think. The prospect of seeing them both again made her happy. Caught up as she had been in feelings of betrayal, rejection and anger, not to mention a whirlwind of passion, she had tried not to think of her family too much; it was easier that way. But everything she had witnessed and learned from Ourania and Alexis had definitely brought about this change in her.

It was time to pay Nicos a visit. She decided she owed him an explanation.

She found him in his studio painting furiously. He didn't hear her walk in, and for a few minutes Anna stood observing him silently. A ripple of desire stirred in her, taking her by surprise. She supposed that love, lust, *Éros*, or whatever you wanted to call it, can't just fade away in a few days. Alexis and Ourania managed to sustain theirs for a whole lifetime. Of course she knew what she felt for Nicos could never be compared to what they went through or their grand passion, or even what she had felt for Max through their life. Nevertheless, Anna had succumbed to that great power, as she assumed Max had done a few months earlier, and for a while she had lost her mind and willingly surrendered her body to the mischievous love god. But her early morning phone call and the revelations of the last few days had a sobering effect on her.

She didn't call out to Nicos, but continued watching him till he sensed her presence. When he eventually turned round, his face lit up with delight.

'Anna!' he cried and walked towards her. 'When did you get here?'

'Only a few minutes ago,' she said as he wrapped his arms round her waist and drew her close. His kiss was gentle and sweet, but Anna held back.

'I missed you,' he said hesitantly, then, sensing her reluctance, 'What's wrong, Anna, are you OK?' Taking her by the hand, he guided her out into the garden.

He made coffee and they sat under the same lemon tree as they had when they had first met. Just like that first day, they talked and smoked cigarettes and ate olives with bread and ripe tomatoes, figs and grapes from the vine until the sun started to move towards the west. She told him everything she'd learned during the last three days and more, and when she cried he held her in his arms and soothed her, and they didn't stop talking until the sun vanished behind the hills and the moon appeared low on the horizon. Anna told him how his love had helped her heal her wounded pride, how his Greek passion, which so unexpectedly crept into her heart, had touched her, and how she would never forget him. Then Anna told him that Max and Alex were coming in two days.

He held her tight and kissed her tears away, shed a few of his own like only Greek men can do, and told her that he understood.

'I never imagined that I would ever have you for myself, Anna,' he said, not looking at her as he rolled another cigarette. 'Maybe there was a crazy moment when I fantasized you might stay, but I knew that the pull of your family would be too strong. I don't blame you.'

'For the first time in my life I didn't think about consequences and about what Max might think or say,' Anna said. 'For once I didn't think about anything except how I was feeling.'

Falling in love with Nicos had been good for Anna. She felt no guilt or regret for what she'd allowed herself to do, only love and gratitude. She knew she'd broken all the rules, Max had too; but who made those rules? Who said that because we love one person we can never love another? Alexis had loved another and so had Ourania, and Anna was sure as hell they were not the only ones in the world to have done that. If she had learned anything over the last few days it was that nothing is absolute and in the end nothing else matters apart from love. She had fallen for Nicos but it didn't stop her from still feeling love for Max. Alexis was right, Anna thought; Love, *agápe*, really is the only enduring thing; its power is endless and it has no boundaries or limits. Respect it, and it will respect you back, handle it with honour and discretion and no harm will be done. Anna never realized that she had so much of it to give; this island, Nicos, Antonis, the moon, the sea, her father, her aunt, everything conspired to make her open up to its possibilities and understand it better and also help her towards forgiveness.

'I'm glad you didn't think too much,' Nicos said, handing her a cigarette.

'Me too,' she replied.

'Sometimes we have to turn the brain off and let the body carry us away,' he said. 'It's better to have something, no matter how brief, than miss it altogether.'

'You mean *"Don't ask for the moon when we have the stars"*?' she said and looked up at the night sky.

'Bette Davis!' Nicos said wide-eyed, his face suddenly breaking into a big smile. *'Now, Voyager*! You know that film?'

'My mother's favourite,' Anna replied, leaning playfully towards him so he could light her cigarette Hollywood movie-style. 'I watched it with her more times than I can count, ever since I was a little girl.'

'Oh Anna!' he said still smiling, and reached across

to take her hand. 'I'm so happy I met you. If only we had met years ago . . .'

Of course, Anna thought, it was a pointless thing to say because if they'd met years ago they would have been different people. For a start she would not have allowed herself to be in this situation, and what's more she was quite certain that Nicos wouldn't have liked her half as much as he did now; she was far too controlled, far too up-tight then to have even considered a clandestine affair.

'I know . . .' he carried on as if he'd heard her thoughts, 'it's a stupid thing to say, we were different people then.'

'I don't know about you, but I like myself better now,' she replied.

'I'm not sure if I've changed much. I've always been obsessed with my work, always been uncompromising. I suppose I still am,' he said, leaning back on his chair and stretching out his legs. 'I've never really allowed anyone to come between me and my studio. I suspect that's why I'm on my own and probably always will be. I like it this way. But your life is good, Anna, it's more balanced than mine. Maybe you had to make compromises but you have love in your life and your children. That is a precious gift, Anna. I always ran away from that; but then again I've made my choices, I have no regrets.'

They sat in silence for a while. They were both in a

good place with each other; there were no bad feelings at all, only good ones.

After a while, when the moon was right above them, so bright in its fullness that it illuminated everything it touched as it masqueraded as a nocturnal sun, they decided to jump into Nicos's car and drive to the Black Turtle. The night of the beach party was upon them and they both had an overwhelming desire to drink ouzo, hear the bouzouki play, and see Antonis and Manos.

That night they all danced till dawn on the beach, swam under the August full moon and promised, just like children do, never to forget each other or this summer.

Anna had no idea how she was going to feel when she saw Max and Alex walk off that boat. Nor was she prepared for it. Her heart pounded and her knees trembled under her long summer dress. The boat from Piraeus was taking an annoyingly long time to arrive, and when she tried to call Alex on his mobile there was no reception. All that day she was in a state of nervous excitement. She spent an uncharacteristically long time deciding what to wear, and what to do with her hair, and far longer than necessary cleaning the house. She filled all the vases with whatever fresh flowers she could find in the garden and helped her aunt in the kitchen to prepare a welcoming meal. Thia Ourania's baked pasta, *pastitsio*, had always been the children's favourite dish.

Anna was more nervous than she wanted to admit, but she was also excited at the prospect of seeing her son and husband again.

'You must have missed them so much, Anna *mou*,' her aunt said while she stirred the savoury meat sauce and Anna busied herself with the béchamel. 'Are you looking forward to seeing Max again?' she asked, searching her niece's face for clues, perhaps in reference to the conversation they had had some time ago. 'Is this the first time you've been apart for such a time?'

'Oh no, *Thia*! Don't you remember? I used to come every summer with Mum and the children.'

'Oh yes. Of course,' she said with a sigh. 'It seems so long ago now.'

'Max and I often spend time apart; he travels a lot for his work, we're used to it.'

'I can't wait to see little Alex, he must have grown so! I wish Chloe was coming with them.'

'I wish so too,' Anna said and felt a pang of longing for her daughter. 'She's camping in France and due to go home soon; but you never know, she might surprise us yet!'

'Have you missed London, Anna *mou*? Are you looking forward to going home?'

Home! That word again. She still hadn't worked out

where that was or what she felt about it. She was perfectly at home on the island. She had missed her family, but London? She didn't think so.

'You are happy, aren't you, Anna *mou*?' she heard her aunt say as Anna stood pondering at her question. 'Max is a good man, isn't he?' she suddenly said, putting the spoon down to look her niece straight in the eyes. 'Alexis says he couldn't have wished for a better son-in-law, but it doesn't matter what Alexis thinks.'

'Oh yes!' Anna interrupted. 'Max is a good man, *Thia*, we've had our troubles, who hasn't, but yes, he is a good man, and yes, I am happy. But sometimes we all need to question our lives, don't we? Or perhaps we shouldn't.'

'Who says you shouldn't?' she said sharply; it was Ourania's turn to interrupt now. 'We are Greeks, aren't we? We must question, we must reflect! After all, *"The unexamined life is not worth living"*,' she said, quoting Socrates, her favourite philosopher.

Anna first saw Alex waiting to get off the boat. He looked taller and thinner than when she had left for the island at the beginning of summer. She couldn't believe that he'd grown that much in less than three months. He was tanned and healthy-looking, his hair, which for the last year or so had been cropped like a convict's – much to Anna's dislike – had grown past his ears and was bleached by the summer sun. Her boy, she thought, looked absolutely gorgeous! He'd grown so much this past year; he was a regular sixteen-year-old heart-throb! He was carrying his rucksack over one shoulder and holding a bright yellow plastic bag in his left hand. Max came behind him carrying only a small holdall, always the master at minimal packing due to years of getting on and off planes. He too looked thinner and a little more drawn than when she had left him but also quite tanned, unlike most of the other tourists around him with their pallid northern skin. *Typical*, she thought, London had apparently waited for her to leave to let the sun shine on it.

Anna stood rooted to the spot, watching them both walk through the crowd towards her. Her heart raced with anticipation. A large group of boisterous Italians were getting off at the same time and for a few minutes they were lost in their midst. Pushing through the mingling crowd, she ran to find them.

'Mum! Mum! Over here!' she heard Alex calling out from somewhere.

'Anna!' Max said, suddenly next to her. Dropping his bag on the floor he put his arms around her and held her tighter than she had ever felt him do before.

'What were you doing, Mum! You were running in the opposite direction!' Alex laughed and ran to give her a hug. He too seemed to hang on to Anna for ever; not since he was a little boy had he given her such a lingering squeeze. Then, out of nowhere, she felt another pair of arms wrap around her from behind and the unmistakable scent of Miss Dior, Chloe's favourite perfume, flooded her senses.

Anna sat with her children on either side of her while they drove up the hill towards the house, basking in their presence and still glowing from Chloe's unexpected arrival.

'You guys . . . you really fooled me well and good!'

'We know how much you love surprises, Mum,' Alex joked.

'Not really,' Anna protested, 'but this was the best kind! Thank you for coming, Chloe, I missed you both so much.'

'I missed you too, Mum,' Chloe said and reached for Anna's hand, her eyes searching her mother's. At eighteen Chloe had picked up on her parents' tensions and her summer had not been worry-free. 'This has been the longest we've all been apart. It's good to be together.'

As the car got closer to the house Anna could see her father and aunt standing at the garden gate waiting to greet them.

'*Kalosorisate!* Welcome!' they both shouted.

'Max! It's so good to see you!' Alexis said as soon as they got out of the car. 'Alex, my boy! And Chloe, my beautiful girl! You have come too. What a wonderful surprise!' he shouted, rushing towards his grandchildren to embrace them.

'You seem to have grown even more!' Alexis said to his youngest grandchild and namesake. 'I will have to stand on my toes in order to kiss you soon, young man.'

'I remember when I used to stand on a chair to kiss *you*, *Bappou*,' Alex replied, kissing his grandfather on both cheeks before turning to his great-aunt. For a few minutes she just stood looking at him in disbelief; finally she walked towards him and, taking his face in both of her hands, kissed his forehead.

'At last I see you again, my little one,' she told him. 'You have grown into a fine young man, Alex *mou*, and you look a lot like your *bappou* when he was your age! And you, my beauty,' she said, looking at Chloe, 'you are the reincarnation of your *nonna*.'

Under the vine the table was already laid out with the appetizers, little plates of *mezethakia*, a carafe of Ourania's own ice-cold lemonade, and a bottle of wine for the customary welcome drink. Anna had especially requested that they hold the big get-together with the rest of the family later to give them all a little breathing space alone, to catch up. The evening celebrations would go on all night, that was a given.

While Alexis and Ourania were busy showing the grandchildren around the house, Max slipped his arm round Anna's waist and led her to the furthest part of the garden. The old wooden bench under the fig tree had been there since Anna was a child. She remembered how she and Max would escape there with a newspaper and a coffee, when all the children had gathered at the house and their noisy games got too much. Some planks at the back of the bench were missing now but the seat still held well. They sat as they had done dozens of times and Max reached for Anna's hands. He cupped them both in his and looked at her. His voice was at first weak but it picked up momentum as he talked.

'Do you think you can ever forgive me, Anna?' he started, but before Anna could reply he continued. 'I have been a fool, an idiot, a cretin. It was a moment of madness.'

'Well, it wasn't exactly *a moment*, Max,' she heard herself protest.

'I know, of course . . . of course. It felt like a moment. It meant nothing.'

Anna found that she was relishing Max's plea for forgiveness and she let him continue for a long while till she decided she had heard enough. He talked about how his illness had affected him, his loss of virility and youth, thinking he was going to die, and that like a fool he had allowed himself to be seduced by flattery and fear and that he pledged to cherish and appreciate Anna and value what he'd nearly lost.

'You and the children mean everything to me, Anna,

I know that now. I always knew. I had a moment of lapsed sanity.' He lifted her hands to his lips. 'Please try to forgive me, Anna, that's all I ask. I have told the university that I won't be doing any more long trips.' He searched Anna's face for a reaction. 'I think we have spent too much time apart and that's all my fault. I let my work take priority over us. We must talk more, Anna, we must never stop again.'

'*Yes, Max, we must talk,*' she told herself and thought of all the things she wanted to say to him. She wanted to talk about her feelings for a change, tell him all she had learned and experienced in the course of this summer and how it had changed her. *Yes, Max,* she thought again, '*you have absolutely no idea just how much we have to talk about!*

'We have a long road ahead of us, Max,' she finally replied, feeling drained as they got up to join the others. She knew it was her turn now to say something, he had had his say, but she had done all the talking and listening she wanted to do for now. Her turn was going to have to wait a little while longer.

Soon, one by one, they gathered together at the table under the vine and Alexis poured them all a drink.

'Welcome back, all of you,' he said, standing up and reaching across to toast each one. 'It was about time we returned to the island, to the old house. We have all been greatly missed, and I assure you that this gathering, my beloved family, will be the first of many more to come.'

'*Stin ygeia mas!*' To our health, Ourania added, lifting her glass, her face aglow with joy.

The last time they were all together like that, sitting around that same table, Rosaria had been with them, and like so often since she'd died a wave of sadness washed over Anna. How could it be that her mother no longer existed? How could she be dead, be gone from her, how can they all still be here without her? They were the testimony of her existence. Alex, Chloe and Anna came from her, they carried her genes. They belonged to her, they all loved her, yet she was gone, banished to live only inside their minds.

Chloe, as her aunt had commented earlier, resembled Rosaria in her physical appearance but also in temperament too. She was tender and kind. Anna saw her mother every time she caught a certain look from her daughter. The same warm brown gaze and laughter that would trickle out of her with such ease, infecting everyone nearby.

'That girl is a radiator,' Anna's friend Sam, Chloe's godmother, would say. 'Everyone is drawn to her, she exudes warmth.' Chloe also possessed a wisdom far beyond her young years. If she hadn't been her daughter, Anna would have wanted her as a best friend. There had been many a time in the past year when she had longed to confide in Chloe, ask for her advice, or cry in her arms. But of course she hadn't; protecting her children from the aftermath of their marital problems was Anna's main goal.

Across the table next to Chloe and Alexis, sat her son. Her baby boy, Alex! When had he become such a budding young man, with as much masculine presence at sixteen as his grandfather at eighty? He looked like Alexis, the physiognomy was shockingly close, but when you looked further the likeness to his father was also apparent. The eyes, not as brown as the rest of them, were tinged with hazel. The hair, too, wasn't quite as dense, dark and curly as the Greek clan, but sleeker and sun-kissed, something of the Anglo-Saxon in him too. *'My little Piscean,'* Anna would muse of him. *'Always in a world of his own.'* He was the total opposite to his Aquarian sister, who was down to earth and practical. When she was pregnant with him, a friend of Anna's who knew about horoscopes had told her, 'You're lucky to be having a Piscean baby, because it will always feel your pain.' That particular trait of Alex's kicked into action big-time when Max was sick, Alex always secretly worrying about his dad and keeping a watchful eye on him. But a Piscean baby has another characteristic that Anna was soon to discover: head in the clouds and an ability to switch off when things got tough. 'You see, Anna,' the horoscope friend had told her with a giggle, 'in due course you will find that there is *reality* as most of us perceive it, and then there is *Piscean* reality.' This aspect of Alex's character actually proved to be beneficial for him during the last year. Even if he was worried about his father's health, when it came to the family issues he was, much to Anna's relief, able to switch off and escape into his Piscean reality.

She was grateful for both of her children. Her family was everything, her most precious possession.

She looked at her daughter and her son, her father and her aunt in turn, and her heart swelled with emotion. Then she looked up at Max and she could see in his eyes that he was guessing what was going through her head. Max's eyes always betrayed him. She couldn't have lived with him for all those years without knowing that about him. Even if he wanted to, they could never conceal his feelings; at that moment, sitting across the table from him, his eyes told her that he too was her family, that she might not have her dear mother any more but she did have everyone else and that she had *him* too if she still wanted him. That he was there to stay, that he was sorry.

Glancing around the table at the most important people in her life, Anna was filled with a sense of history, a sense of belonging, and a word came to mind: *home*. In fact it came to her not so much as a word but more as a feeling.

When her Thia Ourania had asked a few weeks ago

where home was for her she didn't have an answer. Now it was all clear. Now Anna realized that it is possible to be at home in many places; to inhabit many worlds, in our heads, our hearts and in our bodies. To belong to any or all of them at the same time and be happy enough. But perhaps, she thought, in the end what we call *home* is not a place but a feeling.

She looked at Max again. He was her husband, the father of her children, the man she had spent the best part of a lifetime with and the man who had out of the blue announced that he wanted to be with someone else. To her surprise, for the first time since his betrayal, she felt no bitterness towards him, for she realized that in fact Max had set her free. She was free to love another, free to be herself; a self she could never have imagined before. Here they both sat, the same, but different.

She thought of the journey she had been on, of the four kinds of love that she had been blessed to feel. Never in such a short period of time had Anna experienced the intensity of love in all its aspects. She felt the force of *Éros*, for Nicos, the splendour of *philía* for her new-found friends, and the intensity of *storgé* for her aunt and father. Her heart swelled with *agápe* and all its glory for all her family and those who came before her and had suffered so much.

Maybe, she thought, there was even a fifth kind of love, the love of freedom, of opening the cage and setting the bird free. She was no longer the little girl that Max had swept off her feet all those years ago.

This summer she had discovered a new freedom, a new honesty. She was now her own woman. Would Max be able to accept that?

London, Greece, the world; she looked at her son and daughter and was filled with love and pride. Wherever she was in this world, travelling towards a new millennium, she would continue to be a good mother to her children, she would continue to *love*, but this time by her own rules.

Acknowledgements

My heartfelt thanks go to all those who helped, encouraged and believed in me, that not only could I write this novel, but that when I did, it was worthy of publication.

I thank my agent and now also dear friend Dorie Simmonds, who always believed in both me and the book and who has been a continual source of inspiration and motivation for me. I would also like to thank Caroline Hogg and Louise Buckley at Pan Macmillan who loved this story enough to publish it. My thanks also go to my dearest friends Alison Sheriffs Brown and Gill Brackenbury who read chapters as I went along and gave me feedback. To Linda Kelsey, who was the one to encourage me to write a novel in the first place; Trudy Whyle, who was the first to read my synopsis and give me advice before I started writing; my cousin Christina Zira and friends Sally Faulkner and Gill Macdonald, who read and loved it and gave me a glimpse of hope that perhaps it could be published; Anne Boston, who read and edited it for me as an act of pure friendship and gave me the most valuable advice, and Justin Somper and P. J. Norman, who approved of everything.

My thanks also go to the Hornsey Library in Crouch End, and to all my Italian friends, Roberto, Serena, Paolo, and the delightful Mr Costas Kavathas, who shared his childhood memories of wartime on a Greek island with me, and also I cannot forget Thoth, Rafael and Mike.

I thank my parents with all my heart for loving me always and wish that my mother was still alive. I miss her more than words can say but am grateful for my wonderful father who continues to remind me each and every day about the four Greek words for love and many more.

It's time to relax with your next good book

THEWINDOWSEAT.CO.UK

If you've enjoyed this book, but don't know what to read next, then we can help. The Window Seat is a site that's all about making it easier to discover your next good book. We feature recommendations, behind-the-scenes tales from the world of publishing, creative writing tips, competitions, and, if we're honest, quite a lot of lists based on our favourite reads.

You'll find stories and features by authors including Lucinda Riley, Karen Swan, Diane Chamberlain, Jane Green, Lucy Diamond and many more. We showcase brand-new talent as well as classic favourites, so you'll never be stuck for what to read again.

We'd love to know what you think of the site, our books, and what you'd like us to feature, so do let us know.

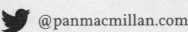 @panmacmillan.com

facebook.com/panmacmillan

WWW.THEWINDOWSEAT.CO.UK